"Simon Brewster wants me to find his daughter."

"What daughter?" Jonas stared incredulously at Abby. "The old man doesn't have a daughter. He's using you because of his own agenda. Brewster does things for his own weird reasons and nine times out of ten, someone gets hurt. Go back to Dallas and forget about him."

"I can't," she whispered, and felt chills run up her spine. She thought of all the years her father had worked for Simon Brewster—all the hard work and loyal service Abe Duncan had given Brewster, only to be tossed aside like an old shoe. And the rumors... Brewster had promised to tell her the truth if she found his daughter. "I have to clear my father's name."

But Jonas wasn't ready to accept her answer. "What if you find out that your father did the things people say he did?"

"No!" She shook her head. "You knew my father. How can you even say it?"

Jonas took a step closer. "Because when you start digging into the past, you'd better be able to handle the consequences."

Dear Reader,

You need to go. That's what my brother J.O. said to me when he was drilling water wells in the Rio Grande Valley. He talked about the large fields of agricultural crops growing there, the Mexican laborers, the seasonal workers and the poverty across the Rio Grande River. The more he talked, the more questions I asked. I could definitely feel a story coming on.

You have to go, he kept insisting. So my husband and I headed for the border. I'd been to Mexico years ago, but this time it was more vivid and real. I looked at the contrast between Texas and Mexico through the eyes of a writer, and a story emerged that I hope you will enjoy.

Abby and Jonas are two very different people, and it took me a while to sort through the trails of their lives. I hope you will find these characters and the area as absorbing as I have. If you do, you will go there, too—if only in *On the Texas Border.*

Thanks for reading my books.

Linda Warren

You can always reach me at P.O. Box 5182, Bryan, TX 77805, or e-mail me at LW1508@aol.com

On the Texas Border

Linda Warren

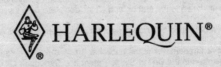

HARLEQUIN®

TORONTO • NEW YORK • LONDON
AMSTERDAM • PARIS • SYDNEY • HAMBURG
STOCKHOLM • ATHENS • TOKYO • MILAN • MADRID
PRAGUE • WARSAW • BUDAPEST • AUCKLAND

ISBN 0-373-71049-6

ON THE TEXAS BORDER

Visit us at www.eHarlequin.com

Printed in U.S.A.

To my brothers—
James Otto Siegert, Bobby Louis Siegert
and Paul William Siegert. Thanks for the love and
encouragement. As we grow older, I hope we continue
to grow together instead of apart and that we always
remember the sense of family our parents instilled in us.

And to the man who went with me to the RWA conference
in New Orleans without one complaint—
my husband, Billy Warren, my Sonny.

ACKNOWLEDGMENT

J.O. Siegert, Tammy and Rodrigo Medina and all the people
who answered my endless questions about Texas and
Mexico with such patience. Any errors are strictly mine.

CHAPTER ONE

"LOOK AT THAT, ABIGAIL," Simon Brewster said as he stood at the huge windows overlooking the Rio Grande Valley. "It all belongs to me...as far as the eye can see."

"Are you proud of that?" Abigail Duncan asked, scribbling notes on a pad while a tape recorder picked up his voice. She was writing Mr. Brewster's memoirs. The eighty-year-old's life had been turbulent and fascinating, and she didn't want to miss a word.

"You're damn right I am," he told her in his gruff voice. "If you've ever known poverty like I have, you'll make sure you never have to live like that again." He paused, then added, "I was nine years old when my father died and my mother and me had to work the fields to make a living. It was during the Depression and there were a lot of days when all we had to eat was bread and honey. I vowed that one day my mother would never have to work again. She was the only person I ever really loved until..."

She waited for his next words, but none were forthcoming. She glanced up to see him staring out the window and realized he was lost in another time. She doodled on the pad, knowing he wouldn't speak until he was ready. She'd been working on his life story for a month and she had come to know his moods.

Her pencil stilled as her mind drifted. She'd returned—after a bitter divorce—to Hope, Texas, her childhood home. She'd lived here until she'd left for college. After getting her degree, she'd moved to Dallas and joined a large newspaper as a reporter.

She had been home two days when Simon Brewster had asked her to write his memoirs. The request had come as a shock because there'd been bad feelings between her family and Mr. Brewster for the past year. Her father had worked for Brewster Farms for thirty-five years, then suddenly Mr. Brewster had fired him. Her father said he hadn't been given a reason for the firing, but the rumor that had circulated around the small town was that Abe Duncan had been caught embezzling funds. That had angered Abby and she'd wanted to find out the truth. But then her father became ill, and Abby had spent her time at home helping her mother to care for him. Nine months later he died. She'd loved her father, and had been devastated by his death. Her mother blamed Mr. Brewster. So did Abby.

When Mr. Brewster offered her the job, she'd turned him down. She had no intention of writing his life story. But then she began to see it as an opportunity to uncover the truth. She knew Abe Duncan had not embezzled a dime, so why had Mr. Brewster fired him after so many years of loyal service? It was time to get some answers. Her mother was adamantly against the idea, but Abby was a reporter, and she had to clear her father's name.

So far she hadn't been able to bring up the subject. The more Mr. Brewster talked about his life, though, the less she hated him. She didn't understand that, but it didn't change her mission.

Feeling uncomfortable, she brushed a speck from her denim skirt, straightened her white knit top and studied the elderly man at the window. He was a formidable character. His gray hair was short and stuck out in all directions. She didn't think he ever combed it. She remembered that from her childhood. When she'd see him in town, his hair was always disheveled, giving him a wild appearance, and all the kids gave him a wide berth. She wasn't a child anymore, but Mr. Brewster was still intimidating. The thought brought her back to the memoirs. She checked her notes to refresh her memory.

"Until what?" she prompted.

"Until my son was born," he muttered. Abby knew better than to ask about his wife because she'd already learned that Mr. Brewster had married her for her land. It wasn't a love match. The son was a different matter, and Abby was reluctant to talk about him. He'd been killed in an auto accident when he was thirty-one years old. Marjorie, Mr. Brewster's wife, had grieved herself to death, and for the past twenty years, Mr. Brewster had been a hard and embittered man.

"I made people pay for his death and I will make them pay until the day I die. Vengeance is mine and always will be," he said in a tone that sent goose bumps up her arms.

She swallowed and asked, "But wasn't it an accident?"

"Drunk teenagers, that's what it was," he roared. "They were jealous of my son and his money and they dared him to a race that night. My son was never one to back down from a dare, but liquor and high speed don't mix. I will continue to seek retribution for their callous behavior.''

Back then Abby had been only a child, but she remembered the accident. Her parents had talked about how sad it was. The whole town had mourned. But she'd thought there were no survivors.

"Didn't the crash kill everyone?" she asked into the silence.

"Not everyone." A sinister smile tugged his lips. "The boys left families, and I made sure those families never worked in Hope, Texas, again. They raised killers and they should be shunned as killers."

Abby swallowed again. This was the side of Simon Brewster everyone had warned her about— the ruthless side.

She glanced at her watch and noticed the time. "Mr. Brewster, it's almost five-thirty," she said. "I've got to go. I promised Mom I'd be on time for supper."

Simon Brewster turned from the window. "We're just getting started," he grumbled.

Abby glanced at him as she stuffed papers and the recorder into her carryall. They went through this every day. He never wanted her to leave. Abby recognized he was lonely. For a man who had so much, he had so little. Hope, Texas, was known as Brewster's valley—miles and miles of fertile land in the Rio Grande Valley between Texas and Mexico. The land yielded vegetables and fruits that were sold all over the United States. Simon Brewster was a very rich man, yet he had no family, except distant relatives who were just waiting for him to die. Everyone said he'd got what he deserved…and maybe he had.

When she'd agreed to write his story, the same people told her she was crazy, and she probably was.

As a child, she'd ridden her bicycle past his mansion with the wrought iron gates. The house was built of white stone and had a red tile roof. Although she'd lived most of her life in Hope, she'd never been inside the house until four weeks ago. It was exactly the way she had thought it would be—elegant and tasteful with a Mexican flavor.

Today they were in his bedroom because Mr. Brewster had been having chest pains, and the doctor had ordered him to take things easy. The room was awesome and the four-poster bed had a headboard, with intricate Mexican carvings, that almost reached the ceiling. A luxurious bathroom and adjoining sitting room gave a sense of space and elegance, but the floor-to-ceiling windows with their spectacular view took pride of place. From his bedroom, Mr. Brewster could see everything that went on at Brewster Farms.

Few people liked Simon Brewster, but most of the town depended on Brewster Farms for a living, so they put up with his bad attitude and bad moods. Just as her father had done. Abe Duncan had never hurt anyone. He didn't deserve what had happened to him. No matter how involved Abby became in Mr. Brewster's life, she never forgot that fact. She would find out the truth…maybe not today, but soon.

"I'll be back tomorrow," Abby said, when she realized her mind was wandering.

A shaggy eyebrow shot up in annoyance. "Every time I'm in a mood to talk, you have to run off. Can't your mother wait?"

Before she could form a suitable reply, there was a knock at the door.

"Come in," Mr. Brewster called crossly.

Jonas Parker stepped into the room. Jonas was the manager of Brewster Farms. He answered only to Mr. Brewster.

"Howdy, ma'am," he said to Abby as he removed his hat, and her toes curled into her shoes. His voice was low and deep and seemed to come from the depths of his broad chest. Jonas Parker exuded raw sensuality.

His light brown hair was bleached blond by the sun. It was parted on the side, and a lock fell across his forehead when he wasn't wearing his hat. His features were masculine and well-defined; his eyes, a clear brown. He was well over six feet, and his body was firm and strong as if he knew what hard work was all about. He wore a chambray shirt, sleeves rolled up to the elbows and faded jeans that emphasized his long legs.

Her stomach tingled with excitement…just as it had when she was sixteen and Brad Hazelton, two years older than her and popular in school, had asked her out. She was appalled at her reaction. She had sworn off men, love and marriage. Evidently her body hadn't gotten the message.

Jonas walked to Mr. Brewster and handed him a clipboard. "Here are the orders for tomorrow," he said. "Twenty eighteen-wheelers will arrive in the morning. We'll have them packed and out of here by five."

Jonas was precise. That's probably the second thing she had noticed about him. He said by five and he meant it. Jonas Parker was a man of his word.

For the life of her she couldn't figure out why she found so many of his qualities attractive. Her hormones were out of whack, she told herself. Time to get out of here.

Mr. Brewster signed the papers. "What vegetables are we shipping?"

"Yellow squash, carrots, onions and the last crop of cantaloupes."

"You see the job's done on time."

"Don't I always?"

"Yeah, I guess. You don't give me much to gripe about."

Jonas took the clipboard from him. "I'm sure you'll find something."

"You're damn right I will," Mr. Brewster snarled. "You work for me, boy, and I expect loyalty and—"

"I'll see you tomorrow," Abby interrupted, not wanting to sit through one of their many arguments. The two men seemed to hate each other, and Abby didn't understand why Jonas continued to work for a man who always tried to belittle him. Of course, Jonas gave as good as he got. And she doubted if anyone could truly belittle Jonas Parker. He was too much of a man.

"Run off." Mr. Brewster waved a hand. "You always do that when I'm on a roll."

Abby slipped out the door without another word. She hoisted her carryall over one shoulder and her purse over the other. She hurried down the winding staircase, eager to get home. A door slammed loudly, and she jerked around them. Her purse slid from her shoulder to the floor, its contents spilling onto the Mexican tile. She hurriedly picked up her wallet, keys and lipstick, and as she reached for a tampon rolled away, a masculine hand, lightly covered with brown hairs, retrieved it.

She straightened to stare at Jonas, and her knees wobbled. A musky, masculine scent filled her nostrils, and her cheeks turned red as he handed the tampon to her. She managed a weak "Thank you." She crammed it in her purse, expecting him to walk on. He never had a conversation with her. He greeted her politely, but that was it.

"Haven't you got anything better to do than listen to an old man's ramblings?"

The attacking words startled her. She slung her purse over her shoulder in a quick movement. "Ramblings? It's his life story. I'd hardly call that ramblings." Her voice was cool, belying the heat building in her.

"But how much of it is true?"

Again, she was startled by the question, but didn't allow her puzzlement to show on her face. "All of it," she responded. "It's his life so I assume—"

He cut her off. "Never assume anything about Brewster. He's asked you to write his memoirs for a reason, and you can bet it has nothing to do with his desire to let the world read about his remarkable life." With that, Jonas walked past her and out the front doors.

It took a moment for Abby to catch her breath, then she quickly followed. If he thought he could throw that at her and leave her standing like an idiot, he had another think coming.

She caught him on the front steps. "What did you mean by that?" she demanded.

He swung around to face her, the clipboard in his hand. "Are you naive, or what?"

"I am not naive," she replied sharply. She'd been away to college, lived and worked in a big city, gotten married and been through a divorce. At thirty, she was anything but naive.

"You're from Hope. Surely you've heard the stories about Simon Brewster."

"Yes, I've heard the rumors," she said stiffly.

She was standing on the top step and looking down at him, which gave her the advantage she needed, since she was five foot three and he towered over her. He took a step up and they were at eye level. His eyes delved into hers.

"Everything you've heard about Brewster is true. Nothing is exaggerated or blown out of proportion. It's all true."

She shrugged lightly. "I'm writing his memoirs, that's all."

His eyes narrowed. "After what he did to your father, why would you want to do that?"

"You knew my father?" she asked hoarsely.

He looked surprised. "You're supposed to be a reporter and you couldn't figure that out?" he quipped sarcastically, and she bit down on her tongue to keep from saying something she'd regret.

She knew her father had worked with Jonas. His question had thrown her off balance.

"We worked together for years," he went on. "Abe was an honorable, decent man, and Brewster shattered him like a piece of glass. Brewster didn't flinch while he was doing it, either, and he never gave your father a second thought."

Abby's stomach tightened in pain, but it didn't keep her from noticing the insinuations in Jonas's voice. Did he know something?

"Why did he fire my father?" she asked quietly.

Jonas shook his head. "Don't know. Brewster uses people for his own means, and he's doing the same with you."

Jonas was wrong about that. Abby was using Mr. Brewster for her own purposes. "What would his reasons be?" she managed to say, trying not to show how his words affected her.

Jonas shook his head again. "Don't know."

Abby shifted her weight to her other foot. "Sounds to me like you're making accusations without any proof. What are you afraid of?"

He didn't respond, just stared at her with guarded eyes.

Her journalist's instincts kicked in. "Are you afraid I might find out something about you?"

He took another step up and loomed over her with barely controlled anger. "I hope you find something on me...something that will get me out of this god-forsaken place and away from Simon Brewster—forever."

With that, he turned and took the steps two at a time. He got into his white truck with the Brewster Farms logo on the door. The door slammed with a deafening sound, and he sped down the driveway to the gates.

Abby held on to the iron railing that curved to the bottom of the steps. Her insides were a hard knot of nerves. She'd been wishing that Jonas would talk to her, but not this way. He was rude and accusing. He made her feel as if she'd betrayed her father. That was the last thing she'd intended. She was going to get justice for her father—one way or the other. And she didn't need Jonas Parker's interference.

As Abby drove to her mother's house, her mind was a jumble. She'd believed that writing Mr. Brewster's memoirs would be easy. He'd talk and she'd write, then they'd discuss her father. But so many other emotions—and people—were interfering. People like Jonas. In her job as a reporter, she'd come up against men like him. The strong, silent types, who never wanted to talk or share emotionally. She was always uncomfortable around them. She had to admit, though, she wasn't a really great judge of men. Just look who she'd chosen to marry.

She'd met Kyle at the paper. He was fun, loving and caring...and he'd swept her off her feet. Within three months they were married. They were happy for a while, but then she noticed he was drinking to excess. She didn't worry too much because they were both dealing with a lot of stress at work. She began to get bigger assignments and awards for her writing. Kyle became jealous and bitter, and Abby began to turn down stories because her achievements angered him so much.

He wanted a child, and she told him that they had to work on their marriage first. She wouldn't bring a baby into a home that was fraught with tension. That only increased his anger. His drinking got worse, and he started staying out late. Then he was fired from the paper. That brought matters to a head. Kyle blamed her for everything that was wrong in his life. He became so enraged one night that he hit her. She packed her things and left. The next day she filed for divorce.

Kyle began calling and showing up on her doorstep, wanting to reconcile, but he had destroyed any feelings she'd ever had for him. She had no intention of ever going back. He harassed her for weeks until she had to get a restraining order. Finally, the divorce was granted, and she headed home to heal.

She forced the depressing thoughts from her mind as she parked behind her mother's car and hurried into the house.

Gail Duncan sat at the kitchen table, flipping through a magazine. "You're late," she said, not looking at her daughter.

Abby got the message. Her mother was upset. She dropped her purse and carryall by the refrigerator and kissed her mother's cheek. "I'm sorry. Things ran long today."

Her mother was in her late fifties and still an attractive woman, with her short, neat graying hair and trim figure. She didn't answer or look up as Abby spoke, just turned a page with a jerky movement.

Abby sat next to her and took her hand in hers. "Mom, you know why I took this job, so be patient with me."

Her mother glanced at her, her green eyes—so like Abby's—swimming with tears. "I don't like you anywhere near that man."

"I know, Mom, but I have to find out what happened with Daddy, and I'm getting close. I think Mr. Brewster will tell me."

Her mother squeezed her hand. "Don't you trust Simon Brewster for a minute."

Jonas had said almost the same thing. But she wouldn't think about him and his insulting words.

"I won't," Abby assured her. "But there has to be a reason he fired Daddy."

"Your father never would say. He said to forget about it, that he was tired of working for Brewster,

anyway. Then he found out about the cancer and—''
Her voice cracked.

"It's all right," Abby said softly. "It's time to get
on with our lives. But before I can do that, I need to
have some answers."

Her mother got up. "You were always like that—
needing to know the who, when, where, what and
how about everything." She took lasagna out of the
oven and brought it to the table. Setting it on a hot
pad, she added, "I guess that's what makes you a
good reporter. But," she continued wistfully, "sometimes you have to let go."

Abby stood and kissed her. "I'll try, but right now
I'm so hungry, especially for your lasagna. I'll wash
up and be right back."

She ran to the bathroom, hoping she was doing the
right thing about Simon Brewster. She knew her
mother was worried that Mr. Brewster was going to
hurt her the way he'd hurt her father. Funny, but
Jonas seemed to feel the same way. *Stop thinking
about him,* she admonished herself.

Maybe she should forget about the memoirs and
let go of the past, like her mother had said. No, she
couldn't. She had to know. She washed her hands,
then stared at herself in the mirror. Her natural blond
hair was in disarray around her shoulders and her
green eyes lacked their usual sparkle. She looked awful. Had Jonas noticed? Probably, she thought, answering her own question. He wasn't blind. But then,
why should she care? A man was the last thing she
needed in her life. Besides Jonas wasn't interested in
her in any way, shape or form. And that was a good
thing.

Wasn't it?

JONAS LEFT HIS OFFICE and walked through the big metal building that housed the offices of Brewster Farms. Juan, one of the warehouse employees, tried to stop him.

"Mr. Jonas, I—"

"Handle it, Juan, I'll be back later," Jonas threw over his shoulder as he made his way to his truck, which was parked out back.

In less than five minutes he pulled up in front of Mick's Tavern in town. He got out of the truck and went inside. The place was a dive—peanut shells littered the worn floor, a jukebox hummed in a corner and a Mexican couple necked at a table that could have used a good cleaning. Jonas came here often to unwind. God, he needed to unwind today. That Duncan woman was beginning to get to him.

"Coke and peanuts," he said to Mick, who stood behind the bar. Jonas and Mick were old friends. Mick had been there for him when no one else had— not even his own parents. In fact, Jonas thought, Mick was probably the only person who'd cared about him when he was a kid.

Mick had married a Mexican woman, and they'd settled in this small border town so his wife could be close to her family. Mick was a die-hard Texan with rough edges and a spit-in-your-eye attitude. He was equally at home with the locals and the Mexicans. Everyone knew that Mick was a good man to turn to in times of trouble. He had helped many other people as well as Jonas.

Not all of Mick's endeavors were on the up-and-up, though. Even as a kid Jonas had figured that out. A brothel was illegal in Texas, yet Mick operated one in plain sight of the sheriff and the town. Jonas knew that Mick had some sort of arrangement with the sheriff. For a certain amount of money, the sheriff turned a blind eye. A lot of illegal activity—drugs, prostitution, smuggling—went on in this town, yet nothing was ever done about it. Brewster was the only one who could put a stop to it—and he chose not to.

Illegal immigration was also a big problem. No matter how tight the security, Mexicans always managed to find a way to get across the Rio Grande undetected. It was routine for illegals to show up at Brewster farms wanting work. Brewster had always hired them, and Jonas continued that practice. If they proved to be good workers, he tried to help them get a Green Card so they could continue to work without fear of being caught. It was a lengthy process, but worth waiting for. Many extended families—parents, brothers, sisters, uncles, aunts and cousins—came to work for Brewster. Once here, they usually stayed—only going home for visits.

Some went farther into Texas or other states. It made Jonas sick when he heard of illegals dying from heat, exhaustion and thirst while hiding from the border patrol. Then there were the ''coyotes''—as the Mexicans called them—who smuggled illegals across the border for a price and transported them deeper into Texas. They jammed as many people as they could into a concealed truck. If the Mexicans didn't die from suffocation, and if the driver managed to slip through the checkpoints without suspicion, they had a ticket to freedom. It was a roll of the dice and the Mexicans took it.

Jonas remembered the first time he had helped to burn the sugarcane for harvesting. Three bodies were found huddled together. No identification, nothing on them, and everyone knew they were illegals. Unfortunately, it was something that happened too often. When Jonas took over Brewster Farms, he warned the Mexicans when the cane was going to be burned. He wanted the word spread on both sides of the border. He then had Juan use a foghorn and circle the fields, informing everyone in Spanish that the burning was about to begin. So far he hadn't had to witness such an awful scene again.

During peak season, temporary Mexican laborers came by the busload with a special pass to work. They couldn't go farther than twenty-five miles from the border and they had to return to Mexico at night. It was a good arrangement and it helped everyone. In the winter months, seasonal workers came from up north to avoid the bad winters. The trailer park was a hive of activity during that time. Some workers came regularly and a reunion took place every year. All in all, everyone got along. Everywhere there was Mexican music mixed with country.

Mick slid an iced cola can and a bowl of roasted peanuts across the bar. Jonas took them and sat at one of the tables, propping his feet up on a chair. He took a swig of the cola and began to break the peanut shells.

Mick came over to the table. A white apron covered his large form. He chewed on a cigar. He never lit the thing, but he always had one in his mouth. "Why do you come in here, Jonas? You never buy any liquor or make use of my girls."

"I don't drink and I don't need to pay for sex," Jonas said, popping a peanut in his mouth. He glanced at Mick. "You got a problem with that?"

Mick held up his hands. "No problem. Just bad for business. In the old days I couldn't keep you outta here."

Jonas removed his worn hat and plopped it on the table. "The old days, Mick? I've forgotten what the hell they were like."

"No, you haven't," Mick said, pulled up a chair and rolled the cigar to the other side of his mouth. "You made a mistake. You were young. Now it's time to say *adios* to all that."

Jonas ran his thumb over the sweat on the cold can. "Yeah, if only it were that easy."

"Brewster can't control you forever," Mick told him. "Not unless you let him."

Jonas looked at his friend.

"You've paid your dues," Mick added forcefully.

Jonas went back to rubbing his thumb over the can. He didn't want to talk about Brewster or the past. It was over, but his dues would never be paid, not until...

Mick caught that stubborn look and changed the subject. "I got two illegals over at my place. They're scared but they need work."

"How old are they?"

Mick sighed. "Why do you always have to ask that?"

"Because I'm not working kids."

Mick chewed on the cigar. "They're both sixteen."

"You wouldn't lie to me, would you?" Mick knew that sixteen was the youngest age that Jonas would allow.

"I haven't lied to you since you were eight years old. I told you the truth even when it hurt."

He had. Mick had always been straight with him, so there was no reason to doubt him. Jonas had a strict rule about children. He refused to work them. Brewster gave him enough leeway to enforce it.

"Send them over," he said. "I think there's a couple of beds in a trailer. Make sure they're aware of the rules—no liquor or drugs on the premises. As long as they behave, they'll have a safe place to work. Tell them to ask for Juan and fill out papers, and they can start work tomorrow."

"Thanks, Jonas," Mick said. "How about another Coke?"

"Sure, why not."

On his way to the bar, Mick asked, "What's Brewster got you in a snit about today?"

"It's not Brewster."

Mick set another can in front of him. "Then, it has to be a woman."

Jonas took a swallow. "Women, Mick? How in the hell do you figure them out?"

"I don't. I just enjoy them."

Jonas laughed. "That's very good advice."

"Then, why the hell don't you take it?"

Jonas didn't answer. Mick wouldn't understand, anyway. Jonas tipped his head back and drank thirstily.

Mick watched him for a moment. "Why don't you get on your Harley and head for parts unknown. What the hell can Brewster do?"

Jonas pushed hair away from his forehead. "In my dreams, Mick...only in my dreams."

Neither spoke for a moment, then Mick said, "Is this about the pretty Duncan woman who's been hanging around the Brewster mansion? She's a nice piece of—''

Jonas stopped him. "Don't talk trash."

"Then, it *is* about Abigail Duncan."

"Brewster's using her, and I can't figure out why."

"It's not your business, is it?"

Jonas gulped down more cola. "No, but..."

"But what? You're concerned for her?"

"No, dammit. She needs to get her ass back to Dallas where she belongs."

Mick chuckled. "Or maybe she belongs in your bed."

Jonas's eyes narrowed on Mick. "Is that all you ever think about?"

Mick chuckled again. "It's good business and it's why you're so wound up. You can't get the Duncan woman out of your head."

Jonas twisted the can. "Your dime-store psychology stinks."

"But I'm right, ain't I?" Mick said gleefully. "Take the woman to bed and get her out of your system. That will solve the problem, and you'll definitely be in a better mood."

Jonas stood, laid some bills on the table, picked up his hat and walked out. Mick was wrong, he told himself. He didn't want to take Abigail Duncan to bed.

Liar! resounded a voice in his head. Okay, she was attractive with her blond hair, green eyes and knock-out body, he admitted, but she was a career woman with a divorce behind her. He didn't need someone like that. His life was messed up enough the way it was.

On the way back to the office, Jonas decided Mick was out of his mind. He also decided he would stay out of Ms. Duncan's life. He'd warned her. Now she could do whatever the hell she wanted.

CHAPTER TWO

THE RINGING OF THE TELEPHONE woke Abby at two in the morning. She groped for the receiver and brushed hair out of her eyes at the same time. "Hello," she mumbled.

"Ms. Abigail Duncan?"

"Yes."

"This is Hope Medical Center. Mr. Simon Brewster has had a heart attack, and he's asking for you."

Abby scooted into a sitting position. "Is he all right?"

"He's still alive, if that's what you're asking, and he wants to see you."

"Me? Why?"

"I've just been instructed to call you."

"Oh." Mr. Brewster wanted to see her. She wasn't part of his family. Maybe it had something to do with the memoirs.

"Ms. Duncan?"

"Yes."

"Are you coming?"

"I...uh..." She hesitated for a moment, then added, "I'll be right there."

Abby hung up the phone wondering if she'd made the right decision. Her mother wouldn't like this, but the man was probably dying. Abby had to see him. She dressed hurriedly in jeans and a knit top. Luckily the phone hadn't woken Gail. Abby made her way out the back door and to her car. Within minutes she was parking in front of the small hospital.

Mr. Brewster was in ICU, and Abby was shown into a waiting area. Three people were sitting in the small room. Abby recognized them immediately. They were Mr. Brewster's so-called family. Edna Kline, tall and heavyset, was Mr. Brewster's sister-in-law. His wife's sister. She had been at Mr. Brewster's house several times while Abby was working on the memoirs. Edna always had her son, Jules, in tow. In his fifties, Jules was short and thin, very unlike his mother. He didn't seem to have a job. Abby knew that Mr. Brewster supported them.

The other person was Darby, a cousin who turned up when he needed money. He was in his sixties and traveled a lot...mostly at Mr. Brewster's expense.

"What are you doing here?" Edna asked cattily, her ample bosom heaving as she got to her feet.

"Mr. Brewster asked to see me," Abby answered, feeling as if it was none of Edna's business.

"Whatever for?" Darby asked. "You're just someone who works for him."

As he walked closer, she got a whiff of his breath. The man had been drinking.

"You'll have to ask Mr. Brewster," she replied evenly.

"Have you got your eye on Uncle Simon's money?" Jules asked nastily.

Before Abby could respond, Edna moved close to her. "Let me tell you something, missy. Take your little notepad and tape recorder and get the hell away from Simon."

"Ms. Duncan," a nurse called from the doorway. "Mr. Brewster will see you now."

"What?" Edna choked. "We've been waiting much longer than she has."

The nurse stepped into the room. "Mr. Brewster asked that you all go home. He only wants to see Ms. Duncan."

"That's ridiculous," Edna hissed. "We're his family." She pointed at Abby. "She's nothing."

"I'm sorry," the nurse said. "Those are Mr. Brewster's wishes."

"Well, I never." Edna expelled a long breath and sank heavily into a chair.

Abby followed the nurse out the door, but not before she heard Jules say, "We have to put a stop to this."

Oh God, Abby thought. She didn't want to be here and she was certainly no threat to them.

The nurse showed her into a darkened room. Mr. Brewster lay in the bed, hooked to machines and oxygen. His skin was pale, his breathing shallow.

"Come in, Abigail."

His voice sounded strong enough. She stepped closer to the bed. "You wanted to see me?"

"Yes, I'm glad you came."

She didn't know what to say, so she said nothing.

His fatigued brown eyes stared at her. "Don't look so scared, Abigail. I'm not dead yet."

"I...I..." She wasn't scared, but words wouldn't come. The room, the machines and the hospital reminded her of her father's last days. He'd been in excruciating pain and his heart had been filled with sorrow—mostly caused by this man.

"I have a favor to ask of you." His voice penetrated her troubled thoughts.

She found her voice. "If it's about the memoirs—"

He stopped her. "No, it isn't."

Abby swallowed. "What is it, then?"

He took a ragged breath. "Many years ago I had an affair with a Mexican girl who worked in my house."

Abby was taken aback by the statement. She had expected to hear a lot of things, but this wasn't one of them. She forced herself to listen.

"She had a child, a girl, whom I refused to acknowledge as my daughter. She left and returned to Mexico with the baby. I don't deserve anything from them, but I have to see my daughter's face before I die."

Abby shook her head. "I'm not sure how this concerns me."

"I want you to find my daughter," was his shocking reply.

"What?"

"You heard me."

"Mr. Brewster, I'm not a detective. You need a private investigator."

"No." He shook his head. "They would drag this out for money and leak tidbits to the papers. I won't have that. You're a reporter. You can do this. The mother's name is Delores Alvarez. Jonas has all the information on her in his files. He'll go with you."

A man moved from the shadows, and until that moment, Abby hadn't even realized Jonas was in the room.

"I'm not going," Jonas said tersely. "I already told you that."

"You'll do what I tell you to do," Mr. Brewster roared, his face turning red in anger.

"Calm down, Mr. Brewster," the nurse ordered.

Mr. Brewster took a couple of deep breaths. "I own you, Jonas," he murmured. "Remember that."

Abby wondered what the old man meant, but didn't have time to ponder it. She could see that Jonas wasn't backing down. A full-fledged argument was about to erupt.

"Mr. Brewster, I'm not searching for your daughter," she told him before the situation got out of control. "I wouldn't even know where to start. There are reputable people who can help you. Besides, you should concentrate on getting better and—"

"You have to do it," he breathed heavily. "You're a woman close to her age. She'll listen to you. Tell her I'm sorry. I just want to see her. That's all."

Abby inhaled deeply, trying to understand this strange request. "Mr. Brewster, I can't, but—"

"No," he cut in, took a breath, then asked, "Why did you agree to write my memoirs?"

Thrown by the question, Abby chewed on the inside of her lip, searching for the right words. Her motive was not altruistic, and she had difficulty telling him that. She didn't understand why. Mr. Brewster had hurt her father, so she shouldn't worry about his feelings.

"What's the matter, Abigail?" he taunted. "You think the truth will hurt me?"

"I..."

"Nothing touches me anymore. My heart is like a rock. I'm not sure what's keeping me alive."

"I keep wondering the same thing," Jonas slipped in.

"You see, Abigail, Jonas knows me, and he keeps waiting for me to draw my last breath. Not because he's after my money but because he wants his freedom. But he will never be free of me...not even when I die."

Abby threw up her hands. "Okay, I've had enough. This is getting weird, and I'm not getting involved." She turned toward the door.

"You agreed to write my memoirs to get information about your father."

She swung around, her eyes huge in her pale face.

"What?" He lifted an eyebrow. "You think I didn't know?"

Abby swallowed hard. She felt as if she were a puppet and he were pulling her strings, manipulating her. She didn't like that feeling...not one little bit.

"Here's the deal, Abigail Duncan," he went on. "You want something, and I want something. Let's hammer out the details."

"You think you can manipulate me?"

His eyes stared into hers. "Yes," he answered. "And I'll tell you why. You're a reporter and you need to clear Abe Duncan's name. I'm the only one who can do that." He paused, then added with a touch of cynicism, "Or the town can go on believing the rumors."

Blood began to pound through her numb body with exhilarating speed. "You're a cruel old man," she said angrily. "How can you be so—"

"Enough," he ordered briskly. "What's it going to be?"

Thoughts ran riot in her head. This was what she'd been waiting for—to hear the reason her father had been fired. She thought of all the years her father had worked for Simon Brewster, all the hard work and service he had given, only to be tossed aside like an old shoe. And the rumors. Abby would do anything to put an end to the rumors.

She raised her eyes to his. "Let's hammer out the details," she said quietly.

"Have you lost your mind?" Jonas shouted.

She ignored him.

"Good," Mr. Brewster said, as if Jonas hadn't spoken. "I knew I could count on you."

Abby wrestled with her conscience. Could she do this? She didn't know a thing about finding people, and she didn't understand why he wanted *her* to find his daughter. There were so many other avenues. But he'd given her no choice. Not if she wanted the truth.

"All you have to do is go into Mexico and find Delores," Mr. Brewster was talking. "Her family doesn't live far from the border. They'll be able to tell you where she is."

"If it's that simple, anyone can do it," she reasoned.

"We've been through this. I want someone I can trust. Someone Delores can trust."

"Are you sure you can trust me?" she fired at him. "After all, I am Abe Duncan's daughter."

"Touché, Abigail." He sighed with admiration. "To answer your question, yes, I trust you implicitly."

"Aren't you the man who told me in his memoirs never to trust anyone?"

"Are you gonna pick at every little thing I've said or are you going to help me?"

She didn't want to help him or have any part in this bizarre mess. But she had to push aside her feelings and remember why she was doing this.

"Why hasn't Delores come back before now?" she asked. "Wouldn't she want the best for her child?"

"I told her that if she ever came back, she'd regret it, and she knew I meant what I said. I'm not proud of the way I acted years ago, but...now that I'm near death, I have this need to see my daughter. She'll be close to thirty, probably with a family of her own."

This was crazy, and when she heard herself say the words, she knew they were the craziest thing she'd ever said. "Okay...I'll try to find her."

"I have your word."

"Yes, you have my word."

"Good," he said, and seemed to relax.

"Why did you fire my father?" she asked, holding her breath as she waited for the answer.

That sinister smile she was beginning to associate with him curved his blue lips. "You don't think I'm stupid, do you, Abigail?"

"No, of course not."

"You find Delores, then we'll talk."

Frustration ran through Abby. She was close—so close—but she should have known better. Simon Brewster wasn't going to make this easy for her.

"What if I don't find her?"

"You will."

"You seem certain of that."

"I know you, Abigail. You won't give up until you find her."

You don't know me, old man, she had the urge to say, but she didn't. She had to keep her emotions clear. "How can I be sure you'll tell me the truth when I find her?"

"You have my word."

"Do you think *I'm* stupid?"

Mr. Brewster started to laugh, but it turned into a cough. The nurse immediately adjusted the oxygen. In a moment he was better.

"You got fire, girl. Your father never had that."

"Don't criticize my father," she snapped.

He ignored her words and asked, "Do we have a deal?"

"No, not until I have some proof that you won't renege on your promise."

Mr. Brewster watched her closely. "I'll leave a sealed letter concerning the information you're after with my attorney. When you return with my daughter, you can read the contents. Will that satisfy you?"

"Maybe," she answered. "But I insist on seeing the letter and talking to your attorney."

"No problem. Do we have a deal?"

He wouldn't tell her a thing until he got what he wanted. It crossed her mind that he'd been planning this all along—but why her? Why had he chosen her to do this? It really didn't matter. She was going to do it…for her father.

"Yes, we have a deal."

"Good," he said, and started to cough again.

Jonas took her elbow and pushed her out the door. He'd obviously decided that was enough for her, for him, for everybody.

"You...promised." Brewster's voice followed them.

"Are you serious?" Jonas asked roughly, once they were in the hall. "A daughter? My God, no one but you would believe that cock-and-bull story."

"I have to find out about my father," she said stubbornly.

"Your father was a good man. Why can't you just leave it at that?"

Her eyes caught his in the dimness of the hallway. "I'm sure you've heard the rumors concerning my father."

"What?" He shrugged. "That he embezzled money from Brewster?"

The words spoken so cavalierly filled her with anger. "My father never took from anybody. He always gave."

"You brought it up, I didn't," he was quick to tell her. "Besides no one believes that trash, anyway."

"But they've heard it, and it's in their minds. I can't stand the thought of my father having that kind of epitaph." With that she headed for the elevator.

Jonas soon caught up with her. "Ms. Duncan, just let it be."

"I can't," she said, and poked the Down button.

"Ms. Duncan, Simon Brewster lives by his own rules. It would be wise for you to go back to Dallas...far away from Brewster."

"I can't," she said again, softly.

That ache in her voice threw Jonas. He was trying to remain detached from the situation, but the hurt in her eyes and the pain in her voice were making mincemeat out of that resolve.

They stepped onto the elevator in silence. Inside, Jonas tried again, "Ms. Duncan—"

"Please stop calling me Ms. Duncan," she snapped. "My name is Abigail. Everyone calls me Abby. I would prefer it if you did the same."

Jonas had a hard time hearing anything she was saying. All he could see were her full lips moving, her eyes sparkling and her breasts pressing firmly against her blouse. Mick was right. Jonas wanted her...right here, right now, in this elevator.

He was in big trouble.

The doors swished opened, and still Jonas didn't move or speak. She watched him with a perplexed expression, probably wondering what was wrong with him.

Jonas reached out to catch the doors as they started to close. The action brought him to his senses. He was acting like a schoolboy, and he was anything but that. He'd had his share of women. He accepted them as they came into his life, enjoying the time he spent with them and then moving on to someone else. From the start of every relationship, he made it clear that there was no future with him. He had screwed up his life when he was fifteen years old, and he wouldn't destroy anyone else's.

He sensed in his gut that Abigail Duncan wasn't a one-night stand or a casual affair. He avoided women like her—women who wanted commitment, family and babies. He had to admit he was attracted to her, but he could handle that without—

He suddenly realized she was waiting for an answer. Clearing his throat, he said, "We won't be acquainted long enough for me to call you by your given name."

Her eyes narrowed to green slits. "I don't care. You're not calling me Ms. Duncan in that tone of voice. You make it sound like I'm old enough to be your grandmother."

Jonas walked out of the elevator, and Abby followed him. God, she was relentless. She was a woman who never gave up or gave in. He was beginning to see that.

As they walked out into the coolness of the September night, he turned swiftly—and she almost collided with him.

"All right, *Abby*," he said harshly. "Are you satisfied?"

No, not quite, Abby thought. "Ms. Duncan" was better than that angry tone. What was wrong with her? Why should she care what he called her? She had more important things to worry about.

As if reading her mind, he added, "You'd better concentrate on Brewster, instead of worrying about what I call you."

She tucked hair behind her ear. "I'm sorry. I think I'm getting a little crazy."

"I'll second that," he quipped.

"Do you always have to be so insulting," she snapped, tired of his rude remarks and insinuations.

There was a pause. Then he said, "Listen, Abby…"

Oh God, her name sounded just the way she had known it would—low, sensual and spine-tingling good. All she wanted to do was taste that sound on his lips. She pulled herself together, trying desperately to steady her roller-coaster emotions. One minute she was low and the next high. What was hap-

pening to her? Why did Jonas Parker have this effect
on her? She shook the question away.

"I've worked for Brewster for twenty years, and
this is the first I've heard of a daughter. My guess
is, there isn't one."

"Why would he lie? Why would he concoct this
elaborate hoax?"

"Like I tried to tell you earlier, Brewster does
things for his own weird reasons, and nine times out
of ten someone gets hurt. Go back to Dallas, make
up with your husband and forget Brewster's deal."

"Stop saying that," she said heatedly. "I'm not
going back to Dallas, and I'm certainly not going
back to my ex-husband."

Jonas took a long, patient breath.

"I have to find out the truth," she added more
calmly. "Can't you understand that?"

"What if you find out that your father *did* embez-
zle money from Brewster?"

"What!" she cried, feeling as if he'd slapped her.

"You heard me."

"No." She shook her head. "You knew my father.
He wouldn't do that. How can you even say it?"

He took a step closer. "Because when you start
digging into the past, you'd better be able to handle
the consequences."

She frowned, hearing a hint of a warning in his
voice. A warning that indicated he might know more
than he was saying. "If you know something, tell
me."

"I don't." He sighed. "Brewster didn't like your
father, and your father wasn't all that crazy about
Brewster. It was something personal between them,
so just let it be."

"I can't," she whispered, and felt chills run up her spine in apprehension of what lay ahead.

"Don't go into Mexico to find this fictional daughter."

The breeze picked up and blew her hair across her face. She quickly tucked it behind her ear again, wishing she had the option of refusing and wishing even more that he'd at least try to see this from her point of view. A siren wailed close by and a couple hurried past them, but neither Abby nor Jonas were in the mood to watch the activity around the hospital. They were too engrossed in each other.

"I have to," she finally said.

A low grumble left his throat.

"What does that mean? You don't think I can do it?"

"Ms. Duncan, I've no doubt you can do anything you set your mind to." The words came out in that insulting way again, and it angered her.

"I will, Mr. Parker, and I don't want your help," she told him. "I've been to Mexico many times. I don't need some rude, arrogant, *insulting* man to watch over me."

As the words left her mouth she wanted to take them back, but she couldn't. She was so infuriated at his attitude.

She couldn't see his face clearly in the moonlight, but she could feel his anger. She instinctively braced herself. She wasn't afraid of him because somehow she knew he wouldn't hit her. She wasn't certain how she knew that, but she did. Maybe it was her experience with Kyle. She was afraid of Kyle because he couldn't control his temper. Jonas had extreme control over everything in his life. She'd only met him a month ago, but intuitively she sensed certain traits about him—like that when he touched a woman it would be with affection and the utmost care. Right now he was angry with her and she'd received the full brunt of that anger with several lashes from his tongue. But that was fine. She could give it right back to him.

"I might be all those things, Ms. Duncan," he said in that infuriating tone. "But I have enough sense to know a scam when I hear it. If you want to play games with Brewster, that's your business. I've made my feelings clear on the whole situation and that's all I have to say." He turned into the September breeze and muttered, "'Night, ma'am," as he walked away.

Abby wanted to laugh and cry at the same time. Even though Jonas was angry with her, he still remembered his manners. She'd never met anyone like him before and she didn't think she ever would again. She inhaled the cool night air. She was very curious about Jonas Parker. Why did he put up with Brewster's ridicule and abuse? Why did he work for a man he seemed to hate? Mr. Brewster had said something about owning Jonas. What did that mean? Her reporter's instinct was on full alert.

"Oh, Jonas, you haven't seen the last of me," she whispered under her breath as she made her way to her car.

WHEN ABBY GOT BACK to the house, she couldn't sleep. She tossed and turned and kept staring at the clock. At six, she grabbed the phone and called Dallas. She had to talk to her friend Holly.

"Hello," a sleepy voice answered.

"Holly, it's Abby."

"Do you know what time it is?"

"Yes, but you're always up early."

"I was out late last night."

"Date or assignment?"

"Assignment."

"I should have guessed." Abby laughed.

"What are you saying?"

"I'm saying we're both dedicated to our work."

"Yeah," Holly said. "But there's this new guy in accounting, and I've got my eye on him." She yawned. "Why are you calling so early?"

"I wanted to run something by you."

"Okay, but I'm not thinking too clearly just yet."

Abby and Holly had been friends since their freshman year in college, and later they had worked at the same newspaper, Abby as a reporter and Holly as a photographer. They lived in the same apartment complex and saw each other daily. Even after Abby had married, they remained close. Abby had told her about writing Mr. Brewster's memoirs and Holly had understood because she knew how much Abby had loved her father. Now Abby explained to her friend Mr. Brewster's odd request.

"Wow," Holly said. "This is totally out of the blue."

"Yes, but I'm going to do it," Abby answered, then asked, "Do you think it's crazy?"

"Not for you. I know how desperately you want to clear your father's name. Just be careful."

"I will, but Mr. Brewster thinks Jonas should go with me."

"The guy with the muscles and unfriendly attitude."

"That's him—the man with 'don't touch' written all over him."

"That's the way you want it, isn't it?"

"Of course" was Abby's quick response.

"You're not saying that with too much enthusiasm. Are you attracted to this man?"

"Oh, please." She started to deny it, then stopped. "Okay, I'll admit there's something there, but it's purely sexual."

"So indulge. You've earned it."

"For heaven's sake, Holly, are you still asleep or what?"

"I must be or I'd never suggest such a thing, hmm?"

They both laughed.

"If you have to do this, do it, but as I said before, be very careful. And if Brewster wants Jonas to go along, let him. What could it hurt? And don't give me that bull about not needing a man. Common sense overrules that notion."

"Oh, Holly, it's so good to talk to you."

"So when are you coming back? Tanya's getting ticked off at her workload and Phil asked if you might return early."

Phil was her editor. He'd granted her a six-week leave of absence, and Abby was going to need every day of that to resolve things in Hope.

"I don't think I can now, but I'll call Phil and explain."

"Okay, and keep me posted on what's happening."

"I will. Now go back to sleep."

"Yeah, right."

After Abby hung up, she sat staring into space. At

least Holly understood why she had to do this. But a tiny doubt lurked in the back of her mind. Was she doing the right thing? Yes, for her father she had to do it. She knew Mr. Brewster was manipulating her. She didn't need Jonas to tell her that. Still, she couldn't let it go. She had to find out the truth.

And now she had to find a way to tell her mother.

CHAPTER THREE

ABBY GOT UP and made her way to the kitchen. As she made coffee, her thoughts ran helter-skelter. Her mother would be upset. How should Abby handle this? Before she could form a plan, her mother walked into the kitchen in her pink flowered robe.

"You're up early," Gail said, and poured a cup of coffee.

"I couldn't sleep," Abby replied.

Gail sat at the table. "You're still not worried that Kyle might come here, are you?"

Abby shook her head and took a seat. Kyle was the furthest thing from her mind. When she first returned home, she'd been afraid that he might follow her, but so far, nothing. Maybe Kyle had gotten on with his life. She hoped so because she had no intention of seeing him again.

"I had this strange dream last night," her mother was saying. "I thought I heard your car leaving and I tried to wake up, but I couldn't. It seemed so real."

Abby squirmed in her chair. God, did her mother have mental telepathy or what? When she was sixteen, she and a friend had skipped school and driven to Brownsville to stand in line for tickets to a rock concert. Somehow her mother had known. The principal hadn't called and notified her of Abby's absence. Her mother just knew by looking at her face.

Surely Abby had matured and learned how to hide those guilty feelings. Maybe not, she conceded. Maturity was no match for her mother's intuition.

She took a sip of coffee. "I did leave last night."

Her mother's hand stopped in mid-motion as she stirred sugar into her coffee. "You did?"

"Yes."

"Where did you go?"

"To the hospital."

A worried look entered Gail's eyes, and Abby hastened to reassure her. "No, there's nothing wrong with me. Mr. Brewster had a heart attack, and a nurse at the hospital called and said he asked to see me."

"Oh." Her mother leaned back. "I guess he wanted to give you some important details on his memoirs."

"No, it wasn't about the memoirs."

"Then, why in the world would he want to see you in the middle of the night?"

Abby fingered her cup. "Mom, do you ever remember hearing about Mr. Brewster having an affair?"

"An affair?" Gail almost choked. "Good Lord, no. Who'd sleep with that old fool?"

"Mr. Brewster's not the most handsome man in the world, but he does have money, and I'm told that's a great aphrodisiac."

Her mother rose and hurried to the sink. "Abigail, where do you get this nonsense? And what does it have to do with why you went to the hospital last night?"

Abby drew a deep breath. "Mr. Brewster says he has a daughter."

Gail whirled around with a shocked look on her face. "A daughter?"

"Yes, he says he had an affair with a Mexican girl that worked in his house over thirty years ago. The girl took the baby and went back to Mexico. Mostly, because he forced her to."

"What has this got to do with you?" her mother asked stiffly.

Abby swallowed hard. "He wants to see her before he dies, and he wants me to go to Mexico to find her."

"You have to be joking."

Abby could hear the anger building in her mother's voice. "Now, Mom, don't get upset until you hear everything I have to say."

Gail folded her arms across her chest. "I'm not sure I want to hear it."

"Mom," Abby implored, hoping for some understanding.

"No, Abby." Gail waved a hand through the air. "You've been on this crusade since your father died, and I know it has something to do with him. I just...just can't take anymore."

"Mom." Abby jumped up and put an arm around her. "Come, sit down and I'll explain."

Gail sat, and Abby faced her. "Yes, it's about Daddy."

Gail threw up both her hands. "I knew it."

"Listen to me," Abby begged. "If I find his daughter, Mr. Brewster will tell me why he fired Dad."

"Abby, Abby." Gail groaned in frustration.

"Don't you want to know?"

Gail looked directly at her. "What good will it do? It won't bring him back."

"We'll know the truth, and no one can ever again say that Abe Duncan embezzled funds from Simon Brewster."

"No one cares about that, but you."

"Don't you care?"

"I want Abe to rest in peace."

"But he's not. Can't you see that? There's a cloud over his grave, and I won't stop until I clear his name."

Gail heaved a big sigh. "I refuse to let you do this."

"What?" Abby drew back in disbelief.

"I will not allow you to go into Mexico to find this…this girl. It's crazy and dangerous."

"I'm thirty years old and I don't need your permission," Abby told her, though it took all her strength to say those words. She didn't want to hurt her mother, but this was Abby's choice.

Gail rose in a jerky movement. "This is how Simon Brewster has you talking to your mother."

"Mom, please try to understand."

"That's what I'm asking of you, Abigail."

Abby took a long breath. "I know you're worried and—"

"That's an understatement. Going to Mexico alone to find…to find—

Abby broke in. "Mr. Brewster wants Jonas Parker to go with me." Abby had no idea why she said that. It just seemed to slip out.

"Jonas Parker!" Gail screeched so high, Abby feared the windowpanes were in danger of cracking.

"What's wrong with Jonas?"

"If you have to ask that question, then you haven't learned anything by living away from home."

"What's wrong with Jonas?" she persisted, wanting to get everything out in the open.

"He lived on the streets when he was a kid. His parents were drunks and they didn't care where he was. Jonas has been in trouble with the law since he was eight years old. He wouldn't go to school. He wouldn't do anything he was supposed to. He was wild and rebellious, and I won't have my daughter associating with people like him."

Abby bit her tongue to keep words from tumbling out. She recognized that her mother was concerned, so she let the last remark pass. "Jonas has a past. So what? He seems to have matured. He has a good job and he's responsible and dedicated. All the workers at Brewster Farms are crazy about him."

"Especially the women," Gail said testily.

Abby inhaled deeply, knowing exactly what her mother was getting at. "Yes, I've noticed that Jonas has an animal magnetism that attracts women. But I'm not looking for a man or that kind of relationship. After what Kyle did to me, I'd just as soon coast for a while. The only thing I'm interested in is finding Mr. Brewster's daughter so I can hear what he has to say about Daddy."

"Brewster has agreed to tell you the truth?" Gail asked in a disbelieving tone.

"Yes."

"And you trust him?"

"No, but I'll make sure he keeps his end of the bargain."

"Abby." Gail sighed. "Nobody gets around

Brewster. He's in control at all times. If you think otherwise, you're fooling yourself."

Abby stood and kissed her mom's cheek. "I know what I'm doing. Trust me. Now, I've got to get dressed." She started to walk away.

"Abby," Gail said.

Abby stopped.

"Please don't get involved in this crazy scheme."

Abby let out a long regretful groan. "Mom, don't do this to me."

"What? Try to make you see sense? I'm your mother. That's what I do. But it's never worked in the past, has it. You've always been so headstrong, making quick decisions without considering the consequences."

Abby knew exactly what her mother was talking about—her quick decision to marry Kyle. Still, she couldn't give in to her mother's wishes. Something inside Abby wouldn't let the past go. She couldn't explain it to Gail. She couldn't even explain it to herself. All she knew was that she had made a deal with Simon Brewster and she had to keep it.

When Abby didn't speak, Gail entreated, "Let it go, Abby. Just let it go."

Abby bit her lip, then said, "I'm sorry, Mom. I can't."

AN HOUR LATER Abby was on her way to her cousin's office. Earl Turner was a lawyer, and she needed his help. Of course, she'd have to talk him into it, which she hoped wouldn't take long.

Earl was the son of her mother's sister and five years older than Abby. They weren't close, but they were family. Earl was the proverbial mama's boy.

He had never married and still lived with his mother.
People teased him that he got his law degree through
correspondence school because his mother wouldn't
allow him to leave home. In actual fact, he'd com-
muted to college and now he was the only lawyer in
this small town. She couldn't imagine why he'd
never broken free and gone to a bigger city, but then,
understanding Earl wasn't one of her top priorities.

Before Abby could enter Earl's office, her friend
Brenda came out of her beauty shop next door. They
embraced.

"It was so good seeing everyone the other night,
wasn't it?" Brenda asked, referring to the school
reunion. Abby had reluctantly attended. Brenda's
brown hair had blond highlights and hung in a soft
style around her face, which enhanced her brown
eyes.

"Yes, it was," Abby admitted, glad she hadn't lost
touch with her friends from high school.

"I can't believe we're all still around here. You're
the only one who ventured to the big city chasing
that dream of yours."

Abby brushed her hair back. "Well, the dream
blew up in my face."

"You're not the first one of us to get a divorce.
Candy, Deb and Miles have one behind them, and
Barry's on wife number three. Luckily, Stuart and I
are still together." Brenda and Stuart had been
sweethearts since eighth grade and they'd married
right out of high school. Brenda had gone to beauty
school, and Stuart had taken a job at Brewster Farms.

"Sometimes, just sometimes," Brenda continued,
"after a day in the shop and running kids here and
there, then going home to cleaning and cooking, I

wonder what it would be like to have a life like yours.''

Abby smiled. "Not nearly as fulfilling as yours. Being a wife and mother has to be very rewarding.''

"I tell myself that, but when Stuart's out with the guys or working late for Jonas, I get a little put out.'' Brenda glanced at her watch. "I've got to go. My youngest has an earache, and I have to get her to the doctor. You have to come and have dinner with us one night. You won't believe how the kids have grown.''

"I will—just call me.''

"Okay,'' Brenda shouted as she hurried to her van.

Abby stood for a moment lost in thought. There was something about coming home and seeing old friends that made one look back. No matter what choices she'd made in life, those friends and times would always be a part of her. Like Brenda, she wondered what her life would have been like if she'd made different decisions. She, too, had wanted to be a wife and mother, but only after she had established her career and was able to enjoy a family. Now, she wondered if it was too late.

ABBY WALKED SLOWLY into Earl's office, which was two rooms in an old building on the main strip in downtown Hope. Not that Hope had much of a downtown—a bank, grocery store, a couple of gas stations, a school, several churches and the clinic and hospital that Mr. Brewster had built with his own money so there would be some medical services in the area. Hope was just a stop in the road before the international bridge, but it was home.

There wasn't a secretary, so Abby went through to Earl's office. He was in his chair reading a newspaper, his feet propped on the edge of his desk. The paper covered his face, but his bald head glistened under the fluorescent lights.

"Good morning, Earl," she said brightly, and pulled a chair forward.

Earl swung his feet to the floor and laid the paper aside. Pushing his glasses up the bridge of his nose, he replied, "Abby, I was thinking of dropping by to see you."

"You were?" She was thrown for a second. Earl wasn't much of a conversationalist.

"Yeah, I need a woman's opinion."

"On what?"

He fidgeted with a pencil on his desk. "Well...I met this woman and I'm...I'm crazy about her." All the while he talked he looked at the pencil, not at Abby.

"That's great, Earl."

Shyly, he raised his green eyes. "You think so?"

"Earl." She sighed. "Have you looked at your driver's license lately?"

He frowned. "What?"

"Look at the date of birth. It will tell you that you're way overdue for a serious relationship."

"Aw, shucks, Abby, it's not that simple."

"Why not?"

"Because Mother doesn't know I've been seeing Carol. She lives in McAllen and works for an attorney. I've been helping him with legal matters in the valley, and Carol and I...well, you know." His face actually glowed a vivid pink.

"I don't see a problem," Abby said.

"Mother doesn't know I've been seeing her," he repeated.

"Still don't see a problem."

"Carol has a five-year-old daughter."

Big problem. Aunt Sybil was going to have a fit.

"If you care for this woman and the child, tell Aunt Sybil and don't give her a chance to talk you out of it. Just do it, like the saying goes."

"You see things so realistically, but I'm all that Mother has and I—"

"Earl, you talk as if Aunt Sybil is in her eighties. She's fifty-nine and teaches school. She drives and plays bridge on Wednesdays and Saturdays. It's not like she's housebound and depends on you for everything."

"But—"

"And she's not alone. She has a brother, a sister and other relatives that live in Hope."

"Yes, yes, she does." Earl was gaining confidence. "She might even like Carol and her daughter."

"That's it, Earl, go for the brass ring or the gold ring or whatever the hell it's called. Go for it."

He smiled weakly. "You're good for my ego."

She scooted forward. "Good, because I came in here for a favor."

"Need a lawyer, huh?"

"Something like that," she admitted, and told him what she wanted him to do. His eyes grew bigger and bigger, and any minute she thought they would pop out onto his desk. He finally pulled out a handkerchief and wiped sweat from his forehead.

"I don't know, Abby, I don't like going against Brewster."

"You won't be going against him," she assured him. "You'll just be helping me."

"I don't know."

"I promise that Simon Brewster won't annihilate you."

"You can't promise that."

"Earl, just help me, okay?" She couldn't keep the aggravation out of her voice.

Earl frowned, and she wanted to reach across the desk and smack him. "Tell you what." She tried another tactic. "If you help me with Mr. Brewster, I'll help you with Aunt Sybil."

Earl smiled his partial smile. "That won't work," he told her. "Since your divorce, Mother thinks you're a loose woman."

She almost screeched "What!" in that high-pitched voice she'd heard her mother use earlier. But she immediately calmed herself. She didn't care what Aunt Sybil thought. She was a narrow-minded, spiteful person. *But you do care,* that little voice inside her whispered. A woman who had never failed—who had achieved everything she'd ever wanted—was now a failure. It took a moment to recover, then her spirit came soaring back.

She *wasn't* a loose woman. Where had that come from? She opened her mouth to give Earl her scathing opinion, when he spoke.

"Don't get all worked up."

"Okay, Earl, you help me, and I won't rip out your mother's tongue by the roots."

"Did anyone ever tell you that you're volatile?"

"Yes."

"Heavens, I wish I had some of your grit."

"If you did, you'd have a divorce behind you and an aunt who thinks you're loose."

He tried his smile again. "All right, I'll help you, but if things get rough, I'm gone."

"Coward."

"Yeah, and I have a yellow stripe down my back to prove it."

"Just keep your clothes on so no one will see it." She fished in her purse for her cell phone and called the hospital.

"You make me smile, Abby."

"Remember that and we'll get through this."

She talked to a nurse and told her to inform Mr. Brewster that she was on her way. She dropped the phone into her purse and glanced at Earl. "Follow me to the hospital. It's show time."

JONAS STOOD AT THE FOOT of Brewster's bed, trying to figure out this man he'd known for years, but he knew he was wasting his time. There was no figuring out Brewster.

"What are you doing here?" Brewster barked when he noticed him. "Don't you have trucks to load?"

"Stuart and Juan are supervising the loading, and Perry's in the office until noon. He has that computer class this afternoon and tomorrow. They can handle things until I get back."

Brewster pushed a button and raised his bed slightly. A nurse immediately adjusted his pillow. "I'm not sure about Perry. He doesn't seem to be working out. Fire him and start looking for another accountant."

Jonas took a patient breath. He had been expecting

this. It had been the pattern since Abe left. Jonas had decided he wasn't going through this again.

"I'm not firing Perry. He's a good accountant, and he's returned to Hope with his family to be near his aging parents. He needs the job, and I trust him. Besides, you just paid for these computer courses."

Brewster's eyes narrowed. "You take orders from me—or have you forgotten?"

"Not for a minute," Jonas answered swiftly. "If you want to fire Perry, you'll have to do it yourself and also find someone to replace him. I'm not doing it again."

"You're getting too big for your boots, boy."

"You can always fire me."

"You'd like that, wouldn't you," Brewster asked smugly. "But it's not gonna happen." He paused, then asked, "So you trust this Perry?"

"Yes," Jonas replied.

"I'll think about it" was the response. "Now, I want to talk about something else."

"Unless it's important, I want to get back to the loading docks."

"Yes, dammit, it's important. I want you to go with Abigail to Mexico."

Jonas gritted his teeth. "I thought I made my position very clear on that subject."

"Yes, you did," Brewster acknowledged sardonically. "Now I'm going to make mine clear. Bottom line—you're going. You can buck it, fight it all you want, but you're going."

Jonas gritted his teeth harder. But they both knew he'd give in. It was part of their agreement, and Jonas always tried to live up to his word. This time, though, it wasn't easy.

Brewster broke into his thoughts. "I've seen the way you look at her, Jonas. She's a very nice-looking woman, and I don't want her crossing the border alone."

Jonas met Brewster's eyes. "Abigail Duncan can take care of herself," he said in a hard tone.

"Yes, yes, she can," Brewster acknowledged. "But you're still going."

Jonas's eyes never wavered. "Then, why get her involved? I can find the girl on my own."

"Dammit, Jonas, do you have to question everything I tell you?" Brewster snapped. "Abigail has to be there. It's the ending to my book, and I want her to witness it firsthand."

"I see." Jonas sighed. "Well, I guess that makes sense. Still—"

"Go with Abigail and find Delores, and get back as fast as you can."

If he had to do this, Jonas reasoned—and there didn't seem to be a way out—then he would at least get something out of Brewster. "I'm still not sure there is a daughter," Jonas said, "but since you insist, I'll go on two conditions."

"Don't try to bargain with me, Jonas."

Jonas continued. "I want a raise for Stuart and Juan. They haven't had one in two years. And Perry stays."

Brewster rubbed the metal bars on the bed. "Is that it?"

"That's it."

"Don't you want a raise for yourself?"

"You pay me a good salary. I have no complaints."

There was a long pause. Jonas waited.

Finally Brewster said, "Okay, consider it done, but I want you to stay until Frank, my lawyer, and Abigail get here."

This was too easy, Jonas thought. Brewster never gave in without an argument. What was he up to? Jonas didn't have a clue, so he concentrated on the positive side. If he could keep his accountant, it would be worth putting up with Ms. Duncan.

But he wasn't looking forward to it.

As Abby and Earl walked down the corridor to Mr. Brewster's room, Abby could hear Earl breathing. She stopped to talk to him, then sighed. "Earl, there's sweat on your brow."

He whipped out a handkerchief and mopped his face. "I'm sorry. I'm nervous."

"There's no need to be," she assured him. "All you have to do is read a piece of paper. I'll do all the talking."

"Suits me fine."

"Ready?"

"I guess so."

Abby tapped on the door, and a nurse let them in. Mr. Brewster was in a special unit with round-the-clock private nurses. Today, in addition to the nurse and the patient, there were two other people in the room. A man she didn't recognize and Jonas.

As she stared into Jonas's turbulent eyes, something kicked awake in her lower stomach. She knew exactly what it was—desire. She had told her mother that she could coast along without those feelings, but when she looked at Jonas she felt as if she were falling into a void of pure need. Hell, maybe she *was* a loose woman.

"Abigail, I'm glad you're here." Mr. Brewster's voice brought her sanity back. "This is Frank Foster, my attorney. He's from McAllen."

"Mr. Foster." Abby acknowledged the introduction at the same time that Mr. Brewster noticed Earl.

"Turner, what are you doing here?"

"Earl is my attorney," Abby put in quickly, "I felt I needed one."

"Fine," Mr. Brewster said, to her surprise. "I dictated the letter to Frank earlier this morning and it's now in his possession. When you return, he'll hand it over to you."

"How can I be sure the letter isn't bogus?"

"You have to trust me."

Abby shook her head. "No, I can't do that. This is too important. I want Earl to read the letter to make sure that you have kept your word."

Mr. Brewster grunted, and the nurse quickly checked the machines attached to him. Then he spoke, "Turner's your cousin. How can I trust that he won't tell you what's in the letter?"

"Earl is my guarantee that the letter is real. That's all."

Brewster thought for a minute. "Okay, he can read part of it, but I don't want him reading the crucial information."

"Fine," Abby agreed.

Brewster turned to Foster. "There's a room down the hall. Take Turner and let him see a portion of the letter."

"Yes, sir," Frank said, picking up his briefcase and heading for the door.

"Turner," Mr. Brewster called, before Earl left the room.

Earl stopped.

"If you tell Abigail anything, I'll make sure you never work in this town or anywhere else again. Do you get my drift?"

"Y-yes, sir," Earl stuttered, and mopped his forehead. Abby feared he was on the verge of melting into his shoes and she'd have to carry him out of here in a wad.

"You'd better," Mr. Brewster warned, as Earl made his escape.

"If that's all, I've got to get back to the office," Jonas said tightly.

"No, dammit," Mr. Brewster bellowed. "I want you to talk to Abigail."

"About what?" Abby spoke up.

"Jonas is going with you," Mr. Brewster informed her.

Abby glanced at Jonas, saw that stubborn light in his eyes and knew he hadn't relented on his own. Mr. Brewster had forced him. "When did this happen?"

"Just now," Mr. Brewster answered.

"Why? He doesn't want to go, and I don't need him to—"

"Doesn't matter what either one of you wants," Brewster broke in. "He's going."

"Then, he can go alone," Abby shot back. "There's no need for me to be there."

"Goddammit, girl, you're trying my patience," Brewster shouted. "You have to be there. You're writing my memoirs. It's the ending—or haven't you guessed that, yet?"

Was that what this was all about? An ending to his book? Or did he really want to see his daughter? Abby wasn't sure anymore.

"And it's the only way you'll find out about your father—or have you forgotten that?" he asked grumpily.

For a moment Abby had lost sight of her main goal. She suddenly remembered Holly's words about it being bull that she didn't need a man. Maybe she was carrying it a little too far. So what if Jonas went with her. She'd get a chance to learn more about his situation with Mr. Brewster, and she was becoming more curious by the second. She would have sworn that Jonas would never change his mind. What kind of hold did Mr. Brewster have over him?

She suddenly realized they were waiting for her answer. She swallowed. "No, no, I haven't forgotten."

"Good, because I'm tired of all this bickering," Mr. Brewster said in a frustrated tone. "You two can work out the details."

Jonas put his hat on his head. "I've got work to do." With that he walked out the door.

"Insufferable bastard," Mr. Brewster muttered. "But his bark is worse than his bite."

Abby stared at the door. "Really, I hadn't noticed."

"Jonas is a hard person to get to know, but he's very loyal."

Abby glanced back at the elderly man. "I see. So how did you get him to change his mind?"

"You'll have to ask him."

She intended to. Yes, she definitely intended to find out what kind of hold Mr. Brewster had on Jonas.

As she pondered that thought, Earl returned and said the letter was authentic. There was information concerning her father and his job at Brewster Farms. It was what Abby wanted to hear. Now she faced the biggest challenge of her life—finding Mr. Brewster's daughter.

Mr. Brewster seemed pleased, and Abby left with Earl, feeling a sense of elation. She didn't know why, unless insanity had completely taken over her mind.

Before Earl got into his car, Abby stopped him. "Could you give me a hint as to what's in the letter?" She didn't want to cause Earl any problems. She was hoping for a clue to justify what she was doing.

"I'm not gonna slit my throat" was his answer. "Not even for you. Just be careful. Very careful."

"I will," she said. "And thanks. I realize this was hard for you."

"Abby, I—" He seemed to reconsider, and instead said, "Don't do this alone. Hire an investigator or something."

Abby rolled her eyes. "Men. You're all alike. Mr. Brewster is insisting that Jonas go with me."

"That's good," he said.

"No, it isn't," she retorted. "I'm not putting up with Jonas's arrogant attitude, and I intend to tell him so."

"Abby…"

But Abby wasn't listening. She got into her car and headed straight for Jonas's office. They had to get a few things straight.

CHAPTER FOUR

STANDING AT HIS WINDOW, Jonas saw her drive up in a white Accord. She slid out of the vehicle in the graceful movement he was beginning to associate with her. She wore tan slacks and a tan sleeveless top. The slacks covered long gorgeous legs, which he had glimpsed several times during the past month. The top emphasized her slender arms, and rounded breasts that drew his attention like a magnet. The blond hair and green eyes completed a package that his hands ached to unwrap. As long as he knew that and no one else did, especially Abby, everything would be fine.

Soon she'd tire of this absurd quest and go back to Dallas where she belonged. As the thought crossed his mind, he recognized it was wishful thinking. He'd already seen that stubborn streak in her and he knew she'd see this through to the bitter end. And now he was caught right in the middle of the whole blasted mess. A place he didn't want to be…a place he'd sworn he wouldn't be. But Brewster was in control—totally. Jonas had given him that control when he was fifteen, and he couldn't change things now. He fought it at times, but he'd learned early on that fighting was futile. He wished he knew what Brewster was up to, though. There was little doubt in Jonas's mind that the old man was up to something and Abigail Duncan was just a pawn. Trying to get her to see that was a waste of Jonas's time, so he might as well accept the inevitable.

ABBY WALKED INSIDE. The big room held three desks and rows of filing cabinets. There was an inner office that she knew belonged to Jonas. Every high-tech innovation was available—computers, fax machines, copiers and a few pieces of equipment she didn't even recognize. In the way of decor, the place was sadly lacking—right down to the exposed concrete under her feet.

Her eyes settled on the desk in the corner...the one her father had occupied for so many years. She felt a tightness in her chest. Someone else's things were on the surface, but she could still feel Abe's presence, his calmness, and she knew she was doing the right thing. No one could stop her now. Not even Jonas's attitude.

Glancing around, she spotted him at the window. "Could I speak with you?"

"No" was the quick answer, as he turned and went into his office.

Undaunted by the brisk manner, Abby followed. "We have to talk."

"I can't right now. I'm real busy." His voice was abrupt and final.

She chewed on her lower lip. *Immovable object.* She now knew exactly what that meant. Well, she didn't need Jonas Parker.

"I don't want or need you to go. I can do this by myself." She eyed him thoughtfully, as he shuffled papers on his desk. "I'm just wondering how he got you to change your mind. Last night you were vehemently against it. And today, just like that—'' she snapped her fingers ''—you agreed to go.''

He kept shuffling the papers as if she hadn't spoken.

''Mr. Brewster has something on you, doesn't he?''

He raised his head, his brown eyes so dark that she could feel their heat. ''That's why you take crap from him. That's why you continue to stay under such unpleasant conditions.'' She paused, then asked, ''What does he have on you?''

Jonas picked up a clipboard and came around his desk. ''As I said, I got work to do.'' The words came out curt, and she knew she wasn't going to get anything out of him...today. She would eventually, she vowed.

''I need the keys to the file room,'' she said, before he could leave the room. ''Mr. Brewster said you had them. I'm looking for Delores Alvarez's family's address.''

He walked back, opened a drawer, threw keys on the desk and pointed down a hall. ''Second door on the right and it's not air-conditioned.''

She picked up the keys. ''Is that supposed to deter me?''

''A hurricane wouldn't deter you, Ms. Duncan.''

So they were back to ''Ms. Duncan.'' It made her want to smack his face.

What was wrong with her? She'd wanted to smack Earl earlier and now she wanted to hit Jonas. That wasn't her. She didn't like hitting. Even when Kyle had hit her, she hadn't hit him back. Because she'd never hit anyone in her life. So why the sudden urges? Urges! That's all they were. Urges brought on by the trauma of her father's death and her divorce. Did that make sense? No, nothing made sense to her these days—especially her interest in Jonas.

She favored men in tailored suits with manners and a sense of humor. Jonas was as far removed from that as one could get. He probably didn't even own a suit, and his sense of humor was nonexistent. He did have good manners, though. Oh hell, she needed to get a grip.

Without a word, she turned and hurried to the file room. She looked at the key ring. There had to be twenty keys on it. Which one?

"It's the third key," said a familiar voice. She glanced over her shoulder and saw Jonas standing behind her with a chair in his hands. "You have to prop the door open with a chair. The lock is old, and if the door closes, you'll lock yourself in."

"Thank you kindly for the information and the chair," she quipped sarcastically.

"No problem," he snapped, and went into the warehouse.

For the next three hours she searched cabinet after cabinet, looking for the name Alvarez. She had never realized how many people had worked at Brewster Farms over the years—thousands, all dependent on Mr. Brewster for a living. Some workers were permanent legal workers, some seasonal, some migrant. Most were Mexican, and she suspected a lot were illegals. Every name imaginable was in the files. She found several Alvarezes, but no Delores. She grew tired and hungry and decided to go home for a while.

Jonas wasn't in the office, so she locked the door and took the keys with her. She had a sandwich and iced tea, then wrote her mom a note saying not to wait up for her. Her mother was a schoolteacher and wouldn't be home until later in the day.

When Abby arrived back at Brewster Farms, she saw Edna's car at the mansion. That was one woman Abby planned to avoid. When Edna, Jules and Darby found out what she was doing, they were going to be furious. A long-lost daughter could ruin their plans for the future.

When she entered the office, Jonas wasn't there. He must be working on the farm somewhere. Avoiding her, she decided, which she didn't mind. She was sure he didn't do the actual labor. He was the overseer who made sure all the vegetables and fruits were picked, packed and shipped on time. Again she wondered how he'd come to work for Mr. Brewster. He certainly didn't want to talk about it. He'd made that painfully clear.

She unlocked the door, propped it open and went back to her task, quickly losing track of time. Workers in the warehouse were hooting and hollering. They must have finished loading the trucks, she thought idly. Then her eyes were suddenly glued to the name she'd been searching for. She had finally found Delores Alvarez's file. Thank God. Excitement darted through her as she sat on the concrete floor and read through its contents. Now she had the address. Delores's parents lived across the border in Nuevo Hope, Mexico. If they still lived there, it should be easy to locate them or someone who knew Delores. She could do this without too much of a problem.

She glanced at her watch and saw that it was almost seven o'clock. Time to go home. As she rose, she heard a *click*. She whirled in horror and stared at the closed door. She ran over and tried to open it. It was locked tight. No worry, she told herself, the keys were in her pocket. She withdrew them and noticed there was no keyhole on the inside. Damn! She beat on the door with her fist.

"Hey, I'm still in here. Hey. Is anybody out there? Help."

Only silence met her frantic cry, and she sank to the floor. *Don't panic,* she kept repeating to herself silently. Someone must have assumed she'd left. No one could see her sitting behind the cabinets. A simple mistake. That's all. Someone would find her. She just had to wait. But she was so thirsty. She licked her dry lips as anger built inside her.

Maybe it hadn't been a mistake. Had Jonas done this to scare her? No, he wouldn't use that kind of tactic. He told her to her face how he felt and didn't mince words. So who had locked her in? Where was everybody? She began to beat on the door again.

"Help. Help. Let me out of here."

JONAS SAT in Mick's Tavern downing Coke. He'd spent most of the afternoon in the sheriff's office getting two of his workers out of jail. Lupe and Miguel were two young hotheads after the same girl. They had gotten into a fight and someone had called the sheriff. Jonas would have left their sorry asses in jail, but he had a crop to pick and he needed them. Besides, they were good boys, who'd simply let their raging hormones get the better of them.

They were eighteen and illegal. That's why the sheriff had called Jonas instead of having them deported. The sheriff never interfered with anything that went on at Brewster Farms. A person working for Brewster only had to worry about Border Patrol and Immigration. Brewster didn't have any control over those departments.

At least the afternoon's activities had kept Jonas busy and away from Abigail Duncan. That was one obstinate, intuitive woman, and he wasn't sure how he was going to handle the next couple of days. He'd given Brewster his word, so there was no way out. But Jonas had a bad feeling about the whole thing, and her prying didn't help. The woman never knew when to stop. And that wasn't the worst of it. He didn't like the way she made him feel. She threatened the control he had worked hard to master. As long as he could stay away from her, everything was fine. But now...

"Drowning your sorrows in Coke, Jonas?" Mick asked as he took a seat.

"Just drowning my thirst."

"You got a different kind of thirst."

Jonas stared at him over the rim of his can. "You think you know me?"

"Sure do, my friend. I've known you since you were a kid, and I can tell you exactly what you're thinking and feeling."

Mick was right. He'd been Jonas's only friend for a long time. "So what am I thinking and feeling?" Jonas asked slowly.

"Abigail Duncan has you all riled up. Ain't seen you this troubled since—"

"Leave it alone, Mick."

At the tone in Jonas's voice, Mick shifted gears. "Brewster has a daughter? Ha."

Jonas's eyes narrowed. "Where did you hear that?" he asked sharply, then answered his own question. "Oh, yeah, you have a daughter and a sister-in-law who work in the hospital. If Brewster finds out they're spreading rumors, they could lose their jobs."

"But he won't find out, will he, my friend?"

Jonas leaned across the table. "Tell them to keep their mouths shut." He settled back in his chair. "Besides, I'm not sure the story is true."

"You got doubts about Brewster?"

"Yep, and there ain't a thing I can do about it."

"What do you want to do?"

"Nothing" was his quick answer. "I don't want anything to do with the damn situation, but Brewster is insisting that I go with her."

"Ah." Mick nodded, chewing thoughtfully on his cigar. "If Brewster is sending you, what does he need the Duncan woman for?"

Jonas twisted the Coke can. "It has to do with the memoirs she's writing. Finding the long-lost daughter is going to be the big ending, and he wants her there to witness all the little details."

"I see." Mick nodded again. "And you're going along as a bodyguard."

"Something like that, but Ms. Duncan doesn't want my help."

"But you'll go, anyway."

"Yeah." He swallowed some Coke. "I told Brewster I would."

"It's probably not a bad idea." Mick rubbed his chin. "A woman alone in Mexico, poking her nose into family matters—it could get dangerous."

Jonas knew that. Mexicans had a strong sense of family, and they didn't like outsiders interfering.

Mick stood. "I gotta get back to work." He patted Jonas on the shoulder. "Good luck, my friend."

As Mick walked away, Jonas watched the activity in the bar. It was after nine and the place was filling up. Jim Colson, the bank president, was dancing with Teresa Gomez. Their bodies were welded together, and soon they'd be in one of Mick's rooms upstairs. Jim had a wife and three kids, and Sunday morning he'd be on the front pew in church singing his praises to the Lord. Jonas, who'd never been part of a real family, didn't understand a man who was willing to jeopardize everything he had.

Of course, no one ever breathed a word of Jim's infidelities. His bank owned the mortgages on most of the homes and titles to most of the vehicles in this town. And Brewster owned the bank. For the first time, Jonas wondered if Brewster really *had* had an affair with a Mexican girl. It wasn't outside the realm of possibility, he supposed.

Workers were piling into the bar to drink, dance and have a good time. It didn't matter that they had to work tomorrow. They lived for the moment. Jonas thought that was a damn good idea. Maybe Jim had the right idea, too. Tomorrow was a crapshoot, anyway.

He stood and laid some bills on the table. "G'night Mick. It's been a long day."

"Jonas."

Jonas fitted his hat on his head and glanced at Mick.

"Don't be so down about this. You'll spend time with a pretty woman and that ain't bad. It's the best way I know to get rid of those tight muscles."

Jonas didn't respond. He just walked outside to his

truck. But he knew what Mick was suggesting. Dammit, he wasn't listening to Mick.

When he reached the office, he saw her car parked in front. That crazy woman. She was still searching through the files. Well, she could search until the cows came home. He was going to bed. He headed for the outside staircase that led to his apartment over the warehouse. He had built it twelve years ago with Brewster's approval. He'd gotten tired of sleeping on a cot in a storeroom.

As he stepped inside, a slight smile eased across his face. His home. The only home in which he'd ever had his own bedroom and bath—a luxury that made him feel rich.

He stripped off of his clothes and went for the shower. Afterward he wrapped a towel around his waist and fell across his king-size bed. He needed sleep to refresh his mind and body, but the natural remedy eluded him. Abigail Duncan kept intruding, with her green eyes, blond hair and tempting smile.

Go away, Abigail Duncan. Go away!

THE SMALL LIGHTBULB grew dimmer and dimmer, and the heat began to build in the confines of the closed room. Abby struggled to breathe normally, but she felt as if she was suffocating, the walls closing in on her. Her body was sweaty and her nerves were stretched tight with fear. Beating on the door had proven fruitless. No one had come to her aid. She had the horrible feeling that she'd have to stay in the room until morning. Her throat was dry, and she desperately needed water. Where the hell was Jonas?

She lay on the dirty concrete with her nose to the crack beneath the door. The minuscule amount of fresh air helped her breathing. Oh God, oh God, she couldn't keep this up. *Please, someone help me. Don't let me suffocate.*

AT ONE O'CLOCK Jonas was still awake. In an angry movement, he jerked to his feet. Damn woman was now interfering with his sleep. He hurried to the living room and looked out the window to the parking area in front of the office. Goddammit, her car was still there. He could see it clearly in the moonlight. This was too much. She was getting her ass out of there and going home. He grabbed a pair of jeans and slipped into them. He didn't bother with shoes or a shirt.

He charged into the office in a fury. Then he saw the closed door, and an uneasy feeling came over him. Had she left with someone? He noticed the shallow light emanating from beneath the door. Nah, she couldn't be in there with the door shut, he told himself. She had more sense than that. But he couldn't shake that uneasy feeling. He walked to the door and pounded on it with his palm.

"Abby, are you in there?"

Abby raised her head. Was she dreaming or was that Jonas's voice? "Y-es, yes," she tried to scream, but her throat was so dry the words came out as a croak.

Jonas's heart stopped when he heard the pitiful sound. What in the hell had happened? He'd deal with that later. First he had to get her out of there.

"Where are the keys?" he asked, praying that she didn't have them on her.

"In my pocket."

"Dammit."

"Jonas," she called feebly. "Please...help me. I...can't breathe."

"Hold on," he shouted.

"Hurry, please."

His heart jackknifed into his throat, and he ran into the warehouse. He found a crowbar and a hammer. It took him about a minute to pry the lock apart, but it felt like an hour.

Abby heard him beating on the outside, and she tried to get to her feet. But she couldn't seem to move.

Finally the door swung open, and precious air gushed into her aching lungs. Gulping breath after breath, her gaze traveled from his bare feet, to the long legs encased in tight jeans, to the naked chest with swirls of brown hair, to his broad shoulders, then to the darkened eyes that were staring down at her with a worried look. He was like a Greek mythological god coming to her rescue.

Jonas dropped to his knees beside her. "Are you hurt? Can you get up?"

She was still lying on her stomach, unable to muster enough strength to do anything else.

"I...I..." She couldn't find words and felt like a complete idiot.

He rolled her over, scooped her into his arms and carried her into his office. She rested against his hard-muscled chest. Where did he get those muscles? Jonas must do more work than she gave him credit for, because she knew he wasn't the workout-in-the-gym type. A tangy, fresh masculine scent greeted her tired senses. If she could just stay like this until—

Jonas sat her gently in his chair, bringing that thought to a screeching halt. She realized her clothes were soaking wet from sweat, as was her hair, which hung in rattails. She must look awful. Jonas didn't seem to notice. He was gazing at her with... Was that concern? Was he worried about her?

"Are you all right?" he asked in a gentle tone, and she knew that he was. There was a heart in that beautiful chest. Oh, yes!

She licked dry lips. "Could I have some water, please?"

He moved to the small refrigerator in the corner and grabbed a bottle of water. With one twist of his strong hand, the cap came off, and he handed her the bottle. She drank thirstily, then rested the cool plastic against her cheek.

"Thank you," she said. "It's cold. That's good. I'm so hot and..."

"You're probably dehydrated."

She glanced down at her soaked clothes. "Yeah, I think I lost a gallon of fluid."

He leaned against his desk and folded his arms across his naked torso. His muscles bulged, and her eyes were mesmerized by the action.

"What happened, Abby?" he asked in his deep, husky voice. He said her name just the way she had wanted him to, the way she had dreamed he could— his voice was sensitive, caring and filled with passionate undertones that made her envision.... Damn, was she light-headed? Jonas Parker didn't want anything to do with her, and she liked it that way. So what was wrong with her?

She took a gulp of water and gathered her wits. "I'm not sure," she replied. "I was sitting on the floor behind one of the filing cabinets reading Delores Alvarez's file, when I heard the door shut. I guess someone thought I had gone home.''

"Your car is outside," he reminded her.

"Oh, yes." He'd made short work of that logic. Now she had to consider the other possibility. "You think someone closed it on purpose?"

Jonas nodded and hoped she was getting the message. Someone didn't want her to find Delores Alvarez.

"Who would do that?" she asked.

He had to be honest with her. "I told you that when you start digging into the past, you'd better be able to handle the consequences. And there are a lot of people who won't want you to find this...this daughter."

She thought for a minute. "I went home and got something to eat and drink. When I came back, I saw Edna Kline's car at the mansion. Maybe she saw mine, too."

"She's certainly one person who wouldn't want a daughter to surface. I'll have a talk with her and try to sort this out."

An obstinate light entered her eyes. "I appreciate the offer, but I can talk to her myself."

"Under the circumstances, I think it would be best if I did."

She swallowed more water. He was right. Edna disliked her and probably wouldn't tell her a thing. For the first time, the idea of accepting Jonas's help appealed to her.

"Thank you," she said appreciatively. "How do you plan to handle it?"

"Don't ask so many damn questions."

"It's the only way to get answers, and you just

saved me from suffocating to death. Don't I owe you my firstborn or something?''

He grinned. He actually grinned. And the effect was mind-boggling. It softened his masculine features and made him seem more approachable.

"I don't want your firstborn," he answered with that grin still on his lips. Then his face sobered. "What I want, you're not willing to give."

"How do you know until you ask?"

Your body, Abby. I want to enjoy every inch of your gorgeous body.

Of course, he didn't say that. What came out of his mouth was "Give up this crazy quest to find this fictional daughter."

She pushed damp hair away from her face. "Jonas, don't ask that of me."

He looked directly into her eyes. "Think about this, Abby. Someone locked you in that room for a reason—to scare you, and it's only a start."

"I can take a little scaring," she said stubbornly.

"Then, why are you still trembling?"

She tried to squelch the tremors inside her, but without much success. She'd hoped that he hadn't noticed, but her body had been pressed against his. He could hardly miss the fact that she was a quivering mass of nerves.

"I...I..." Even to her own ears she sounded like a babbling idiot.

He took the empty bottle out of her shaking fingers. "Give it up, Abby. Go back to Dallas and get on with your life. It's not worth all this."

She was so tired of people telling her what she should do. Anger pumped through her veins, and the trembling eased immediately. "Stop saying that," she said. "You have no idea how I feel."

"I know Abe wouldn't want you to put your life in danger."

His startling response angered her more. "I know he deserves better than the rumors that are circulating about him."

"Nobody pays any attention—"

"Don't use that line on me. Everybody listens to rumors. I experienced it firsthand. My mom sent me to the grocery store, and I met two women she works with. They were very nice and friendly, offering their condolences and saying how much they liked my father. I forgot something so I had to go back in the store. The ladies were in the checkout line, and I could hear them talking. One said, 'I wonder if Gail told her daughter why Mr. Brewster really fired Abe,' and the other answered, 'I'm sure she didn't. No woman wants to tell their daughter that her father was fired for embezzling funds.'" Abby took a long breath. "I wanted to confront them. Instead I walked away, unable to handle the pain their words caused me. Several days later, I overheard a similar conversation at the bank. People are talking and believing those cruel rumors, and I don't care what I have to go through, I'm going to put a stop to them."

Her eyes sparkled, and a vein worked steadily in her neck. Jonas was captivated by the motion. Abigail Duncan was fire and ice—and everything a man desired. And he wanted her. That was all too obvious by the tightening in his groin. He moved toward the refrigerator to get more water. As he opened the door, cool air washed over his heated body. Oh yeah, that was what he needed. That, and a ton of ice.

He sucked in cold air and walked back to her. He handed her the bottle.

As she took it, she said, "I know you think I'm crazy, but…" She took a couple of swallows of water and glanced at the desk her father had occupied. "I can feel his presence in this room, and he doesn't deserve…" She swallowed and looked at him. "Try to understand. I have to do this."

He stared into her eyes and felt himself wavering like a sixteen-year-old—and wanting her with that same ferocity. He could control it. He had before and he would now.

"It's time to go home," he said tiredly.

She stood, then immediately sank limply into the chair.

Jonas was instantly at her side. "What's wrong?"

"The room's doing a crazy dance."

"Take a deep breath."

She did as he instructed. "I'm okay now," she told him.

"No, you're not." He made a quick decision. "You can't drive in this condition. Let me get my shoes and shirt, and I'll drive you."

"Okay," she agreed meekly.

Jonas was back in record time. She stood, and he took her hand. They walked slowly to his truck.

When they drove up to her house, Abby turned in her seat. "Thank you, Jonas."

The way she said his name made his stomach roll over. He inhaled deeply, knowing he was fighting a losing battle.

"Can we call a truce?" she asked tentatively.

He looked at her. "Since we're thrown together

against our wills, it's probably a good idea. We'll talk tomorrow about going to Mexico.''

She seemed about to object, then stopped. ''Thank you,'' she said, and before he realized what was happening, she reached over and kissed his cheek.

He drew back as if she'd slapped him. ''Don't do that,'' he snapped.

''Okay, okay,'' she said, obviously startled by his reaction. *Great,* he thought. *Now she'll think I'm repelled by her kisses.*

Jonas got out of the truck. He had to, or he was going to take her in his arms the way he wanted to—and he knew she wasn't ready for that. Not that she ever would be. Abigail Duncan had no place in his life. He had to remember that.

In silence he walked her to the front door. She'd left her purse in the file room, so she had to use the key in the flowerpot.

''Thank you, Jonas,'' she said again as she stepped into the house.

Jonas marched to his truck. He had the urge to gun the motor and burn rubber. But he had outgrown that behavior. He only wished he had outgrown this deep frustration inside him, too. Abigail Duncan was making him crazy.

CHAPTER FIVE

WHEN JONAS GOT BACK to the office, he went into the file room and retrieved Abby's purse and Delores Alvarez's file. He took them to his desk, locked Abby's purse in a drawer and sat down. He stared at the file. If he opened it, there was no turning back. So it was time to stop fooling himself. Time to face his lust for Abigail Duncan. For that's all it was— lust, pure and simple.

He'd heard Abe talk about her for years. He'd seen her at a distance several times and he'd seen her up close at Abe's funeral, but he hadn't actual met her until she'd come to work for Brewster. "Nice to meet you, Mr. Parker," she had said in a soft titillating voice, and his insides had coiled tighter than an eight-day clock. He'd never met anyone like her. She was beautiful, smart and sophisticated, and so far removed from his world that it was laughable. He'd made a vow right then and there that he'd stay away from her. It had worked...for a while.

His hand went to his cheek. Dammit, he couldn't believe how he'd reacted to her innocent kiss. Like a teenager. He wondered what she'd say if he told her he'd never been kissed like that before—gently, affectionately—not even by his mother.

The moment her soft lips had touched him he'd felt a need that had long been buried under pain and heartache. A need to love someone. He'd had to get away from her as quickly as he could because he couldn't give reign to those emotions. She wouldn't understand him or his past. No woman would.

He fingered the file. If Abby would give up this insane notion of avenging her father and return to Dallas, his life would settle into its usual routine again and he wouldn't have to deal with his unwelcome feelings. But Abby wasn't leaving, he knew that. Even after spending hours in a locked room, she wasn't backing out.

The door had not closed by itself. Couldn't she see that? It was dangerous to continue this crusade. But there wasn't much he could do.

He opened the file and started to read. Delores lived a few miles across the border. At least her parents did. Since family was important to Mexicans, he'd bet Delores wasn't far away. That disturbed him. So close, yet she never came back to ask for support from Brewster even after his son had died. Why? If her daughter was Brewster's heir, why hadn't she done anything about it?

Brewster was a bastard and he could be a mean son of a bitch when he was in one of his moods. He might have put the fear of God into her. Still…Jonas had trouble accepting that. Somehow the pieces didn't fit.

He decided to call it a night. Maybe after a few hours sleep, he'd be able to think more clearly.

JONAS WOKE UP with a start. Someone was pounding on his door. He opened one eye and glanced at the clock. Six o'clock. Dammit all to hell, he'd overslept. He was always in the office by five.

"Mr. Jonas. Mr. Jonas. Come quick," Juan yelled through the door.

Now what? he thought as he slipped into jeans and made his way to the living room.

He yanked open the door. "This had better be important, Juan."

"Mr. Stuart wants you," Juan said, and hurried down the stairs.

Jonas followed at a slower pace. Stuart Banks stood at the bottom with a worried expression on his face. Stuart was younger than Jonas, but they were friends. Medium height with a spreading middle, Stuart had reddish-blond hair and blue eyes. Jonas spent a lot of Sundays at Stuart and Brenda's house. He knew Brenda had been a high school friend of Abby's. He'd often heard her talk about Abby and her success in the big city.

"I sent Juan to get you," Stuart said. "Thought you should see this." He pointed to Abby's car, which was still parked out front.

Good God, all four tires were flat. Jonas walked closer and knelt down to inspect one. It had been slashed with a sharp object. Dammit. He stood slowly.

"Someone has it in for Abby," Stuart remarked.

Yeah, that was the gist of it. Jonas pushed both hands through his tousled hair and told Stuart about last night's incident and Brewster's deal with Abby.

"Jonas, what's going on?"

"I wish I knew."

Stuart frowned. "I can't believe Abby's doing this, but I know how she feels about Abe. I don't think I'll tell Brenda. She'll only worry."

"Yeah," Jonas said. "I'd better get dressed, and you go call the sheriff."

"Okay, and trucks should be pulling in at any minute."

"I know. Let's try not to get behind. Pull Pablo and Roberto from the fields. We have a full day ahead of us and we'll need all the help we can get."

"Sure thing," Stuart said, and turned toward the office.

"Stuart." Jonas stopped him. "There'll be a raise on your next paycheck."

Stuart's eyes widened. "How in the hell did you accomplish that?"

Another deal with Brewster. "Brewster's tough about some things, but he knows how hard you work around here."

Even though he and Stuart were friends, Jonas had never told him—or anyone—about the deal he'd made with Brewster when he was fifteen. No one knew but Brewster, the sheriff, Mick and Jonas.

"Thanks, Jonas. With three kids, I can sure use it."

Jonas was aware of that. He tried to make sure all the top people had good salaries to support their families. As long as they did, they stayed in Hope, Texas. Jonas didn't want to lose Stuart or his friendship. So he hadn't had much choice but to go along with Brewster's wishes. The smile on Stuart's face was thanks enough.

"Call the sheriff, and I'll be down as fast as I can."

Jonas hurried upstairs and dressed for the day. He stared at the telephone. Should he call her? She'd still be sleeping, he reasoned, and after last night she needed her rest. She had to be told what had happened to her car. He'd give her some time, then he'd call.

As he started out the door, the phone rang. He jerked up the receiver. "Yeah."

"Jonas?"

"Abby?"

"Yes, you sound upset."

He ignored her observation. "I thought you'd be sleeping in."

"No, I couldn't sleep much. Every time I close my eyes I got this suffocating feeling."

Tell her. Tell her.

"I was wondering if I could ask a favor."

Through his own indecision he heard the tentativeness in her voice. "Sure."

"My mom had to go in early to school. I know you're busy, but could you pick me up so I can get my car?"

Silence.

He knew Abby was waiting.

"If it's a bother, I can…"

He found his voice. "No, no, it's not a bother. Do you mind if I send Juan over? I have something to do. I'll be here when you arrive."

A long pause.

"Fine," she finally said.

Was that disappointment in her voice? "Abby."

"Yes?"

"I'll talk to you when you get here."

"Okay."

She hung up the phone with a strange feeling. Jonas sounded put out. She should have called Earl, but she had this urge—one of those urges again—to see Jonas. Well, she'd get over it.

JONAS WAS CURSING HIMSELF. He should have told her and he should have gone to get her, but the sheriff wouldn't be too pleased if Jonas wasn't here when he arrived. Jonas grabbed his hat and walked downstairs, scowling.

He sent Juan to get Abby and told him not to say a word about her car. As Juan hurried to his truck, the sheriff drove up. Bob Fisher emerged from the vehicle. He was a tall stout man. His size alone deterred most people.

Jonas met him at the door.

"What the hell's going on, Jonas? Stuart called. He said you got trouble?"

"You could say that, Sheriff," Jonas replied, and strolled to Abby's car. "Ms. Duncan's tires were slashed last night and she was locked in the file room. I found her about one o'clock this morning."

The sheriff removed his hat and scratched his head. "Holy Moses, I guess the rumor I heard is true."

"What did you hear?"

"Brewster wants her to find some daughter he says he has."

Jonas didn't need to wonder where Bob had gotten his information. He hadn't heard a rumor. Brewster had told him. The sheriff and Brewster were tight. They controlled most of what went on in this small town.

"That's about it."

"What's that old man gonna come up with next?"

"I don't know," Jonas said. "But he's got people jumpy."

"I'll say," the sheriff agreed. "Don't touch anything. I'll get my boys over here to get prints. Maybe someone left a calling card."

"I hope so."

"Where's Abby?"

"She's on her way."

"Good, I need to ask her some questions."

As the sheriff was talking on his radio, Juan drove up with Abby. She wore jeans and a pink knit top. She looked wonderful except for the lines around her eyes. She began walking toward him, then she noticed her car and halted. Her hand went to her mouth. Jonas immediately went to her.

"What happened to my car?"

"Someone slashed your tires," he replied, wanting to hold her, to comfort her, but not doing either. The inclination startled him. Those emotions weren't in his nature. He was a loner. He'd survived by being a loner...never getting too close to anyone. "I called the sheriff," he added abruptly. "That's why I couldn't come get you."

Her eyes caught his. "Why didn't you tell me?"

"Didn't think it would do you any good to worry."

"I guess not," she said quietly, and moved closer to her car. "Who would do this?"

"I was hoping you'd tell me." The sheriff walked up behind them.

Abby turned to face him. "Hi, Sheriff," she said. "I don't have a clue who would do this to my car."

"Jonas says you were locked in the file room last night."

"Yes, I was," she said.

Two deputies drove up, diverting her attention.

"Let's go to Jonas's office and talk, while my boys do some checking," the sheriff suggested.

Before Abby could answer, Juan called to Jonas. "Mr. Jonas, we've got a truck backing up to the dock."

"I'll be right there," Jonas said, then spoke to the sheriff. "I'll be in the warehouse if you need anything."

"You have any idea what's going on here, Jonas?"

Jonas's eyes narrowed with a chilling look the sheriff didn't miss.

"Now, don't get me wrong," the sheriff was quick to add. "You were scared straight when you were fifteen and I know that hasn't changed. I admire the man you've become. It took a lot of courage to turn your life around. All I'm asking is for a little help. You know this farm and the workers better than anyone."

"All I know is Brewster has stirred things up with this absurd story, and Abby's caught in the middle," Jonas said.

"Yep, yep, yep, kinda looks like it," the sheriff muttered. "Seems someone doesn't want Brewster to have a daughter."

"Seems that way."

The sheriff stared directly at him. "You wouldn't be one of those people, would you, Jonas?"

Jonas met his look squarely. "You were just spouting what a good man I've become. Was that hogwash?"

"No, I meant it. I'm only testing the water."

"Well, test it somewhere else. I've got work to do." With that, Jonas turned and headed for the warehouse.

"Jonas." Abby was surprised to find herself running after him. She'd always been an independent person, even when she was little. Now she needed Jonas, and that scared her more than the slashed tires or being locked in a room.

When he looked at her, she didn't know what to say. *Don't go. Stay with me.* Those words hovered on her lips.

As if sensing her nervousness, he said, "I'll be back. Talk to the sheriff."

She nodded and moved toward the sheriff, feeling like a fool. A helpless female fool. She didn't need a man to take care of her. She could take care of herself. So...why was she so afraid?

For the next hour she talked to the sheriff, while his men took prints off the file room door and her car. She told him Edna Kline had been at the mansion that afternoon and that she and Jules and Darby didn't like Abby's involvement with Mr. Brewster.

The sheriff said he would talk to them. He tried to reassure Abby by telling her that the culprit was probably only trying to scare her. Well, he or she had succeeded. But that didn't mean Abby would give up the quest to find Delores Alvarez.

Soon the sheriff and his men left, and Abby went in search of Jonas. She opened the door to the warehouse and stopped. She'd forgotten how huge the place was. Several houses could fit inside it. She shivered—the place was kept at a cool temperature to ensure the vegetables and fruits stayed fresh. Their pungent scent drifted to her. She remembered that smell from her childhood visits to her father. He'd get her an orange or whatever fruit they were shipping. She'd never tasted anything as good as the fruit she'd eaten during those special times with her father.

An eighteen-wheeler was backed up to the dock and workers were methodically loading one-hundred-pound bags of onions onto it. Jonas worked alongside them. He swung bags onto a dolly with ease. Obviously that was how he got those muscles, she thought. She was learning a lot about Jonas Parker, and so far, there wasn't one thing she didn't like—except maybe the fact that he seemed to be immune to her.

As the doors slammed shut on the truck, a man sitting in a corner drinking a soft drink got to his feet. He handed Jonas a clipboard with some papers. Jonas signed the papers and gave the man a copy. They shook hands, and soon the big truck was pulling away. Another was waiting in line.

Abby noticed Stuart giving directions to the truck driver. When he saw her, he waved. She waved back.

Jonas came over. "How'd it go with the sheriff?"

"Fine. He thinks someone is just trying to scare me."

A worker shouted something in Mexican Abby didn't catch. Jonas barked a response. A chorus of "*Sì, sì, sì,*" resounded in the warehouse.

"Let's go inside," he said. "I need water."

She got the feeling that the worker's remark had been about her and that Jonas had put a stop to it. She didn't ask because she really didn't care to know. She followed him into the office. He grabbed bottled water out of the refrigerator.

"Want some?" he asked.

"No, thanks, I've been drinking water all night. I think I'm waterlogged now."

He sat on the edge of a desk and removed his hat. Blond hair fell across his forehead. His eyes held hers. "Ready to give it up?"

She sat on the edge of her father's old desk. "No."

He shook his head. "You're one stubborn woman."

"I'll admit I'm scared, but I'm more determined than ever. That doesn't make any sense, I know. I just have to find Delores Alvarez." She held up one finger. "And that's all I have to do. Find her and tell her Mr. Brewster wants to see his daughter. If the girl wants to see him, well, that's her decision. My job is to inform them of Mr. Brewster's wishes."

"The Mexican grapevine will do the job for you." If Mick's daughter and sister-in-law knew, it wouldn't be long before Delores's relatives and others in Mexico knew.

"Delores probably won't trust the grapevine, but maybe she'll trust me." She raised her eyes to his. "I can do this, Jonas. I know I can."

He didn't say a word.

"Then Mr. Brewster will tell me about my father. He'll tell me what I need to hear…what this whole town needs to hear. You do understand, don't you, Jonas?"

He swung off the edge of the desk and threw the bottle into the trash with a booming sound. The ache in her voice got to him. Oh God, he could fight it and deny it all he wanted, but that didn't change the way he felt when she said his name. He was venturing a step down an untraveled road, a road he'd sworn he would never take, where emotion was stronger than reason.

He turned to her. "You do realize this could be dangerous."

"Of course, it already is," she admitted.

"Once we cross the border it will get worse. The Mexicans will resent your interference."

"I know that."

"Really? When was the last time you were in Mexico?"

"About five years ago."

"Things haven't improved. In many areas there's poverty, heartache and suffering on every corner. That's why people swim the Rio Grande for a better way of life."

"I know that, too."

Silence.

She took a breath and asked, "When can we go?"

His gaze held hers. "Maybe tomorrow." Obviously Abby had accepted the fact that he'd be going with her.

She jumped off the desk. "Thank you, Jonas."

The light in her eyes was brighter than anything he'd ever seen in his life, and he felt its warmth. Oh yeah, he felt it in ways he didn't want to. But there wasn't much he could about that, either.

He glanced toward the warehouse. "I have a lot of work to do today, so we'll discuss it later. I'll get Bernie at the garage to send a tow truck for your car. Any preference for tires? I doubt yours can be repaired."

"The same as those that are on it."

"Okay, I'll get Juan to drive you home, and I'll

call when your car is ready. I should be through by
then and I'll take you to get it.''

Abby started to say her mom could take her when
she got off work, but something stopped her. She
liked Jonas taking control, and that shook her. She'd
never liked it when Kyle tried to control her. But
with Jonas it was different. He wasn't out to prove
he was stronger or dominant. He did it because he
cared and...*oh, was she in trouble!* Jonas didn't care
for her. He didn't even want her to touch him. So
she'd better face reality. She was attracted to Jonas
in ways she'd never been attracted to any other man.
She couldn't explain it, but at least she could admit
it.

She glanced at the empty office. ''Where is everyone? There was no one here yesterday, either.''

''Perry, the new accountant—number five to be
precise—is in McAllen taking a computer course.
Gloria, the secretary, is out with the flu. They'll both
be back tomorrow.''

The first part caught her attention. ''Mr. Brewster
hasn't found anyone suitable to replace my father?''

''He finds them, but they don't stay long, which
means a helluva lot more work for me.''

''Why do you stay, Jonas?'' she asked, hoping to
catch him off guard.

''That's my business.'' He didn't even blink at the
direct question.

''The sheriff said that—''

''Don't pry into things that don't concern you.''

As good a put-down as she'd ever had. The subject
was off-limits. He'd made that perfectly clear, but it
wasn't going to stop her. She'd find out sooner or
later.

He studied her for a moment, and she felt vulnerable under his intense stare.

"Just concern yourself with finding Delores Alvarez and be sure you're doing this for your father and not yourself," he said.

She chewed on her lower lip. "Partly, I *am* doing it for myself," she told him honestly. "I can't live with the rumors."

For a moment, she thought she saw admiration in his eyes.

"Mr. Jonas," Juan hollered from the warehouse.

Jonas reached for his hat. "I've got to go. I'll get Juan to take you home."

"Thank you, Jonas."

"I hope you get what you want," he said.

She did, too.

WHEN ABBY REACHED HOME, she collapsed onto her bed and fell asleep almost immediately. Even though she was disturbed by the events of last night, she had an inner calm about the ordeal ahead of her. If Mr. Brewster was using her for a reason of his own, that was okay. She would know the truth about her father. That's what mattered to her.

She woke up relaxed and ready to handle the situation. She heard her mom in the kitchen and glanced at the clock. It was almost five. She'd slept the whole day. Why hadn't Jonas called? Surely her car was ready by now.

She slipped off the bed and staggered into the kitchen. Her mother turned from the sink. "Oh, you're awake. Do you feel ill?"

"No, I feel fine," Abby replied, getting a soft drink out of the refrigerator.

"Then, why are you sleeping in the middle of the day?"

"I really don't want to get into it."

"I think we're gonna have to," her mother said. "Jonas Parker called and said to tell you that your car is ready and that he'd be by in a little while."

Abby took a sip. She really hated to get into another argument, but she couldn't ignore the censure in her mother's words.

When Abby didn't respond, Gail asked, "What's wrong with your car and why is Jonas coming here?"

Abby took a deep breath and wondered where to start. "I got in late last night."

"I know. I waited until ten and then went to bed. I had to get up early this morning." She paused. "Don't tell me you were with Jonas."

"In a way."

"My God, Abby, that man is so wrong for you. He's uncouth and rough and he spends his time at Mick's Tavern. Everyone knows what goes on down there—girls and sex. Not at all the type of young man you should be seeing."

Abby felt her temper rising at her mother's words. She knew Jonas had a wild past, but he'd changed— even the sheriff had said so.

"Well, he practically saved my life last night, and I'm more than a little grateful to him." For the first time she wondered what had made Jonas come to the office at one in the morning.

"Oh my God, what happened?" Gail sat at the table facing Abby with a terrified expression.

Abby swallowed. "Someone locked me in the file room, and Jonas found me early this morning."

Gail put both hands over her mouth in shock.

"And someone slit my tires."

"I knew something like this would happen," Gail said heatedly. "Give up this nonsense with Brewster. It's too dangerous. You can see that now, can't you?"

"Yes, it's dangerous," Abby admitted. "But I have to find the daughter."

"Abigail."

"Mr. Brewster put the information about why he fired Daddy in a letter. I had Earl read it to make sure it's not bogus."

Gail closed her eyes in exasperation. "Why did you have to get Earl involved? Now Sybil will be asking what's wrong with you, like before. I think you're having a nervous breakdown, and you should get some help. This isn't you."

Like before.

Loose woman.

Earl's words came back to her, and she knew it was time to discuss Aunt Sybil. "Did Aunt Sybil say something about my divorce?"

"It doesn't matter," Gail muttered uneasily.

"What did she say?" she persisted.

"Abby."

"What?"

"That...that you should have tried harder to make your marriage work, and she said you were probably seeing someone else. You can't pay any attention to Sybil."

The hand in Abby's lap clenched into a fist. "Do you feel the same way?"

"Of course not."

But Abby had to ask, "Do you think I didn't try hard enough?"

"Abby, I wish you'd go back to your job and forget about your divorce, your father and Simon Brewster. I want you to start living again and put all the bad things behind you."

Her mother hadn't answered the question, and that didn't escape Abby, but she had to get one thing straight. "You want me to go back to Dallas?"

"Yes," Gail answered emphatically.

Abby frowned. "Kyle's in Dallas. Are you saying you want me to go back to Kyle?"

Her mother looked shocked. "You're putting words in my mouth."

"But you're implying it."

"I am not. You're not understanding what I'm saying at all."

"I think I am."

Abby rose. She had never dreamed her mother had ambivalent feelings about her divorce…would never have known if Earl hadn't said something. Her mother probably thought she slept around, too.

Gail caught Abby's arm. "Listen to me. I'm your mother and I support you wholeheartedly. But his mother called to tell me Kyle's in AA and he hasn't had a drink in months. I told June it was none of my business, but she keeps calling. I'm not sure what to say to her anymore."

Those words only made matters worse. Abby pulled her arm free. "You can tell Kyle's mother that your daughter doesn't like being slapped, and Kyle can go to AA twenty-four hours a day for all I care. It took two weeks for the bruises to heal, and I will never *ever* put myself in that position again." Having said her piece, she headed for the living room.

"Abigail, come back here. You're twisting everything I say. I would never want you to stay with someone who hits you, and I told June that."

Abby didn't stop. She was so hurt and angry that she couldn't speak.

"Abigail, I want to talk to you."

Abby grabbed her purse and made for the front door. As she did, the doorbell rang. She yanked opened the door and breezed past Jonas, down the steps to his truck.

Jonas stared after her with a perplexed expression, then his gaze swung to Mrs. Duncan.

"She's upset," Mrs. Duncan explained.

"I noticed."

"She hasn't been the same since her father's death and her divorce. I'm so worried about her. Please talk her out of this craziness of finding Brewster's daughter."

"I already tried and it didn't work," he replied, not sure what was happening but not wanting to get between Abby and her mother.

"She's always been headstrong and now I can't even talk to her."

"She's determined. I'll say that."

Gail shook her head sadly and went back to the kitchen. Jonas closed the door and headed for Abby, feeling as if he'd stepped into a hornet's nest.

CHAPTER SIX

JONAS CLIMBED INTO THE TRUCK. Abby sat with her hands clamped tightly in her lap, staring straight ahead.

As Jonas's hand reached for the key, she asked, "What did she say to you?"

"Nothing much."

Her head jerked toward him, her eyes steamy. "I thought you were the one person who wouldn't lie to me."

"Hey." He held up a hand. "I'm not lying to you. I'm giving you time to calm down."

She took a couple of deep breaths and knew she hadn't been this angry in a long time. She felt so betrayed by a mother she'd thought understood her, loved her and would always be behind her one hundred percent.

"She's just worried about you," Jonas said.

"Yeah." She sighed, then asked again, "What did she say to you?"

Jonas drew a quick breath and told her the truth. "She said you haven't been the same since your father's death and your divorce."

"Did she tell you I didn't work hard enough to save my marriage...that I should have stayed with a man who hit me—because he's sorry?" Abby knew her mother hadn't actually said that, but she hadn't actually denied it, either.

Jonas's eyes narrowed. *Her husband hit her?* The thought triggered his own anger. "No, she didn't mention that."

"Seems my whole family believes I didn't try hard enough. My aunt Sybil believes I sleep around...that I'm a loose woman. When I think—" She threw both hands out in front of her as if to stop the bad thoughts.

She inhaled deeply. "I'm sorry," she said. "I'm very ticked off at the moment."

"Really? Could have fooled me." He grinned, hoping to lighten her mood.

Questions about her husband clamored in his head. By nature, he wasn't a curious, interfering person, but he wanted to hear about her marriage. He had wondered why a man would leave her. Clearly, she had left the marriage—and with good reason. He couldn't fathom why her mother would even hint at her staying with such a man.

At the sight of her sad expression, he made a decision. "You need some downtime. Have you had supper?"

"No. I'm not hungry."

"Well, I've had a long, tiring day and I am hungry. I was thinking of stopping at that Mexican café by the bank. They have good food."

"I'm not in a mood to be around people."

Way to go, Parker, Jonas thought. He'd just asked the woman out and she'd politely refused. What did he expect? Now his ego was somewhere in his boots.

"Could we get some takeout and eat in a quiet place?"

His ego rebounded. "Sure, we can buy some soft tacos and eat at Brewster's Park. The town went to a lot of trouble and expense, so we might as well make use of it."

"Sounds fine," she said. "What about my car?"

He started the engine. "Bernie put the key under the mat, so we can pick it up at any time."

"What took so long to put on four tires?"

"He didn't have your tires in stock. He had to make a trip to McAllen to buy them."

"Oh."

"He called earlier, but I couldn't leave until about an hour ago."

"It's okay, I slept all day, anyway."

"Thought you might," he said as he drove up to the café. "Anything special you want?"

"The tacos will be fine...and something to drink."

"Okay," he said and got out.

She leaned her head back against the headrest, wondering how her day had turned out like this. She had overreacted...dramatically. She should have talked to her mother in a more reasonable manner. Did Abby have doubts about her divorce? No. Had she tried hard enough to save her marriage? Yes, she had a clear conscience about that. The special bond she and Kyle had once shared had been irrevocably broken. Their marriage was over.

Soon Jonas was back, and within minutes they were at the park. It was a family park with swings, slides and picnic areas. A huge statue of Mr. Brewster stood in the middle surrounded by decorative flower beds that the city maintained—a monument to the man who owned the town and everyone in it.

They made their way to a picnic table. Jonas

spread the food out, and Abby gaped at the enormous quantity. "We can't eat all this," she said, and held up a bag of peanuts. "Peanuts?"

"Yeah, don't you like peanuts?"

"Yes, but not with tacos."

He sat on the concrete bench. "I guess it's a personal thing. I used to love putting peanuts in my Coke when it came in a bottle—but it's hell trying to get peanuts out of a can."

She smiled slightly and reached for a taco. "I can imagine."

He handed her a Coke, and they ate in silence for a while. Before Abby realized it, the food was almost gone.

"I thought you weren't hungry," he teased.

As she licked her fingers, she said, "My taste buds were momentarily blindsided by anger."

"Yeah," he agreed as he watched her tongue dart over her fingers. All he could think about was tasting her tongue, feeling it in… He quickly wadded papers into a ball and stuffed them in a bag. He opened the bag of peanuts, popped several into his mouth and took a long drink of Coke.

She watched him for a second, then reached for the bag and did as he'd done. He raised an eyebrow.

"You're right," she said. "It is good. I remember doing this as a kid. I'd forgotten how good it tastes."

After a moment, he asked, "Feeling better?"

"Much," she said, and glanced around. The sun was slowly sinking; soon it would be dark. The park was empty. Everyone was at home with their families. *Families.* At the moment Abby wasn't feeling too good about hers. Suddenly she had a need to talk. Jonas, being a man of few words, probably didn't want to listen to her, but what she told him would stay between them. He didn't gossip—another thing she liked about him.

"My mom and I got into a discussion about my marriage and divorce."

"I figured that." He took a sip of his drink.

"I thought she understood, and it was a shock to learn that she doesn't. That's what hurt." She paused. "To be honest, my mother never really knew Kyle. He was always on his best behavior when we came home on the odd weekend. She never knew how selfish, petty and cruel he could be. So I guess it's understandable that she doesn't fully understand the situation."

"No," Jonas said, to his surprise. "It's *not* understandable when someone hits you." The words slipped out before he could stop them. He knew what it was like to be hit, and he never wanted anyone to feel that pain, especially her.

She didn't seem to hear him. She was locked in her own inner turmoil. "When I first met Kyle, I thought he was the man of my dreams. He was so attentive and considerate of my feelings and he understood that I wanted a career. We worked in the same field and everything seemed perfect. I married him three months after we met. The real Kyle soon emerged. He was jealous of my success at work and accused me of sleeping with every man I spoke to. Then he started drinking and became violent. He'd hidden his temper while we were dating, but after we were married, he made no attempt to control it. At times, I was afraid of him."

She took a long breath. "I learned later that Kyle's drinking problem began long before we were married. Another thing he hid from me. When he lost his job, that was the straw that broke the camel's back, to use the cliché. I tried to be supportive, but he was impossible to live with. One night I came home late from an assignment, and he accused me of sleeping with the photographer. He was in a rage, and I had to get away from him. I told him I was leaving and started to pack a bag. That was like putting gasoline on a fire. He hit me so hard I saw stars and fell to the floor. As soon as I could get to my feet, I walked out the door. I haven't looked back.''

She ran both hands through her hair. Damn. She couldn't believe she was telling Jonas all the sordid details. But once she'd started talking, she couldn't seem to stop. ''I'm sorry,'' she said. ''I shouldn't have unloaded on you.''

''It's okay,'' he said quickly. ''I have broad shoulders.''

And did he ever. Gorgeous, strong shoulders.

She blinked and searched for something else to say. ''I guess we should talk about finding Delores Alvarez.''

Jonas twisted the Coke can. ''You did the right thing, Abby.''

She stared into his eyes. All her friends told her that, but it felt good to hear him say it. ''Thank you, but sometimes I feel like a failure.'' She hadn't even realized that was bothering her until the words left her mouth. Maybe that's why she'd reacted so strongly to her mother's comments.

''It took a lot of courage to get out of a lousy relationship. Many women stay because they lack that courage. Consider yourself lucky.''

He sounded as if he knew what he was talking about. "Have you ever been married?"

"Nope."

As if the questions were getting too personal, he got up and carried the bag to a trash receptacle. Her reporter's instinct wouldn't let it go.

"But you know someone who was in that kind of relationship?"

He straddled the bench with a brooding expression. Did she really not know? Hell, she had to. His family had been the gossip of the town for years.

His eyes met hers. "I'm sure you've heard the rumors about my family and I'm also positive your mother has warned you about me."

Abby desperately tried to hide a flicker of acknowledgment, but knew she had failed.

"I see that she has," he said in a hard tone.

Abby hated to see that expression on his face—the one that blocked out the world and everyone in it. Funny how she was beginning to recognize his moods. And she intended to change this one.

"Yes, my mother warned me about you," she admitted truthfully. "But I haven't listened to my mother in years. I'm not sure I ever did. I always make up my own mind."

Jonas didn't say anything, just gazed off across the park.

"All I know is that you were a wild teenager and in trouble with the law, but I can see you've gotten your act together...even the sheriff said something about it today."

He still didn't speak.

"Jonas, I really don't know anything else, especially about your family. I know you are friends with

Stuart and Brenda. They've mentioned you from time to time, but neither has said anything about your childhood.''

He finally looked at her. "The whole town knows. How could you possibly not know?''

She shrugged. ''I was a kid and I didn't pay any attention to those kind of things. Tell me about your family. Maybe it will jar my memory.''

''I don't think so.''

''I could ask around, but I'd rather hear it from you.''

His eyes darkened. ''You're relentless and—''

She stopped him. ''So you may as well tell me.'' Abby saw his indecision and decided to give him a nudge. ''I'm guessing since you were a wild teenager, you came from an unhappy home.''

''That's putting it mildly.''

Abby thought about what had prompted this conversation. ''Your father hit your mother?''

''Yeah,'' he admitted quietly, and she had to strain to catch his next words. ''He beat her on a regular basis, and when he grew tired of that, he beat me and my sister.''

''Oh, Jonas, I'm so sorry,'' she said, but he didn't respond. He kept talking.

''When I was twelve, he beat her to death. He then started on me. I hid my sister in a closet so he couldn't find her. A neighbor called the police. He ran away before they could apprehend him. Two weeks later the police told me he was killed in a bar in Las Vegas. I wasn't sad. I was happy. Happy he couldn't ever hurt my sister or me again.''

Abby tried to swallow the lump in her throat, but

all she felt was pain in her heart for the little boy who had suffered so much.

His eyes swung to her. "So you see, your mother was right. I come from bad blood, and you'd be wise to stay away from me."

"I don't believe that for a minute."

He was speechless. All he could do was stare at her. There was no revulsion or disgust in her eyes, just empathy. He hadn't expected this. She couldn't be that open-minded. Could she?

Abby stared back at him. "What happened to your sister?"

"She was put into foster care. A couple from Wyoming adopted her, and she's very happy. At first I was sad they had taken her. Now I'm glad she got out of this place and had a chance at a real life."

"Do you hear from her?"

"Yeah, on my birthday and holidays I get a card and a phone call."

Abby wasn't finished with the questions. She needed to know what had happened to him after they'd taken his sister.

"And you? Did you stay in foster care?"

"No, I hated it," he answered harshly. "I ran away three times. The last time, I made sure they couldn't find me."

"You lived on the streets?"

He didn't miss the incredulous tone. Now he would tell her about the real Jonas Parker and it would put a stop to the questions...and everything else. She wouldn't want anything to do with a man like him. That was the way he wanted it. The way it had to be.

"Yeah, I spent my days evading the sheriff and

the social workers. Mick at Mick's Tavern had a storeroom with a cot, and he let me sleep there. He also gave me food. Whatever else I needed I stole.''

He watched her closely, but he didn't see the effect he wanted. All he saw was sadness and compassion. Dammit all to hell. What was wrong with this woman? She wasn't doing anything he expected. He was trying to warn her and she wasn't getting the message.

Abby knew exactly what he was trying to do—scare her off. It did just the opposite. Her heart ached for him, and she thought of her own childhood—happy, with two loving parents who were always there for her. She definitely had to apologize to her mother. But Gail had to understand that it was Abby's life and she would make her own decisions. They would work out their differences…like always. They were mother and daughter, and nothing could shake that—not even Kyle.

Jonas crushed his soft drink can in his hand. The sound brought her concentration back to him. He threw a leg over the bench and dropped the can into the garbage. Abby got the hint—he was through talking. She wasn't.

"How did you come to work for Mr. Brewster?"

He picked up his hat. "It's late. We'd better go."

End of conversation. She knew better than to pressure him because Jonas was a man who didn't back down under pressure.

The gentle breeze played with the swings. The creaking sound reminded Abby of her childhood. "How long since you were on a swing?"

He frowned at her. Before he could reply, she jumped up and ran to a swing. She sat on the seat, gripped the chains and kicked off. Higher and higher she sailed—forward and back—faster and faster.

"Come on, Jonas," she called, her voice brimming with laughter.

Jonas put his hat on his head and walked closer. Dusk had settled in, but it was a bright night and he could clearly see her. Her green eyes sparkled and her face was full of mischief. He felt himself being pulled toward her infectious voice, her fun-loving smile, and as much as he wanted to walk away, he found he couldn't. Truth be known, he didn't even want to. He wanted to experience everything that was her. *Okay, that's enough,* he chastised himself.

"Jonas, catch me," she cried playfully, and then she was flying through the air toward him.

In a split second, he raised his arms, but it was too late. She catapulted into him, knocking him to the ground. His hat flew off and he lay winded with Abby on top of him.

"You were supposed to catch me," she laughed into his startled face.

"I tried, but you were too fast," he managed to say, very aware of her soft body pressed into him. Her delicate perfume filled him and her feminine curves triggered other responses. Responses he was determined to ignore.

"Haven't you heard the rumors about me? I'm a fast woman."

"Abby, I don't think..."

She moved against him, stopping him in midsentence. "Don't think," she warned and stared down at him. She wanted to be as close to him as possible, see the light in his eyes and that gorgeous grin on his lips. She'd had these feelings for weeks, and tonight she was acting on them. She'd never done anything like this in her life—not even with Kyle—but she was going to make Jonas kiss her. He had to...willingly. She wasn't leaving the park until he did.

Her face was a few inches from his, and her blond hair softly caressed his cheek. He breathed in her fragrant scent and knew he was lost. All he could feel was her body, her hair, her scent, and he ached to taste every inch of her. He'd been dreaming of it for weeks, and now...he couldn't. He couldn't take what she was offering because... Why? As she moved on him, all logic left him.

God, he wished she'd stop that. He had to think. He had to—

She gently kissed his cheek, and he tensed. It didn't stop her. She touched his other cheek.

"Abby," he groaned.

"Yes," she whispered against his skin.

The soft titillating voice broke his control. His hands slipped beneath her hair to her face. He stroked her cheeks and pulled her gently to his lips. The kiss was slow and sensuous, igniting a flame in Abby that had been dormant for a long time. She moaned and opened her mouth, giving him full access. He took, tasted and gave with such exuberance that she lost herself in the moment. She'd known he would kiss like this...warm, tantalizing, with an earth-moving intensity. The night wrapped around them as the kiss went on.

Suddenly, he tore his lips from hers and scrambled to his feet. He grabbed his hat. "We'd better go." His voice came out low and hoarse.

Abby sat on her backside, staring at him in stunned

muteness. Jonas walked to the picnic table and gathered the remaining trash. How could he kiss her so passionately and act as if it was nothing? He'd made her feel attractive and desirable for the first time in ages. And she'd needed that...

What was she doing? She was using him. She had tempted and cajoled him into kissing her without any thought as to how it would affect him. She wasn't looking for a relationship or any kind of involvement. Her emotions were too bruised. She was attracted to Jonas and his rugged sensuality, but she was too old to be playing these teenage games. Jonas deserved better than that.

"I'm sorry," she said, and stood slowly. "I shouldn't have done that. I don't normally do such things."

"Forget it. It's not important." His voice was brisk and he didn't look at her.

"I guess my mother's right and I'm not myself."

He looked directly at her. "Then, give up this crazy idea to avenge your father."

Silence.

"I can't," she finally said. "I have to do it."

"I just hope it's something you won't regret."

Like kissing me, he meant. She pushed that thought aside, and asked, "When can we go to Mexico?"

"I've got trucks coming in tomorrow, but the next day seems fine. The faster we get this over with the better."

He sounded as if he couldn't wait to be rid of her, and she didn't like that. But she didn't want to analyze her feelings. She had to put aside her attraction for Jonas. They were going to Mexico to find Delores. That was the important thing. Finding out the truth about her father was her goal and nothing would divert her.

Her hand went to her tingling lips. Could she forget Jonas's kiss? Sure, no problem, she told herself. She'd been kissed before.

But not like that.

CHAPTER SEVEN

THE DRIVE TO HER CAR was silent, and she knew she had crossed a dangerous line with Jonas. She had jeopardized their relationship by her need to make him notice her. Those feelings were tied to her divorce. She recognized that. She'd been spouting that she didn't need a man for so long that she'd come to believe it herself. But the truth was, she longed to feel attractive and desirable again. Kyle had destroyed a portion of her self-esteem, and she had a desire to recapture her self-confidence.

Jonas was so different from her. He had character and strength, and there was no way a woman could make him feel less than he was. He was secure in his masculinity. She had no right to tempt him, especially after he had made it clear how he felt about her. She probably should apologize again, but she had a feeling he didn't want to hear it. Oh, what had she done? She'd made a bad situation worse.

She was glad when he pulled up beside her car. "The key is under the mat on the passenger side," he said in a wooden voice.

Obviously he wanted to get away from her, but she couldn't go until they were clear on one subject. "Just because your parents had problems doesn't make you a bad person."

"You don't know everything about me," he replied roughly. His elbow was on the door and one hand was on the steering wheel. That hand clenched over and over. He wasn't in a good mood—that was obvious.

"Maybe I don't," she admitted in a low voice. "But I know you could have done anything you wanted with me back there in the park. That doesn't say a lot about me, but it says a great deal about you."

He didn't say a word, and she knew he wouldn't. Still, she couldn't get out of the truck.

"Will I see you tomorrow?" Heavens, that sounded pathetic even to her own ears.

"I've a busy day ahead."

She swallowed, her pride on the outer edge of nowhere. "We have to talk about Mexico. If you don't want to go, I'll understand."

"When I get free, I'll call."

"Okay," she said slowly, taking that to mean he was still going. She had no choice now but to get out. She opened the door and stepped onto the pavement. She glanced at him. "Thank you, Jonas."

Damn, why did she have to say that? Her soft lilting voice was getting to him. Hell, everything about her was getting to him.

Just go, Abby. Go home to your safe, secure world and remember that heated kisses in the night don't mean a thing. They don't mean a damn thing.

WHEN JONAS HAD SEEN her drive safely into her driveway, he headed for Mick's. But he knew that wouldn't ease the frustration she had created inside him. He turned the truck toward Brewster Farms.

He wasn't the man for Abigail Duncan. She

needed a man in a three-piece suit who had an important office job with a salary to match. A man who didn't have calluses on his hands and who knew what fork to use at the dinner table. She didn't need someone to mess up her life...she had enough to handle. And so did he.

They were attracted to each other—definitely. He couldn't deny that, but he sure as hell could do something about it. He'd stay away from her. Fast on that thought was one he couldn't escape. The trip to Mexico. Dammit and damn Brewster for getting him involved. Maybe he could think more clearly tomorrow when his senses weren't so affected by her scent, her touch. Tomorrow things would be different. He'd be in a different frame of mind.

He went to his apartment above the warehouse, took a cold shower and plopped down on the sofa in front of the big screen TV. He turned the volume up loud, blocking out any thoughts of Abby.

WHEN ABBY ENTERED the kitchen of her mother's house the lights were on, and she knew her mother was waiting for her.

Gail rushed through from the living room. "Abby, sweetheart, you're back," she said and hugged her tightly. Abby returned the hug.

"I love you. You're my baby," Gail murmured with tears in her voice. "I would never want anyone to hit or to hurt you, and I know you tried hard to make your marriage work. Please don't think otherwise."

Abby moved toward the table and sat down. "I'm sorry I lost my temper," she said. "But I did try to save my marriage. I put up with more than you'll ever know."

"Oh, sweetie." Gail kissed the top of her head.

"There's nothing to salvage from my marriage, and I'd appreciate it if you'd stop talking to June."

"I'll tell her not to call again," Gail said and took a seat. "I never liked the woman, anyway."

"Then, it shouldn't be a problem."

"No," Gail agreed. "How about some tea?"

"Sure," Abby answered absently, wondering where Jonas had gone after leaving her. Her mom said he hung out at Mick's Tavern. Did he take advantage of the services offered by the girls who worked there? She didn't like the feeling that came over her at the thought. She was becoming too fixated on Jonas and his life.

Her mother placed a glass of iced tea in front of Abby. She squeezed her eyes shut for a second to block out the image of Jonas's rigidly masculine face, then took a quick swallow. Cool—soothing, just what she needed.

"Have you been with Jonas all this time?" Gail asked as she took a seat.

"Yes." Abby looked directly at her.

"Abby—"

"Don't start, Mom," she cut in. "I'm old enough to make my own decisions about Jonas."

"Yes, you are, sweetheart, but your emotions are so battered, I'm afraid you'll do something you'll regret."

Abby took another sip. "I won't regret doing anything with Jonas." As she said the words, she realized that they were true. She didn't know a lot about Jonas, but she knew he wouldn't hurt her.

"Abby!" her mother said in shock, but Abby didn't respond. Instead she asked a question.

"Did you know Jonas's parents?"

"Oh my, yes. He was a mean drunk and she was a— Well, she had Jonas when she was sixteen and she wasn't ready to be a mother. She left him with anyone who would keep him and went running around trying to have a good time. When her husband would find her, he'd beat her and take her back home. Finally one night he beat her to death. Those poor kids were caught in the middle."

"It's so sad. I don't understand why the authorities didn't do something."

"This is Hope, Texas, sweetheart," her mother reminded her. "Nothing gets done here. They couldn't even keep Jonas in foster care."

No, he'd lived a heart-wrenching existence on the street. He shouldn't have had to live like that.

She shook her head. "How did Jonas start working for Mr. Brewster?"

Gail shrugged. "I'm not sure. That was when your grandmother was ill and I was away helping take care of her. I asked Abe about it, but he said only that Brewster had hired the Parker boy and was treating him like a slave. He never said anything else. Of course, your father wasn't one to ask questions or listen to gossip."

"I didn't get that from him, did I?"

"No, you've always loved to ask questions. I think you get it from Sybil."

"Oh, please, don't tell me I'm like Aunt Sybil."

Gail smiled and patted her hand. "Genes are something you can't deny, sweetheart."

The words had a chilling effect on Abby. Jonas

believed the same thing. His father was bad so there-
fore he was, too. But that wasn't true. She went to
bed with that thought in her head. There had to be a
way to convince him otherwise. The idea rattled her.
Jonas was taking precedent over avenging her father.

She grabbed her pillow and held it close. Tomorrow she'd concentrate on Mr. Brewster and Delores
Alvarez, but tonight she'd think about Jonas.

THE NEXT MORNING she called Holly and told her
that Jonas was going with her to Mexico. Holly
thought it was great. Abby didn't mention the incident in the park. That was too personal to share just
yet. She then called her editor and explained that she
couldn't return any earlier than planned.

Later, she went to the sheriff's office to see if he'd
found out anything about her car or the file room
door. He hadn't. Neither had he gotten around to
questioning Edna, Jules or Darby. Abby got the feeling he wasn't going to do a thing. Evidently she did
not rank as a top priority. So much for the law in
Hope, Texas.

Afterward she drove to the hospital to see Mr.
Brewster. She found him sitting up in bed looking
much better. He was still on oxygen, and machines
were monitoring his heart, but he appeared to be his
normal cranky self.

"Abigail, come in, come in," he said when he saw
her.

She walked closer to his bedside. "You seem better."

"I ain't dead yet. Disappointed a lot of people.
But it's just a matter of time—even I know that."

Abby wasn't sure. Mr. Brewster was the type of

person who stared death in the eye and laughed. He seemed immune to pain and suffering; nothing touched him, not even the thought of dying. Well, maybe that wasn't true. He didn't want to die until he saw his daughter. That had to mean he had a heart in his body somewhere.

"Jonas told me what happened," he said. "Are you all right?"

That concern in his voice startled her, then angered her. "No, I'm not all right," she said heatedly. "It was awful being locked in that suffocating room, not to mention having my tires maliciously slashed. This is getting dangerous, but you can put an end to it right now."

He frowned. "How can I do that?"

"By telling me about my father and forgetting about your daughter. She hasn't wanted to see you in thirty years and she probably doesn't want to see you now."

He gave a gruff laugh. "That won't work, Abigail. We have a deal."

She didn't have a ready response. She wanted to walk out the door and keep going, but her feet wouldn't move. A force stronger than her kept her rooted to the spot. She would keep her word even though she was beginning to have doubts.

"Someone got nervous," Mr. Brewster was saying. "Thought their inheritance was in jeopardy. But I can do whatever the hell I please with my money. I'll make that very clear to everyone, so you don't have to worry."

"But I am worried," she told him. "I hope you're not using me for some sadistic reason of your own."

"Ah." He brushed away the thought with a wave of his hand. "You've been listening to Jonas."

"Is he right?"

"No, he's not right," he bellowed. "Jonas thinks he knows me, but he doesn't."

"He probably knows you better than anyone."

"Yeah, we've been together a long time."

Silence.

Abby was stunned. Was that actually emotion for Jonas she'd heard in his voice? It couldn't be. They were sworn enemies. That was one of the first things she'd learned when she'd come here. She had to dig deeper.

"You said you owned Jonas—"

"It's a long story, Abigail, and it doesn't concern you."

That's what Jonas had said, and she was getting tired of hearing it. She wanted answers.

"Oh, I think it does," she informed him. "Suddenly I'm in the center of your life—somewhere I don't want to be—so everything about you concerns me."

"If you're that curious, get Jonas to tell you."

"I will."

"Good luck. Getting anything out of Jonas is like pulling teeth."

"Have you ever tried a little care and kindness?"

He lifted a shaggy eyebrow. "No, never entered my mind."

"How did you get him to change his mind about going to Mexico?"

"Just turned the screws a little."

"That means you have something on him, and it doesn't bother you to use it when it suits you."

He nodded. "When you get to be my age, you use everything at your disposal."

She stepped closer to the bed. "So what do you have on him?"

"Abigail," he grunted. "Don't try to trick me. I'm a master at it."

She'd just bet he was. A master at deception and deceit, too. People were pawns to him. Knowing that, why couldn't she make herself walk out the door?

He broke into her thoughts. "I gave Jonas tomorrow and the next day off. So get this done quickly. I can't afford to give him any more time than that."

Abby's eyes narrowed. "Doesn't Jonas have any free time?"

"Whenever I say he can."

"And he accepts that?"

"Hell, no. Jonas never accepts anything graciously. He gets mad and leaves every now and then, but he always comes back. I can count on it."

"You sound very sure."

"Yep, I am, so don't be putting silly notions in his head."

"Like what?"

"Like, well, you know. Just don't do it. Jonas belongs here."

She was taken aback. There was that note in his voice again—a note that said he cared, which was ludicrous because Mr. Brewster didn't care about anyone.

"Why are you still standing there?" he barked. "Go find my daughter before my ticker gives out."

"I will," she replied calmly. "But you understand I can only do so much. If she doesn't want to see you, I can't force her."

"The deal is, Abigail, you talk to Delores and tell her what I said. Whatever happens after that, I will accept."

"Fine, then, we're in agreement. I'll see you in a few days, hopefully with your daughter." She turned toward the door.

"Oh, you'll find her. I have no doubt about that."

She swung around. "Why are you so sure?"

"Money, Abigail. It will be the deciding factor."

Abby frowned. "You want me to offer her money?"

"Of course not, but money to Delores is like sugar to a fly. It will draw her back, and I will get my wish."

"You're a cruel old man."

He nodded. "So I've been told."

Abby walked out of the room feeling again as if someone were pulling her strings. She was so absorbed in her own thoughts that she didn't see Edna Kline until Edna called her name.

"Just a minute, missy, I want to talk to you." Edna practically bounced after her. The big hat on her head wobbled with her agitated movements. When she reached Abby, she grabbed her by the arm and pushed her into a waiting room. "I warned you to stay away from Simon."

Abby pulled her arm free. "I think you did more than warn me."

"What are you talking about?"

"I'm talking about locking me in the file room and slashing my tires."

"Oh, please." Edna bristled. "Jonas mentioned that, but believe me I'm not that juvenile."

Abby stepped close to her. "Somebody is, so now

I'm warning *you*. Stay away from me." She moved
toward the door, but Edna blocked her way.

"I can't do that until you stop encouraging Simon.
A daughter in Mexico?" She laughed caustically. "If
he believes that, he must be getting a touch of Alz-
heimer's. It's ridiculous, and you're not doing him
any good by indulging his stupid fantasy."

Abby watched the color fluctuate in Edna's
cheeks. "A daughter would really cut into your inheritance, wouldn't she?"

"There isn't a daughter," Edna screeched.

"We'll see," Abby said and walked away.

"You'll regret this," Edna shouted after her, but
Abby didn't turn back.

ABBY WAITED THE REST of the day for Jonas to call,
but he didn't. She had dinner with her mom and
waited. By seven, she'd had enough. She grabbed her
purse and told her mother she was going out. Gail
had a barrage of questions, but Abby didn't answer
any of them.

She headed straight for the warehouse. She had on
jeans and a white knit top. Maybe she should have
changed—but what for? she asked herself. Jonas
wouldn't notice.

She couldn't believe he hadn't called. He'd said
he would, and Jonas always kept his word. Something had to be wrong.

As she drove up, she saw Juan standing by an old
truck. She asked where Jonas was, and he pointed to
the stairs on the side of the warehouse.

"Does he live there?" she asked.

"*Sí*," Juan answered and got into his truck.

Up until that moment she'd had no idea where

Jonas lived. She'd assumed he lived in a house. But where? She'd never gotten that far in her thinking. No wonder he was here all the time. He never left. Why did he put up with this? she wondered.

She climbed the stairs slowly, and found a solid wood door. It was ornately carved, and she knew it came from Mexico. Tentatively she tapped the brass knocker.

There was no answer. She heard soft music. That meant he had to be home. She tapped again. The music stopped and the door was yanked open. "Juan, if you—" Jonas paused when he saw her.

Abby's breath caught in her throat. Jonas stood there in nothing but a towel. His hair was wet from the shower and there were droplets of water on his naked body.

"Abby." Her name came out in a rush.

"Jonas, I'm sorry, I didn't—"

"Come in. I'll get some clothes on." He disappeared from her sight.

She stepped into Jonas's home and glanced around. There was a large living area and a kitchen. Cream-and-green Mexican tiles covered the floor. The walls were cream and the moldings were a delicately carved wood that set off the room. The beams on the ceiling were the same dark wood.

The furniture was hunter green and a large multicolored area rug enhanced the living area. On one wall was an entertainment center with a large TV. A picture of a little girl hung on another wall, and Abby walked over to study it. This had to be his sister. The only family he had.

Jonas returned in jeans and a T-shirt, no shoes and his wet hair slicked back. Clothes didn't still the tingling in her stomach. Something in her reacted so strongly to him. It had happened the first time she'd met him, when he'd said "Howdy, ma'am" in that deep Texas drawl.

He strolled to the refrigerator and got a chilled bottle of water. "Want one?" he asked as he twisted off the cap.

"No, thanks," she answered, and moved closer to the kitchen. The countertop was cream with a green border and the backsplash had fruit and vegetables painted on the tiles. Who had helped him decorate this apartment? she wondered. A woman? She couldn't believe the jealousy that swirled through her. Jonas probably had more women than she could count, and his personal life had nothing to do with her. Not one little thing. Why couldn't she believe that?

"I'm sorry I didn't call, but I just finished for the day," he was saying. "It was one of those days when if anything could go wrong, it did. One of the trucks wouldn't start after we loaded it, and other trucks were waiting to pull in. I had to call Bernie to get it going. Tempers were getting a little heated. We had to work through lunch to make up the time."

He was talking fast but he couldn't stop. It was disconcerting having her in his home. He didn't want her here.

"You haven't had lunch or dinner?" she asked.

"Not yet."

Without even thinking about it, she marched into the kitchen. "I'll fix you dinner."

"No, you don't have—" He stopped when she opened the pantry as if she had known exactly where it was.

She pulled out spaghetti and sauce. "Do you have any hamburger meat?"

"It's frozen."

She noticed the built-in microwave over the cook-top. "No problem. I can defrost it in minutes."

Jonas gave up and sat on the green leather bar stool, watching her move about his kitchen. Her blond hair was clipped behind her head and emphasized her beautiful green eyes. The jeans showed off her slim hips and legs. Her breasts were outlined by the white sleeveless top, and he remembered how they had felt last night against his chest.

As much as he didn't want her here, having her in his home gave him a warm feeling. He liked the feeling a lot. Dammit all to hell, he liked it too much. With other women, he'd always been able to put the skids on when things got complicated. Why couldn't he do that with Abby?

CHAPTER EIGHT

ABBY PREPARED THE SPAGHETTI in record time. There wasn't anything to make a salad out of, but she found fresh broccoli. She steamed it and made a cheese sauce. When she finished, she placed the meal on the bar in front of him.

"Do you have any wine?" she asked.

"I don't drink" came the response.

"Oh." She was disconcerted for a second, then thought of something. "So why do you go to Mick's?" The words came out before she could stop them, and when she saw the look on his face, she wished she could snatch them back.

"How do you know I go to Mick's Tavern?" His voice was low and stiff.

She shrugged. "I guess I heard it somewhere."

"Last night you said you hadn't heard any rumors about me."

She didn't want to lie to him, but she didn't want to hurt his feelings, either. Debating between the two, she decided Jonas could take whatever she said. "I haven't heard any rumors, although my mom told me, so I guess that *is* a rumor."

"What did she say?" he asked quietly.

She took a deep breath. "That you hang out at Mick's and probably use the services he offers."

"I see," he said, and picked up his fork. "I hate

to disillusion your mom, but I don't drink and I don't pay for sex.'' He seemed to be saying those words a lot these days.

And she'd bet he never had to, either.

"Well," she said to hide her nervousness, "what would you like to drink?" She opened the refrigerator. "You have Coke and water."

"Coke will be fine."

Abby put ice in glasses and set a cola in front of him. She remembered seeing peanuts in the pantry, and she got a bag and sat beside him. She snacked on peanuts and drank Coke, while he ate his dinner.

A million questions were buzzing through Abby's head, but she'd wait until after he'd had his meal. Later, they put the dishes in the dishwasher together, and Jonas picked up his Coke and peanuts and headed for the living room. She grabbed her drink and followed. He sat in the large oversize leather chair, while she sat on the sofa.

"Are you ready to go to Mexico tomorrow?" she asked.

He glanced at her. "I was hoping you'd change your mind."

She met his look. "I'm not going to do that."

"Not even after being locked in the file room?"

"No." She twisted the glass in her hand. "Mr. Brewster thinks it was someone in his family, and he said he'd put a stop to it."

"And you believe him?"

Her eyes shot to his. "You're trying to talk me out of going, aren't you?"

He didn't say anything, and his silence angered her. "Fine." She jumped to her feet. "I'll go alone." She moved toward the door.

He caught her before she reached it. "Good God, you've got a short fuse."

"Maybe," she admitted tightly, and remembered Earl had told her almost the same thing. It used to take a lot to make her angry, but these days any little thing set her off. And there didn't seem to be anything she could do about it. "I'm just getting tired of everyone trying to keep me from doing this."

He could see that nothing was going to stop her...absolutely nothing. "Come back and let's talk."

She trailed behind him to the sofa and sat down.

"We have to be very careful," he said.

"I realize that."

"I'm not sure that you do," he replied. "You said you've been to Mexico many times. Where did you go?"

"I once went with some friends to Matamoros for a weekend, and my friend Holly and I went to Cancún for a week. But my parents and I have shopped in Nuevo Hope ever since I can remember."

"That was as a tourist, and Mexicans welcome tourists with open arms. That's how they survive. This will be different. You'll be asking questions, poking your nose into private affairs. Mexico is a poor country, but the people are proud and rugged individuals and they don't take kindly to foreigners asking personal questions. We don't want to step on any toes."

"Sounds as if you know the people well."

"I've worked Mexican laborers for years, some legal, some not, and I've been to Mexico to meet some of their families. They're proud of the ones that come here and are able to get a Green Card and work and make good money to send home. Others keep trying to come here and many lose their lives. But it doesn't stop the illegal immigration because everyone wants a better way of life."

"I'm aware of all that." She could see that Jonas was very passionate about the Mexicans and their plight.

"Sorry, I didn't mean to get carried away—but are you prepared for the heat, the dust, unpaved roads and the general poverty?"

"As much as I can be."

"Good. We won't need a tourist card to spend a day, and we'll walk. It's too much of a hassle to take a vehicle over there. The driving is horrendous, and there are basically no traffic rules."

"Walk?"

"You got something against walking?"

"No," she replied shortly. "I assumed we'd be driving."

"We won't," he snapped. "From what I read in Delores's file, her parents live just outside Nuevo Hope. Some streets are marked, some are not. With a little luck, her family shouldn't be too hard to find."

"Then, we should be able to do this in the one day?"

"Yes."

"By tomorrow night I could know why Mr. Brewster fired my father."

He watched the bright anticipation in her eyes for a moment, then said, "I've always learned to expect the unexpected."

She bit her lip. "You still think Mr. Brewster is up to something?"

"Yeah, I do. I know him, Abby, and he doesn't do anything without a reason."

"Then, why do you continue to work for him? He treats you terribly." The words came out sharper than she had intended, but she wanted an answer to that question.

"That's my business," he said woodenly, and got up to carry his glass into the kitchen. The subject was clearly off-limits, but that had never deterred her before.

"I'd still like to know," she said softly.

Her voice did crazy things to his resolve. He could feel himself wanting to tell her, and that unnerved him. He never talked about the past, but maybe if he told her, she'd see Brewster in a new light. Maybe she'd give up this crazy plan to avenge her father. He was afraid, though. Afraid that she'd see *him* in a new light, too. A light that would send her running away from him forever—which could only be a good thing, he told himself. There was no room for her in his life. Hell, he didn't have a life, so why was he even worrying about what she might think of him.

He walked slowly back to the sofa and sat down again, propping his bare feet on the coffee table.

Abby kicked off her shoes and curled her feet beneath her. "How long have you worked for Mr. Brewster?"

Silence.

"Jonas?" she prompted.

Continued silence.

She bit her lip, wondering how to get past that ironclad control. Just when she thought he wasn't going to say a word, he spoke.

"Twenty years, to be exact. I started when I was fifteen."

Fifteen! She remembered he'd said he lived on the street as a teenager. Could that mean...? "Did Mr. Brewster take you in?"

"Something like that."

She wanted to shake him. Mr. Brewster was right. Getting anything out of Jonas was impossible. She inhaled deeply. "Well, did he take you in or not?"

He looked at her. "You aren't going to stop, are you?"

"No," she said. "You want me to believe that you're a bad person, so tell me just how bad you are."

"Too bad for you, Abby," he said softly.

"I doubt that. I—"

"You don't know me."

"I know—"

"I killed Brewster's son."

Had she heard him correctly? Yes, she had. There was no mistaking those words. They hung between them, and she wanted to slap them away—but first she had to understand what they meant.

"Mr. Brewster said his son was killed in an accident with drunk teenagers. Everyone died at the scene."

"Not everyone."

She swallowed. "What happened?"

Jonas didn't look at her. But the fact that her voice wasn't filled with disgust or shock—just a desire to know—made him long to share the trauma that had changed his life. The accident and the events that followed were buried deep within him, in a place no one had ever touched...until now. Words surged to his throat, and he heard himself speaking.

"The Justice of the Peace pronounced everyone dead at the scene, and that's the story that went into all the papers. But when they got my body to the morgue, they discovered I was breathing. They rushed me to the hospital."

"So you were with the kids who crashed into Mr. Brewster's son?"

"Yes."

"Were you driving?"

"No, I was only fifteen, but I hung out with guys who were older. Eddie, the driver, had souped up his 1975 Mustang, and he and his friends were cruising. They saw me and asked if I wanted to have some fun. They'd stolen some beer in McAllen and they were already pretty high. We drove to Alamo Creek and finished off the beer. Eddie decided to show us how fast the Mustang would go. We hit speeds over a hundred on Alamo Road. Then this white Jaguar came up behind us and tried to pass. Eddie wouldn't let him. Finally Eddie allowed him to pull alongside us. It was Brewster's son. Everyone knew who he was. He was cursing Eddie, and Eddie rammed his car. They did that back and forth for at least a mile, each cursing the other. The farther we went, the faster we went. Then a truck appeared from the opposite direction, and all I remember is the screech of tires, the crashing of metal and the screams...nightmarish screams."

Abby didn't say anything. She was locked in that young boy's world of terror.

"I woke up in a hospital in pain and shock. No one expected me to live, and at times I didn't want to live. I was so scared." He stopped for a second. "I guess I was in the hospital about two weeks when Brewster came to see me. He didn't say a word. He just stared at me and walked out. The sheriff had been to see me, too, and asked a lot of questions. I answered everything truthfully, and the sheriff said I was in a lot of trouble because Brewster wanted someone to pay." He paused again. "Brewster came every day after that. He never spoke. He would just look at me and leave. Then one day he asked how I was feeling, and I told him better. He said that was good because I had to pay for his son's death."

He drew a deep breath. "You asked me why I go to Mick's Tavern. He was the only real friend I had back then. He gave me a place to sleep and food to eat when I was on the streets, and he and his wife came to visit me several times in the hospital. Mick told me that the sheriff and Brewster were after my hide, but there wasn't a whole lot they could convict me of. I tried to believe that, but Brewster scared the hell out of me. When I was able to walk again, I kept waiting for the sheriff to take me away. Then one day Brewster came into my room and started talking about his son. He said he had been thirty-one years old and planning to get married. He was ready to settle down and manage Brewster Farms. Brewster added that I had taken everything away, everything that mattered to him, and he would make sure I'd never have a day's peace. He'd already fired the families of the other boys who'd been in the car, so I knew he wasn't bluffing."

Abby held her breath as she waited for his next words.

"On his next visit, he told me I'd be leaving the

hospital in a few days and I could either go to jail
or work for him. I had no idea what he was talking
about, but I didn't have to wait long for him to explain. I had taken his son and now I would replace
him. I would work for Brewster with no privileges
until the day he died. That way he could keep an eye
on me and make my life a living hell. Still, working
at Brewster Farms seemed a whole lot better than
being locked up. But in the days, weeks and months
that followed, it became very clear that I'd sold my
soul to the devil to stay out of jail.''

Abby held a hand over her mouth to keep from
gasping out loud. Finally, she understood why Jonas
Parker stayed at Brewster Farm's, why he took so
much crap from Mr. Brewster. He was paying off a
debt that wasn't even his.

"You could have left years ago, and Mr. Brewster
couldn't have done a thing,'' she said into the still-
ness.

"Yeah.'' He leaned his head against the back of
the sofa. "I realized that in my early twenties—probably the same time I realized I was an adult. But I
didn't go. I stayed. I just kept thinking about how
much he'd lost. His wife died soon after the accident,
and I felt I owed him. Besides, I'd given my word
that I'd stay until he died.''

So much more about Jonas became clear. Why he
worked from sunup to sundown. Why he drove himself so hard. Why he was quiet and brooding at times.
He'd survived through sheer grit and character. All
the feelings she had for him culminated in that moment. Was this love? she wondered. No! It couldn't
be. She had only known him a few weeks. She was

just feeling sympathetic—his story had touched her heart. As it would any woman's.

"Oh, Jonas," she whispered.

He turned his head to look at her. "It wasn't so bad—well, the first year was, but after that things got better."

"What happened?"

It was so easy to talk to her, and his words flowed freely. "Brewster had a storeroom cleaned out and a bed and dresser put in it. That was my home for the next few years. I worked in the fields from daybreak to dark, and Brewster didn't pay me a dime. I didn't complain. I felt I deserved it. Then Brewster made me go to night school and get my high-school diploma. I worked all day and went to school at night. When I graduated, he started to pay me a salary. I guess it was a test to see if I could stick it out. Later he sent me to college at night to take crop management and business courses. I'd always hated school, but I found myself wanting to learn more. Finally Brewster brought me in from the fields to the warehouse and then to the office."

"Did you ever think of running away?"

"Lots of times, but I learned early that you can't outrun the pain and that there's a price to pay for the wrongs you do in this world."

"You didn't do anything wrong." She had to say it.

"Oh yes, I did," he answered quickly. "I've got bad blood in my veins. Liquor is what drove me back then. I stole it from Mick and anywhere else I could find it. When Eddie offered me free beer, I jumped at the chance and went along with whatever they wanted to do. That's the type of person I was, and I have to fight every day not to become him again.''

Unable to stop herself, Abby moved to wrap her arms around him. He stiffened immediately.

''Abby.'' The word came out as a low groan, but he made no effort to touch her.

She held him tightly. ''You are not bad,'' she murmured. ''And nothing you say is going to convince me of that.''

JONAS WAS STRUGGLING not to touch her, not to turn his head and capture her lips. He should have known she wouldn't react the way he'd wanted her to. She should be walking out the door, not torturing him. Damn, she felt so good, and the fragrant scent of her hair played hell with his control.

''I…'' Words failed him, as she kissed him below his ear. His head tilted toward the gesture, needing it more than he thought possible.

''The sheriff was right the other day,'' she whispered against his skin. ''He admires the man you've become. Everyone does, me included. It took a lot of courage to turn your life around.''

He was drowning in her words, going down so fast he had trouble breathing.

She ran her hands through his hair. ''Jonas.''

''Hmm?''

''Kiss me.''

''Abby.''

''Kiss me and mean it. Don't hold anything back.''

He turned his head, his lips inches from hers.

Her hand trailed down to his chest. ''Kiss me from here…your heart.''

When she touched him, that organ—and others—

sprang to life. Jonas reached up and removed the clip
from her hair, and it fell to her shoulders. He cupped
her face and gently took her lips. She quivered, and
his mouth opened over hers in a slow languorous
exploration.

She moaned, and his hands traveled to her breasts.
He tentatively touched them, then pulled her tight
against him, breathing heavily into her hair.

"Jonas," she cried.

"Shh." He kissed her hair, struggling with his
feelings. He wanted her, but when they made love,
he didn't want it to be out of some misguided sense
of sympathy on her part. He wanted more from her,
for her...for them both. He wanted... He couldn't
even say the word in his head. But he could feel his
heart opening slowly, experiencing something that
had to be...what? *Love?* Was this how real love felt?
When you wanted to be with someone totally and
completely, sharing secrets and emotions you never
dared to share with anyone else? Was love thinking
of her more than you thought of yourself? He shook
his head, not wanting to dig any deeper into his emotions.

"Have you ever ridden a motorcycle?" he asked,
to turn his mind to other things.

She drew back and gazed into his darkened eyes.
"No."

"Would you like to?"

"Depends."

"On what?"

"If I have to ride it alone."

A grin touched his face. "Most definitely not."

"Then, yes, I'd love to ride with you."

The way she said it curled his stomach into a warm

ball, and he gently disengaged his body from hers.
"My Harley's in the warehouse. Let me get my boots
on."

Abby wrapped her arms around her stomach as he
disappeared into the bedroom, missing his warmth,
his strength. She knew that this time he'd stopped
kissing her not because he wanted to, but because
he'd had to. They weren't ready to take that big step,
even though her body said otherwise. This wasn't
about physical gratification. It was about something
much deeper. Something worth waiting for.

Jonas returned wearing his boots and carrying two
helmets. "Come on," he said eagerly. "Let's hit the
highway."

She slipped into her shoes and quickly followed
him out the door. In the warehouse, he removed a
cover from a black-and-silver motorcycle. Abby
didn't know anything about motorcycles, but two
things registered—big and expensive.

"Shouldn't we have leather jackets or something?"

He grinned as he swung his leg over the seat and
started the engine. The sound was deafening in the
warehouse. He nodded to her, and she put on the
helmet and climbed up behind him. He flipped on
the lights and gassed the motor. Her arms tightened
around his waist. They rolled out of the warehouse
and soon were flying down the highway into Hope.
The wind cooled her body, and the darkness of the
night enveloped them...just her and Jonas.

The streets were almost empty at this hour. The
thought crossed her mind that if anyone saw her with
Jonas, it would be all over town by tomorrow. She

didn't care. She hadn't been this happy in a long time.

Twenty minutes later, they were back in the warehouse. Abby jumped off and removed her helmet. "That was wonderful. It's like flying and feeling free and...oh, I don't know, but it was great."

Jonas smiled at her, got off, adjusted the kickstand and carefully covered the motorcycle.

They walked out into the warm September night. "I don't think you'd better come up," he said quietly.

She didn't have to ask why. They had a big day tomorrow and they both had to have clear heads. Tomorrow. She had to concentrate on what that meant for her. It wasn't easy when she could still feel Jonas's lips on hers.

"What time should we leave in the morning?" she asked as she made her way to her car.

"I'll pick you up at eight," he replied.

"Okay." She turned to face him. "I'll see you then." She made herself get into her car. "Thank you, Jonas."

"You're welcome," he answered.

You're very welcome ran through his mind as he strolled to the stairs.

Inside his apartment, he sat on the sofa and felt something beneath his hand. He picked it up. Her hair clip. He twirled it between his fingers, feeling her presence, her scent, and hoped he was doing the right thing...for Abby.

CHAPTER NINE

THE NEXT MORNING Abby was up early. She hadn't slept much. Thoughts of Jonas had kept her tossing and turning. When she finally dozed, her dreams were troubled ones of her father, Jonas, Mr. Brewster and the impending trip to Mexico.

She made her way to the kitchen for coffee. Her mother was already there, dressed and ready for work. She eyed Abby's tousled hair and short night-gown.

"You were out late last night, Abigail."

Abby poured a cup of coffee. "I was with Jonas. We were making plans to go to Mexico."

Gail sighed. "Abby, I just don't understand why you have to do this."

"Mom, please, we've been all through this," Abby said. "I have doubts about Mr. Brewster, too. That's why I had him write that letter. That's all that interests me—reading the letter and knowing the truth. I plan on printing it in the *Hope Herald* so everyone can read it. I'm also going to run it in my paper in Dallas."

"What if it's something you don't want to hear?"

Abby's eyes narrowed. "What are you saying?"

Gail didn't answer. She put her cup in the sink and turned slowly around.

"Mom."

144 ON THE TEXAS BORDER

"You have this image of your father as a saint, but he was human just like everyone else."

Abby jumped to her feet. "Don't say anything bad about Daddy."

Gail blinked back a tear. "I'm not saying anything bad. I'm trying to make you listen. Can't you see I can't take any more? You have to stop this."

The silence was suffocating, and for the first time Abby weakened in her resolve. Everyone was trying to talk her out of going...even Jonas. Why couldn't she listen? How could she hurt her mother like this?

She walked over and hugged Gail. "I'm sorry."

Gail held her tight. "Don't go, Abby. Don't go."

Abby shook her head and stepped away from her mother. "Jonas and I are leaving this morning. I'll be back as soon as I can. Try not to worry." With that, she headed for her room.

"Abby." Gail's voice sounded as if she was close to tears.

Abby stopped and waited.

"Be careful, sweetheart. Please be very careful," Gail murmured.

"I will," Abby replied, and walked toward her bedroom...and the unknown future.

SHE DRESSED QUICKLY in a pair of old jeans and a cotton shirt. She pinned up her hair and didn't use any makeup. She didn't want to draw attention to herself.

Jonas arrived at precisely eight o'clock. He was wearing his usual jeans, chambray shirt, boots and hat. He looked so handsome that her heart missed a beat. She eyed his lean frame and remembered how that hard body had felt against hers.

"Are you ready?" she asked, mostly to change the direction of her thoughts.

"As ready as I'll ever be," he answered sardonically, and followed her down the walk to his truck.

She didn't mistake his tone but she didn't say anything until she'd climbed into the vehicle. "Don't start," she warned, and buckled her seat belt. "I've already been through this with my mom and that's all I can handle."

"I wasn't going to say a word," he said as he pulled the truck away from the curb and headed toward the international bridge. "I've already learned that you have a head like cement."

She frowned at him. "That's not much of a compliment."

"It wasn't meant to be." Then, as if he realized he may have hurt her feelings, he added, "But you cook very well. Thanks for supper last night."

That didn't quite make up for his earlier insult, but she decided to be gracious. "You're welcome."

They didn't speak again until they drove into the parking area at the bridge. People were already walking across, and several vehicles were waiting to be cleared by Customs.

"Did you see Mr. Brewster this morning?" Abby asked, unbuckling the seat belt.

"Yeah, and he was a little too excited. He's convinced we'll find his daughter."

"He seems to know how this will end before we even start," she said in a low voice.

"That's what bothers me," Jonas said.

"Well, let's go find Delores Alvarez and get some answers."

"Leave your purse in the glove compartment," he

instructed, as she started to get out. "One less thing to worry about. Put your ID and some money into your pocket."

She did as he suggested, and he locked the bag away. They got out, and Jonas paid the man in the booth to leave his truck in the parking lot. Then they paid the tourist toll and started over the bridge. Abby stared through the chain-link wire into the muddy green Rio Grande River.

An eerie feeling came over her as they walked from Texas into Mexico. Mexican children not more than five years old had climbed the fence and hung from it with one hand, while begging with the other. Others were standing with both hands out. Abby reached into her pockets.

"Don't even think about it," Jonas said. "If you give them a penny, they'll follow wanting more. It's how their parents make a living."

"I know. It's so sad."

"It's life here, so get used to it."

His voice was gruff, but Abby knew that he sympathized with the plight of these kids. Life here was very different. Vendors filled the crowded street. Fresh fruit was peddled on every corner and gift shops overflowed with jewelry, precious metals, leather goods, colorful pottery and embroidered cloth. Most of the customers were Americans. Tourists spilled into the tiny stores looking for bargains. The drugstores were particularly busy. Medicines cost less on this side of the border, and prescriptions weren't needed. All one had to have was the name of the drug. Nothing here was regulated.

They had to thread their way among the crowds to get through the small town. When they were almost at the edge of town, an old woman, with gray hair twisted into a knot, held out a denim jacket in front of Abby. "You buy, you buy?" She smiled, and Abby saw that she had no teeth. Abby studied the jacket. It had beautiful embroidery work on the front and back; delicate flowers interwoven with leaves and petals.

Abby touched the lovely jacket. "It's very nice."

"*Sì, sì,* you buy?" The old woman smiled broadly.

"Abby, we're not here to shop," Jonas said sternly.

"Just look at this," she pleaded.

"Abby." There was a warning in his voice now, but she ignored it.

"How much?" she asked the woman.

"Twenty dollar," she replied in her broken English.

"Abby."

"The jacket is exquisite," she said. "It's all hand done, and it must have taken her days to embroider it."

She fished a twenty out of her pocket and paid the woman. Then she noticed Jonas remove his wallet and shove something into the woman's hand.

"Oh, *señor, gracias, gracias.*" The old woman beamed.

Jonas nodded.

"What did you give her that made her so grateful?" Abby asked, as they moved on.

"Nothing" was the short answer.

"Jonas…"

"Are we gonna shop or are we gonna find Delores Alvarez?" he said in an aggravated tone.

"Don't be so grouchy," she retorted. "You're acting just like Mr. Brewster."

He swung around to face her, and they came to a complete stop. His brown eyes were almost black. "Don't you ever say that to me—ever."

Abby wasn't afraid. She was just taken aback. It wasn't like him to be so short-tempered. But before she could respond, he apologized.

"I'm sorry. It's just that this place always upsets me. So much poverty. So much misery."

"It's all right," she assured him. "I shouldn't have said that. It was thoughtless."

Without another word, he turned and walked away. She quickly followed. She knew exactly why he was upset. He was afraid of his anger—afraid that he was like his father.

She ran ahead and faced him, but he wouldn't stop. She jogged backward talking to him. "Jonas, stop so I can talk to you."

He kept walking.

Finally she grabbed his arms with both hands, forcing him to stand still. She felt him tense. She looked into his eyes, but he was staring off into space. It didn't stop her.

"You're allowed to get angry," she told him. "I said a stupid thing, but I knew you weren't going to hit me. You would never do that. You're nothing like your father."

A breath came from the bottom of his chest, and he pulled away from her. "Stop analyzing me, Abby, and leave me—"

"No, I'm not leaving you alone," she snapped as if she were reading his mind.

"Why? Am I a challenge to your journalist's instincts? Is that's why you kissed me and asked me to kiss you?'' His voice was as cold as steel.

She shook her head. "No, it wasn't like that."

His eyes narrowed. "Then, tell me how it was."

Her eyes didn't waver from his as she grappled for the words to tell him. She felt ashamed and foolish, but she wasn't going to let him believe something that wasn't true. "Kyle put a dent in my self-esteem," she said reluctantly. "I didn't feel attractive or desirable anymore. I didn't want anything more to do with men, but—"

"But what?" he prompted.

She drew a hard breath. "But when I looked at you, all those negative feelings disappeared, and I wanted to be desired again...by you. That was selfish of me, when you had made it very obvious you didn't want me."

If only she knew.

The tightness in his chest eased and he realized they were standing in the middle of the sidewalk with people jostling them, giving them dark stares. He stopped scowling. "Why are we talking about this now...and here?"

She shrugged. "You were upset, and I wanted you to know that everyone gets angry. It's a human re-action. It doesn't make you a bad person as long as you don't take that anger out on someone else. You would never do that. You're very gentle and consid-erate, and you're always in control. I've never seen anyone with so much self-control."

"But I'm so afraid that someday I will lose it." He'd spoken without thinking. Something about her made him reveal more than he wanted to. And this was definitely not the time or place to talk. He took

her arm and began walking. "We'll discuss this another time. Right now, we need to find Delores Alvarez."

"Jonas?"

"Later, Abby."

He was very glad when she relented. He'd deal
with the promise he'd just made...later.

THEY LEFT THE PAVED STREETS of the town. Now,
when a vehicle passed by, the dust from the dirt road
was almost suffocating. Outside the town, most of
the dwellings were lean-tos and shacks. Occasionally
there was a small concrete or stucco house. Laundry
hung on bushes and fences. The poverty all around
was heartbreaking.

Some roads had street signs, others didn't, but they
found the road where Delores's parents lived. The
house wasn't much more than a shack, but it had a
front porch. The yard was bare but for some wild
cactus. A dog growled from beneath the porch, as
Jonas knocked on the door.

The door opened a crack, and an old man peered
out.

"Donde esta Delores Alvarez," Jonas said.

"Vete, vete," the man said and tried to close the
door, but Jonas stuck his boot in the crack.

"Es muy importante," Jonas added.

"Hace mucho tiempo que se fue," the man mumbled.

"A donde se fue?" Jonas persisted.

"No se. No esta aqui."

Though the man spoke quickly, Abby caught most
of the conversation. Delores had left a long time ago,
and he didn't know where she was.

Jonas stared at the man an extra second, then removed his foot. The door was immediately closed. They walked away.

"Do you believe him?" Abby asked when they were out of earshot.

"I'm not sure. He could be telling the truth, or maybe someone paid him to keep quiet."

"But why?"

"I have no idea, but we'll try a few of the neighbors. They might know something."

They walked over to one of the concrete houses. A woman sat in an old wooden rocker pasting strips of red, yellow, green and blue papers on a whimsical piñata that would later be sold in town. The yard was dirt, and there was an occasional flower among the cactuses.

"Tu conoce a Delores Alvarez?"

"Sì."

Abby felt a moment of jubilation.

"Tu savis donde esta?"

"No, hace mucho tiempo que se fue."

The woman continued to paste the strips. Abby recognized that the woman had said virtually the same thing as the old man. Delores had left a long time ago, and they didn't know where she was. They tried several more houses and got the same response. It was very frustrating. Suddenly a man pulling a cart loaded with watermelons appeared around a curve. The load was so heavy that the man was struggling to pull it along.

Jonas stopped him. *"Cuanto?"* he asked.

Abby knew Jonas was asking how much the melons were.

The man wiped sweat from his brow with the

sleeve of his shirt. He held up one finger. "*Uno* dollar."

Jonas handed the man a five and took a melon off the cart.

"*Sì, sì, señor, gracias, gracias.*" The man was bobbing his head in delight.

"*Tu conoce a Delores Alvarez?*" Jonas asked quickly.

The man's face changed dramatically. He picked up the cart and trudged away shaking his head.

"Dammit," Jonas cursed, and stared at the melon in his hands.

"What are you gonna do with that?" Abby asked, laughter edging her voice. She had to laugh or she was going to cry.

A young woman with two boys about ages eight and nine came by, and Jonas gave the melon to them. They smiled and carried it into town, where they'd probably sell it.

Jonas smiled wryly. "Well, at least we're boosting the economy."

"That's about all we're doing," she remarked.

By mid-afternoon the temperature was unbearable, so they walked into town and bought Cokes, chips, peanuts and candy bars.

With the goodies in a bag, they made their way out of town again to an oak tree, and sat in the shade beneath its branches. They munched on the junk food, discussing what to do next.

"No one will tell us where she is," Abby muttered.

"They're all saying the same thing—*left long ago*—as if they've been told exactly what to say."

"I don't understand why someone would do that,"

Abby said. "This could only be a good thing for Delores and her daughter. They could have a better life."

"Yeah, it doesn't make sense," Jonas agreed. "Unless—"

"Unless what?"

"Unless Delores thinks that this is just some game of Brewster's."

"He sounded so sincere about a daughter, though."

"Yeah, I was beginning to believe him, but now I have a feeling something else is going on."

"What could it be?' she asked forlornly.

"I don't know," he answered, and got to his feet. "But if Delores doesn't want to be found, we won't find her. The Mexicans will make sure of that."

"I thought this would be easy and I'd find out about my father, but now Mr. Brewster is never going to tell me." A bitter taste settled in her mouth. She had defied everyone for nothing. Her father would forever be the man who had embezzled money from Mr. Brewster.

Jonas reached out as if to give her some comfort. She put her hand in his, and he pulled her to his feet.

"It will be dark in a couple of hours, so we'd better head back for the bridge," he said.

Before she could respond, a young boy, not more than fifteen, came running up to them. *"Señor, señor,"* he called to Jonas. *"Te digo por dinero donde esta Delores Alvarez?"*

Abby caught Delores's name. He'd said he knew where Delores was and he'd tell them for money. Her heart began to beat a little faster.

"Cuanto?" Jonas asked.

"Cien dollares."

Jonas eyed the youth's eager face. *"Lleva me a Delores Alvarez."*

"Dinero primero." The kid held out his hand.

Jonas shook his head. *"No dinero hasta veo a Delores."*

The kid's dark eyes snapped angrily. *"Bastardo gringo,"* he muttered and ran off.

"Jonas, don't let him get away," Abby cried. "He knows where Delores is."

"He doesn't. He's just trying to make a hundred dollars."

Abby knew Jonas was right. When he'd insisted on seeing Delores first, the youth had gotten angry. But it was hard to let go of that tiny hope.

Jonas retrieved her jacket from the ground and handed it to her. "But it's all very disturbing. Evidently the whole town knows we're looking for Delores. Instead of the grapevine opening doors, it's closed them. That doesn't make sense. Something's not right."

"So what do we do?"

"Maybe we'll come back tomorrow and give it another try. Someone in this town has to be willing to talk."

Her heart lifted. "Thank you, Jonas. Thank you."

He recovered his hat from the ground. "Don't thank me yet. I haven't done anything but waste a day of my off time."

"I'll make it up to you. I promise."

He stared into the green of her eyes, losing himself in the pledge he saw there. No mattered what happened, he would find the answers she needed. It was a vow he made to himself...to repay her for these feelings she was bringing to life inside him.

CHAPTER TEN

THEY STARTED WALKING down the dirt road into
Nuevo Hope. Abby felt a lot better. At least they
weren't giving up. And tomorrow might prove pro-
ductive. Several vehicles passed, and Abby could
taste the dust in her mouth. She was ready to get
back to civilization.

An old truck came up behind them, and they had
to move into the ditch to allow it to pass. Still, it
barely missed hitting them.

"Stupid fools," Jonas muttered, as they made their
way onto the road again.

The truck stopped ahead of them, smoke billowing
out of the tailpipe. It backed up and turned around.
The driver gunned the engine and roared toward
them at high speed.

"What the hell!" Jonas said, an instant before he
caught her hand and began to run.

The truck kept coming—closer and closer. Abby's
breath was locked in her throat and her legs were
tight. When it was inches from them, Jonas grabbed
her around the waist and jerked her into the ditch.
They rolled down a ravine into a cornfield.

Abby was winded and shaken. It took a while for
the world to right itself. She lay on top of Jonas, her
heart hammering loudly in her ears.

Jonas raised his head. "Are you all right?" he asked.

She nodded and moved onto her back, taking several gulps of air.

He looked down at her. "Are you sure?"

"No, but I don't believe anything's broken." She'd lost her clip, and her hair had fallen across her face. Her clothes were filthy, and her head was beginning to pound.

Jonas sat up, brushing debris from his clothes. "I don't know what the hell that was all about. They were either trying to scare us or kill us, and I sure as hell don't like either option."

"Kill us?" She managed to sit up. "But why?"

"I wish I knew, but we certainly have someone's attention."

She shook dirt and grass from her hair and clothes. "Could it possibly have been an accident?"

"No, the truck came right for us and it wasn't stopping."

She knew that, but had hoped for a less scary explanation.

"The license plate was so dirty, I couldn't make it out," Jonas said. "I guess we'll have to stay here for the night. It won't be safe on the road. They could be waiting."

She looked at the dried corn, tall weeds and desolate landscape. A shiver darted through her. "Here?" The word slipped out weakly.

"You have a better idea?"

"No," she snapped, and got to her feet just to prove that she could. Her legs were wobbly, and she immediately sank to the ground. "I didn't think it would be like this." Damn, she sounded like a whining baby. Where was all her strength? She had been through rough times before. She had been a member of an investigative report team for a while, and they'd handled stakeouts, long hours and unsavory characters. But it wasn't like this—where her next breath could be her last.

"I told you from the start," he said in an even tone that irritated her, "when you start digging into the past, you'd better be able to handle the consequences."

"Thanks for telling me 'I told you so,'" she mumbled, and lay back on the grass, trying to breathe normally, more upset with herself than with him.

She felt Jonas move away, and turned her head to see where he was going. He walked up the ravine and retrieved her jacket and his hat. He returned and dropped the jacket beside her.

"Good thing you bought it," he said. "It will be the only cover you have tonight, and it will get pretty cool by morning." Having said that, he lay on the grass and placed his hat over his eyes.

Her irritation grew. "Are you going to sleep?"

"Yep."

"But it's barely dark."

"We don't have any food and there's nothing to do but get some rest. We'll need all our strength in the morning."

"I'm not tired, and I don't see how you can go to sleep with everything that has happened."

He didn't answer and the silence became unbearable.

"Jonas."

"Hmm?"

"You'd said we'd talk later."

"This isn't later."

"What is it?"

Again, he didn't answer, and she wanted to shake him. She sat up and moved closer to him. Her knees brushed his waist. He stiffened automatically, and she didn't miss it.

"Who do you think doesn't want us to find Delores?" she asked.

"Could be anyone—Edna, Jules, Darby, even Brewster."

"Mr. Brewster's the one who sent us here."

"He has a weird sense of reasoning. Sometimes I don't think he even realizes how cruel he can be. Life's a game to him and he plays to win. He might want to see how far you'll go to find the truth when in reality there might not be a truth at all. He's manipulating you, but I think you already know that."

She wrapped her arms around her waist to still the trembling inside her. "Yes, but I was hoping we'd both get something out of this."

"Don't count on it."

"You're very cynical."

"Maybe," he admitted. "But I'm also realistic."

"So you still think there isn't a daughter?"

"I'm not sure what to think right now." He adjusted his hat. "Get some rest. The questions can wait."

Silence fell again, and she grabbed her jacket and held it to her. Without a second thought, she curled up beside him and rested her head on his chest.

"Comfortable?" he asked sarcastically.

"Yes, thank you."

"Then, go to sleep."

She tried, but all she could think about was how

nice it was to be close to Jonas. She listened to his even breathing and the steady beat of his heart. Her cheek and hand were on his chest, and she could feel those hard muscles. She loved how... Her thoughts came to a halt. There was that word again. *Love.* Could she love Jonas? Could it happen this quickly? What was she thinking? She had fallen for Kyle just as fast, but this was different—an overwhelming, consuming emotion every time she was near Jonas. She wanted to know him inside and out, ease his pain and be there for him when he needed someone.

These feelings had begun weeks ago, and the moment he'd kissed her, they'd blossomed into something real and overpowering. *She loved Jonas.* With everything that was going on around her, that one thing stood out in her mind. She knew Jonas wasn't ready to hear those words from her—love was foreign to him—but she'd change his mind someway, somehow.

Her fingers slipped between the buttons of his shirt.

"What are you doing?" he asked immediately, and removed his hat.

"Seeing if you're awake."

"I am *now.*"

Jonas felt her gentle caress permeating his whole being, weakening his control. She was the only person who'd ever been able to do that, and he wasn't sure he liked it. Being in control was a creed he'd lived by for the past twenty years. As long as he was in control of his emotions, no one could ever touch him and cause him pain again.

But Abby was slowly opening the door to his heart with her warmth, persistence and unfailing loyalty.

He saw all of those qualities in her love for her father and in the compassionate way she listened to Jonas talk about his past.

"Jonas," she murmured faintly, breaking into his reverie. "I'm so afraid. I've been afraid before—when Kyle hit me and when my father died—but this…this is a new kind of fear."

His hand slid under her hair to her neck and rested there. "Don't worry," he said calmly. "At first light, we'll be out of here before anyone knows we're gone. Then we'll confront Brewster and demand some answers."

Abby relaxed, soaking up his strength. Once again, she was surprised at how much she'd come to depend on him. She'd never needed anyone this way before. Maybe her mother was right, and she wasn't herself. Certainly her life wasn't going the way she'd planned.

"Have you ever dreamed or fantasized?"

He'd fantasized plenty since he'd met her, but he was sure that wasn't what she meant.

When he didn't answer, she went on. "I never had any fears or doubts about my life. My friends used to tease me about my big dreams. But my parents instilled in me strong values and a sense of self-worth. I knew early what I wanted to be, which college I'd go to and where I'd work. I'd fall in love with a wonderful man. We'd get married and have a boy and a girl. We'd raise them together, sharing responsibilities while maintaining our careers. And at night we'd share a passion that would not diminish over time." She gave a fake laugh. "That's such a bunch of crap, but it's every little girl's dream and it was mine. My dream became ashes in the wind, as my grandmother used to say.''

Jonas listened, sensing that she needed to talk.

She rubbed her face against him again. ''Oh, I can't believe how much I'm babbling.'' She turned to look at him through the darkness. ''What do you dream about?''

''Freedom,'' he said without thinking. ''I dream of having my freedom...of being free of Brewster.''

''Oh, Jonas.'' Her hand touched his face. ''My problems seem so petty compared to everything you've been through.''

He swallowed hard at her soft caress. ''We all have problems. That's life and it's not a blank page. Some things are written for us, others we write ourselves. It's how we handle the latter that makes us who we are.''

''I hope some good things happen for you,'' she said, and snuggled against him. ''You deserve them.''

''You, too,'' he replied earnestly. ''And don't let any man make you believe that you're not attractive or desirable. You don't have to make a pass at me to prove it, either.''

''You think...I'm attractive and desirable?''

''Don't fish for compliments,'' he said. ''You should know by the way I react to you that you are.''

''Then, why do you fight it?''

''Because your mother is right. I'm not the kind of man you should be seeing, kissing or doing anything with.''

''I'll be the judge of that—not my mother.'' She reached up and kissed his cheek. ''I kiss you because I want to and because I find you desirable, too.''

Unable to resist, he turned his head, and his lips met hers with a need that surpassed anything he'd ever felt. She responded with an eagerness that excited and aroused him beyond reason. "Abby, Abby," he groaned, his mouth finding hers again as his hand stroked her abdomen.

Suddenly a light flashed from somewhere above and everything stilled. Jonas held his breath. He could hear Mexican voices. He rolled to his side, holding Abby tightly against him. The voices continued, but he couldn't make out a word. They were too far away.

"What are they saying?" Abby whispered.

"Shh," he ordered, and watched the light. Soon it moved on. He let out a ragged breath.

"What were they saying?" Abby asked again.

"They were talking so fast, and the words were slurred. Evidently they've been drinking. All I could make out was *gringo, stupid* and *bitch*. So I assume they were looking for us."

"Oh, Jonas, are we ever gonna get out of here?"

"They'll go somewhere to sleep off the drink, and we'll be gone before they wake up." He reached for her jacket and pulled it over her. "Maybe we'd better go farther into the cornfield to make sure they don't find us."

They stood and fixed their clothes, then slowly threaded their way through the corn. Weeds clung to Abby's jeans and dried stalks hit her in the face. She tried not to think about mice, snakes or other creatures that might be lurking out of sight.

Jonas finally stopped and pulled her down to the ground beside him. "Try to sleep. Morning won't be far away."

Sleep! That was the last thing on her mind. She curled an arm around his waist and rested her head beneath his chin. Her body still ached for him—fear had not replaced desire. It had only forestalled the inevitable. Of that she was sure. She held that thought to her heart as she started to count sheep....

JONAS DIDN'T SLEEP MUCH. He dozed off a couple of times then jerked instantly awake, listening for any sound or movement that might indicate impending danger. He'd told Abby not to worry, but he couldn't take his own advice. If the men were paid enough money, they'd do anything...even make sure he and Abby didn't make it back to Texas. Who would go to such lengths? Four people came to mind, the same four he'd mentioned to Abby. Edna, Jules, Darby and Brewster. The first three had a strong motive—greed. But what would Brewster get out of this elaborate scheme? Did it have something to do with Abe?

Jonas remembered the many arguments between Abe and Brewster. Now he wished he had listened more closely to what they'd been arguing about. All he remembered was Brewster complaining that Abe was getting lax and slow, costing Brewster money. None of it was true. No one was more responsible or dedicated than Abe. That last day Abe and Brewster had a heated argument. Jonas heard their angry voices from his apartment, but he didn't go down. The next morning Jonas noticed that Abe's desk had been cleared off, and Abe never returned to work. At the time, Jonas had felt that it was Brewster's business—not his. Looking back now, he realized he should have made it his business. Maybe he could have saved Abby all this heartache.

He didn't really know that. Certainly Edna, Jules and Darby had a much better motive than Brewster for silencing Abby, but Jonas couldn't shake his uneasiness about Brewster. He realized it was fueled by the years of antagonism between them. If Brewster was trying to hurt Abby because of an old grievance against Abe, then Jonas vowed he would walk away from Brewster Farms without a second thought. He would take his freedom sooner than Brewster expected, even though that freedom didn't seem nearly as appealing...without Abby.

The thought rocked him. He and Abby had no future, he reminded himself. They were two people attracted to each other and that didn't mean squat. When this was over, she'd go back to Dallas and her world, and he'd do whatever the hell he had to.

His arms tightened around her in protest. For the first time, he had to admit that it would be nice to have someone in his life...someone like Abby. But he knew it wasn't meant to be. His fate had been sealed long ago.

The wind picked up and rippled through the corn. A dog barked in the distance. Jonas glanced at the sky. The heaviness of night was giving way to the lightness of pre-dawn. He eased away from Abby and walked a short distance to check things out. He wanted to leave as soon as possible.

ABBY WOKE UP feeling a strange emptiness. As soon as her mind began to function, she knew what the problem was. Jonas was gone. She scrambled to her knees as panic swept through her. Then she saw him coming through the corn, and her whole body trembled with a sense of relief...and more...an awareness that went beyond anything she'd ever known. How had she ever lived without knowing Jonas—his touch, his warmth, his deep sense of pride? A few days ago she'd just wanted him to talk to her. Now she wanted so much more.

Jonas halted a few feet away from her. He saw the fear in her eyes and dropped down beside her. "Abby, what is it?"

She swallowed. "I thought you'd gone."

"I wouldn't leave you here. Don't you know that?"

"Yes," she said, and dragged both hands through her disheveled hair. "But when I woke up, I had this horrible feeling, and you weren't here..." She threw both arms around his neck. "Hold me, just hold me."

He held her tightly, enjoying this moment. "We have to go," he said, and leaned away. "It will be light soon."

"Why do you always do that?"

"What?"

"Pull away from me."

"Abby." He sighed. "This isn't the time."

"Yes, it is," she told him. "Are you seeing someone else?"

He drew back. "No."

"A woman decorated your apartment," she continued, hating the jealousy she could hear in her voice.

His eyes narrowed. "How do you know that?"

"A woman's instinct."

"I see," he said, and watched her thoughtfully for a second. "I dated a woman for a while who has an interior decorating shop in McAllen. She helped with the apartment.''

''Was the relationship serious?''

''It was a physical relationship, Abby,'' he replied. ''We both knew that from the start. She wanted to take things further, but I don't have a future to offer anyone. Brewster owns me, just like he said. I thought you understood that.''

''Brewster does not own you,'' she declared fiercely. ''Not unless you let him. And it's time you realized that.''

''Abby.''

''It's true, Jonas. You can't stop living because of an accident you weren't responsible for.''

He stood and held out his hand to her. ''We'll talk about it later. Now we have to go.''

She placed her hand in his, and he helped her up. She was beginning to hate that word. *Later.* She was afraid there was never going to be a later for them.

CHAPTER ELEVEN

THEY MADE THEIR WAY through the cornfield and to
the top of the incline. Abby was dirty, grimy and
hungry. She had started this trip wanting answers,
but she was beginning to recognize that she might
never get those answers. She wanted to clear her father's name so no one would ever think badly of him.
But her mother was right. Abby was also doing this
for herself because she wanted people to remember
Abe the way she did—loving, kind and honest.

Now she had a different perspective. Her father
wouldn't want her endangering her life or Jonas's.
Could she give up the quest? A day ago she would
have said no, but with these new feelings for Jonas...
She shook her head. First, they had to get out of
Mexico.

They walked down the dirt road toward Nuevo
Hope. At this hour nothing stirred, except a jackrab-
bit that jumped out in front of them and almost
scared her to death. She was jumpy, with good reason. She didn't know what was going to be around
the next bend, but she kept walking. She just wanted
to see Texas again.

They were almost in Nuevo Hope when a truck
suddenly came out of nowhere and slid sideways to
a complete stop in front of them. Dust blanketed
them. As it cleared, two Mexican men got out. The

first things Abby noticed were the switchblade knives in their hands. Fear engulfed her, and she couldn't move. All she could do was stare at the two men in horror. What did they want with her and Jonas?

The bigger man stepped forward, the silver blade glistening in his hand. He smiled, showing a set of yellow teeth with gold caps. "You lost, *gringo?*"

Jonas moved in front of Abby. "No, are you?" he countered in a calm tone.

The man laughed, but it didn't reach his eyes. He spoke to the other man. "Gringo's funny."

"*Sì.*" The other man grinned, his eyes on Abby.

He seemed fascinated with her hair. Revulsion crawled along her skin and she moved closer to Jonas.

"What do you want?" Jonas asked, steel in his voice.

The smile left the big man's face. "The woman, *gringo.* I want the woman."

Jonas felt Abby tremble, but he kept his eyes on the man. "Over my dead body."

The first man snickered. "That won't be a problem."

"You don't want to do this," Jonas said.

"Why?" The man laughed again. "Because you're Brewster's henchman don't mean nothing here. You're in Mexico now, *gringo.*"

So he knew Brewster and he knew who Jonas was—but Jonas was positive he'd never met the man before.

"Nothing to say, farm boy?"

"Let us pass," Jonas said, his eyes never leaving the man.

The man motioned to his partner. Before Abby

realized what was happening, the shorter man made a grab for her, but Jonas's fist came out and knocked him to the ground.

"*Bastardo gringo, mata lo,*" the man muttered, holding his jaw. Then he quickly got to his feet. He wielded the knife in his hand, an evil look on his face.

"Ah, *gringo,*" the big man said. "Now you've made Pepe mad. He's mean when mad."

Jonas watched the two men as they slowly advanced on him. "You want money? Name your price. We'll make a deal."

"No deal," the first man said. "Your money's in Texas and the woman is here. Now it's time for you to die." As he said the words, they both jumped on Jonas and wrestled him to the dirt. The big man came up with his arm locked around Jonas's neck, the knife to his throat.

Abby was petrified. Before she could do anything, Pepe grabbed her. He held her around the waist, her arms pinned to her side. He smelled of sweat, whiskey and stale tobacco. Her stomach churned.

"Ah, *gringo,* are you ready to die?" the big man snarled.

"Do what you want with me, but let the woman go," Jonas said.

"What we want with a man? My compatriots pay much to be with a woman like her."

A gasp left Abby's throat. She couldn't give in to fear. She had to help Jonas or the man was going to slit his throat. The mere thought gave her courage. There had to be a way out of this. She needed something...a weapon of some kind. She caught sight of a broken tree branch on the ground, but there was no way she could get to it, unless... Yes, she could use her hand.

She looked at Jonas, hoping he'd keep his eyes on her. He did. He winked, and she knew he was fixing to do something. Before the thought left her mind, Jonas drove his heel into the man's chin. The Mexican groaned but didn't let go.

At the same time Abby brought her hand to the arm around her waist, dug her nails in and scratched as hard as she could. The man let out a curse and loosened his grip. Everything happened quickly after that. Abby fell to the ground, gripping the branch with both hands. With all her strength, she slammed it against the man's head. He collapsed to the dirt, moaning and holding his head.

Jonas shoved his elbow into his captor's stomach and twisted away. The man came after him, and they wrestled to the ground. Abby hoisted the branch again, poised to strike. But there was no way to be sure she wouldn't hit Jonas. So she held her breath and waited to see who would come out on top, but she was well acquainted with those muscles in Jonas's arms and legs and she knew there was no way the Mexican could win this fight. She was right. Soon he rolled the man over, straddling him, the knife to the man's throat.

"Okay, *amigo,* now we're gonna do this a different way," Jonas growled.

Blood suffused the man's brown face. "Ah, *gringo,* we meant you no harm. It was just fun."

"Yeah, right," Jonas snapped. "Who's paying you?"

"No—"

The knife touched the man's skin, and Abby saw a trickle of blood.

"Please, please, don't kill me," the man cried.

"Then, tell me the truth, and I'll let you go."

"No se."

"What do you mean you don't know?" Jonas's hold tightened.

"Por favor. Por favor. No me matas."

"Start talking, and I won't kill you."

"Victor Rios gave me *dinero* to keep you away from Delores Alvarez. *No se* who pay him. That's the truth, *gringo."*

Jonas knew Victor Rios. He'd been fired by Brewster for stealing, and after that he'd been into all sorts of shady deals...in Texas and Mexico.

"Why do you want the woman?" Jonas asked, not sure what to believe.

"She make me big *dinero,* and Rios didn't care. He only paid me to keep you away from Delores."

"You bastard." Jonas wanted to smash his fist into the man's face, but he didn't.

"It's true, *gringo.* I swear."

"Since you seem to know Delores Alvarez, where is she?"

"Rios will kill me."

Jonas brought the knife to his jugular again. "Where is Delores Alvarez?"

"Por favor, gringo," the man begged.

"You can die now or later," Jonas told him. "Your choice."

The man took several gulps of air. "She runs a cantina...on the edge of town."

"Does she know we're looking for her?"

"*Sí*, but I told her and everyone that if they talked, I'd slit their throats."

Jonas wasn't sure if he was telling the truth, but there wasn't much he could do. At least now he knew someone was paying Rios, and he'd take it from there.

"Abby," he called, "get into the truck and start it."

Abby dropped the branch, noticing the other man was still grunting in pain. She climbed into the truck and turned the key. The engine backfired a couple of times but kept running.

Jonas swung his leg over the man. "*Adios, amigo,*" he said and ran for the truck. Along the way he threw the knife into the bushes.

As soon as Jonas was in the passenger seat, Abby pressed the gas pedal and they roared away. The truck bounced on the dirt road like a rubber ball, but Abby didn't stop until she saw Nuevo Hope.

She pulled over to the side. Her insides began to quiver, and she had to take several deep breaths to still her nerves.

Jonas watched her for a moment. "You okay?"

She shook her head. "No, I'm getting angrier and angrier by the minute. Who paid Rios? Who would do this to us? This is not a game. What those men wanted to do with me..." She shuddered, unable to finish the sentence.

"It's over," he assured her. "And now..."

"Now what?" she asked.

"I was going to say we get the hell out of here, but I want to find Delores Alvarez and see if that bastard was lying or not. Are you game?"

"Oh, Jonas." She reached out and smoothed his

hair from his forehead. "I don't want you to get hurt because of me."

He caught her hand. This time he didn't push her away. She noticed his knuckles were bruised. "You're hurt," she said miserably, and moved along the seat to kiss his hand.

"I just skinned them rolling on the ground with that slime."

He grinned as she kissed his knuckles again. "They're much better now."

"Oh, Jonas, I could've got you killed."

"Don't worry. I'm fine."

She leaned back against the seat. "You were right. I have a head like cement. When I started this, all I could think of was absolving my father." She paused and stroked his hand. "Now I know that it doesn't matter what people think of him. It only matters how I feel about him in my heart."

"You finally realized that?"

"Yes, when that man was holding that knife to your throat, I knew this was senseless. I shouldn't have put you or myself in that position. My father wouldn't want that."

"Can you really let it go?"

She blinked back a tear. "If you help me, I can."

Eyeing her determined face, he said, "Why don't we find out if Delores is where the man said she is…just to justify all we've been through. And to see whether Brewster's daughter really exists."

Her eyes brightened. "Yes, let's do that."

Ten minutes later, they found the cantina right on the edge of town, just like the man had said.

"This must be it," Jonas said as they entered.

A youth, not more than twelve years old was

sweeping the concrete floor. Tables were scattered throughout and there was a bar at one end.

"Tu conoce a Delores Alvarez?" Jonas asked the boy.

"Sì," the boy nodded. He stopped sweeping and glanced toward the ceiling. *"Esta dormida."*

Abby recognized that the boy had said Delores was upstairs sleeping. Her heart began to race. He'd answered without even thinking. Obviously he was so young he hadn't gotten the message that he wasn't supposed to talk. They'd found Delores. Now Abby could hardly wait to hear what the woman had to say.

"Por favor desperta la." Jonas asked the boy to wake up Delores.

The boy shook his head. *"No, no puedo."* Evidently he'd been given orders to let her sleep.

Jonas pulled out a twenty-dollar bill. *"Es muy importante,"* Jonas said.

The boy snatched the twenty and ran toward a small staircase in the back.

"Do you think she'll come down, or try to get away?" Abby asked.

Jonas walked over to the only window and looked out. "There's no way out from upstairs, so she'll have to come down, and we'll be waiting."

Mexican curses erupted from upstairs. Suddenly the youth came running back, picked up the broom and began sweeping again. Jonas was about to ask him a question, when a woman appeared at the top of the stairs. All she had on was a black slip. Her black hair was tangled and matted around her face. Her heavy makeup had caked and run during sleep. Her face was tired and old.

Delores stumbled down the stairs. "What the hell do you want?"

"Delores Alvarez?" Jonas enquired.

"*Sì,*" she said, and spat something at the boy. The discolored lace on the slip barely covered her large breasts, and she made no move to cover herself.

The boy brought her a bottle of whiskey, and she sat at a table and took a swig from the bottle. She wiped her mouth and said, "Go back to Texas, *gringo.* I have nothing to say to you."

She spoke good English, and Abby was glad. At least they could talk. Abby walked forward. "Please, it's very important."

Delores took another swallow of whiskey. "I know why you're here. Brewster says I had his daughter." She laughed, spitting whiskey on the table. "If that was true, do you think I'd be in this place turning twenty-dollar tricks?"

"You didn't have an affair with Mr. Brewster?" Abby asked.

"No, Brewster never bothered the Mexican girls that worked for him."

Abby wanted to ask if she was sure, but knew the question was unnecessary. Delores had nothing to gain by lying.

"Why did you leave Brewster's employment?" Abby had to have some answers.

"I was pregnant, and Brewster didn't want pregnant girls working in the house."

"So you were pregnant?"

"*Sì, señorita.*" She smiled slyly and shouted something in Mexican. Five girls appeared at the top of the stairs, all scantily clad. "These are my daughters," Delores added. "Do any of them look like Brewster?"

They all had dark hair and eyes and brown skin, and Abby had to admit that she didn't see any trace of Mr. Brewster in them.

Delores shouted something again, and the girls disappeared. "I didn't have Brewster's daughter, *señorita.* He lied to you."

"Why would he lie? Please, tell me the truth."

Delores swallowed more whiskey and watched Abby with cunning eyes. Jonas recognized that look. He reached in his pocket and pulled out his wallet. He laid a hundred on the table.

"Is the truth worth that much?"

"Ah, *gringo,* you're very generous." Delores smiled at Jonas, and Abby didn't like the way she was sizing him up, as if she was wondering what he was like in bed.

Delores tried to take the money, but Jonas held it up. "The truth first."

Delores grabbed the whiskey bottle again. After several swallows, she said, "Before I left I found Brewster in bed with that woman who worked in his office. His wife had left him, and he didn't want anyone to know about the affair. He said he'd cut my tongue out if I told. He wanted his wife and son to come back to Brewster Farms."

"What woman?" Abby asked.

"A prissy thing who thought she was better than the Mexican girls."

"What was her name?"

Delores shrugged. "Don't remember her name. It's been too long."

Abby laid her palms on the table and leaned in

close to Delores's worn face. "How would you like to make ten times that amount?" She gestured to the hundred in Delores's hand.

Delores's eyes widened. *"Sì, señorita."*

"You come to Texas and tell this story to Mr. Brewster, and I'll give you a thousand dollars."

Delores frowned.

"You have a Green Card to go into Texas, don't you?"

"Sì, I've worked in Texas."

"All you have to do is tell Mr. Brewster your story, and I will handle it from there."

"I don't want trouble. Someone paid Rios to keep you from me. That means trouble."

"When I get back to Texas, I'll find out who paid Rios, everything will be out in the open and you'll be a thousand dollars richer." Abby glanced around the seedy room. "That beats twenty dollars a night here, doesn't it?"

"Sì."

"All I want is the truth from Mr. Brewster, and I can get it with your help. Please, Delores."

Delores eyes darkened as she thought it over. "How do I know you'll pay me?"

Abby reached into her pockets and drew out a handful of twenties. She laid five in front of Delores. "You come to Texas, and I'll give you the rest."

"Sì, I'll come." Delores made up her mind.

Abby let out a long breath and straightened. "Nine o'clock tomorrow morning at the Brewster mansion."

"Sì, señorita, I be there."

Jonas stepped closer. "And if you don't show, Delores, I'll come looking for you."

Delores's smile broadened. "I might like that, *gringo*."

"No, you won't," Jonas assured her. "You just be there."

With that, Abby and Jonas walked out of the bar. The town was coming alive. Vendors and patrons were spilling everywhere. Jonas and Abby didn't speak. There was too much noise and activity. Through the turmoil in her head, Abby thought of the old lady who'd sold her the jacket, then realized she didn't have it. She stopped in her tracks and faced Jonas.

"I dropped my jacket when those men accosted us."

"We can't go back," he said practically. "We have to get out of here."

"I know." She sighed. "But I loved that jacket."

"Maybe we'll see the lady again and buy another one."

They didn't. The old woman was nowhere in sight.

Soon they spotted the international bridge, and Abby forgot about the jacket. She was eager to set foot on Texas soil. They paid the toll and went through Customs without a problem. Within minutes they were at Jonas's truck. Abby breathed deeply and looked around. The flat landscape was basically the same—mesquite, cactus, fields of crops, and several fruit and vegetable stands. But this was home, and she felt safe. Still, she couldn't shake an eerie feeling of foreboding.

Jonas paid the man in the booth and they got into the truck. They sat for a few moments in silence.

"Jonas, I don't understand any of this."

He glanced at her. "I don't, either, but Brewster

is up to something. I knew that from the start. He took an interest in you too quickly, seeking you out to write his memoirs almost as if he was taunting you.'' He paused. ''And why did he want you to hear Delores's story? He knew what she was going to say. What does this have to do with your father?''

''Nothing. Maybe he's just playing a game like you said, getting a kick out of seeing me run through hoops to get the truth, which he had no intention of giving me. I wish I had realized that a couple of days ago.''

Jonas started the engine. ''This isn't over, Abby. Brewster may think he's won, but he's in for a surprise.''

''What do you mean?''

''If he's toying with you out of spite, I'm walking away...something I probably should have done years ago.''

''Do you mean that?'' She couldn't keep the shock out of her voice.

''Of course, I mean it,'' Jonas replied. ''I've put up with a lot from Brewster, but I'm not putting up with his hurting you for no reason.''

Abby wanted to snuggle against him, but she knew the time wasn't right. Still, they were making progress, and soon she'd be able to tell him how she felt. She consoled herself with that thought as they drove toward her house.

Jonas parked at the curb and switched off the engine. ''I don't know about you, but I need a shower and some clean clothes.''

She smiled. ''That's my number one priority.'' Her face sobered. ''Do you think Delores will show tomorrow?''

"We'll have to wait and see."

"I suppose," she mumbled, knowing there was nothing she could do now but wait. Her eyes caught his. "Thank you, Jonas."

That special grin lifted his lips. "Why don't you come over here and say that?"

He didn't have to ask her twice. She moved to his side, her eyes never leaving his. "Thank—"

He smothered the words against her lips, and she wrapped her arms around his neck, giving herself up to his kiss. She ran her hands through his sun-bleached hair and realized he didn't have his hat on. He'd lost it, too. The thought was only momentary, as urgent desires swamped her. His lips moved over hers with an expertise that left her aching for more.

His mouth trailed to her neck and warmth suffused her entire body. All she wanted was Jonas. "My mother's at work. We could take that shower together," she whispered without shame.

"Abby," he groaned, kissing her nose, her cheek.

"Don't say no," she begged.

"I'm not, but I..." He stopped, and she brought her eyes to his. "Isn't that your mother's car?" He was staring toward the garage, and Abby could see the back of a car.

"Yes, it is," she admitted with a groan. She sagged against him. "She probably took off from work because she's worried about me. I'm sorry, I've got to go, but we'll finished this another place, another time."

Before she got out, he said, "Wait," and handed her her purse. Then he added, "My place tomorrow night, and I'll have lots of hot water."

"I'll be there."

WHEN ABBY ENTERED the house, silence greeted her, and she thought that maybe her mother had ridden to school with someone else. Then Gail appeared from the kitchen, a concerned frown on her face. A pang of guilt hit Abby. Her mother obviously had been sitting here worrying ever since Abby left.

"Sweetheart, you're back," Gail cried, and ran across the room to envelope Abby in a tight hug. "I'm so glad you're home."

Abby drew back. "Why aren't you at school, Mom?"

"School?" Gail shook her head. "I couldn't concentrate with you gone on this ridiculous trip so I took a couple of days off. I wanted to be here when you returned. I was so scared." As she talked, she scowled at Abby's appearance. "Why are you so dirty?"

"It's a long story, and I'll explain later. Right now, I want a bath and some food."

"Okay," Gail said. "You get cleaned up, and I'll fix us something to eat. Then we'll talk."

Abby was glad of this reprieve to get her thoughts together. If she had to hear another *I told you so,* she wanted to be clean and fed. She stripped off her clothes and turned on the tap. As she waited for the tub to fill, she noticed several bruises on her body. *Lesson learned,* she thought, and slipped into the hot water. Oh, it felt like heaven. There was just one thing missing…Jonas. How she wished he was here, massaging her aching body. Then she'd massage his and… Damn, her racy thoughts were fogging up the room. That was the way she felt about him, though— hot, eager and excited.

She reached for the shampoo and washed the dirt

out of her hair. Her thoughts veered in another direction. If Delores showed up—and Abby knew that was a big if—how would Mr. Brewster react to being caught in a lie? Would he admit to pulling a hoax? No, he probably wouldn't, she decided. He'd try to turn it to his advantage. However, she wasn't taking any more from him. If she didn't get the answers she wanted, she'd leave…as she should have done when he'd first mentioned his fictitious daughter. Admitting defeat wasn't easy, but tomorrow Mr. Brewster might get a taste of his own medicine.

Abby crossed her fingers and whispered, "Please, Delores, don't let me down."

She quickly dried herself, slipped on a white terry-cloth robe and headed for the kitchen. Her mother had the table set, and Abby couldn't believe her eyes. Gail had prepared a full meal of meat loaf, mashed potatoes, green beans and salad.

"When did you do all this?" Abby asked as she took a seat.

"This morning," Gail replied. "I had to keep busy. When you didn't come back last night, I couldn't sleep, so I planned a meal. I made peach cobbler for dessert."

Abby picked up her napkin and placed it in her lap. "I'm sorry you were worried."

Gail brought iced tea to the table and sat down. "That's a mother's job."

"But Mom—"

"Eat, Abby, then we'll talk."

Abby did exactly that. She couldn't ever remember being this hungry, and for a while, not a word was spoken. As she ate, she thought of Jonas.

"I wish I had known you had all this food cooked. I would have invited Jonas in."

"I'm sure Jonas is more comfortable going back to..."

"To where?"

"Abby, I don't want to argue."

"Then, don't say anything disparaging. Jonas doesn't deserve it."

Gail pushed the food around on her plate with a fork, but she didn't say anything. Abby was grateful. She didn't want to get into an argument about Jonas so soon. There would be plenty of time later for her and Gail to talk.

"Did you find Delores Alvarez?" Gail enquired quietly.

"Yes, after a long ordeal, we did," Abby answered, and went on to tell her mother what had happened.

"Oh my God, Abby, you could have been killed," Gail muttered in shock, her face a grayish white.

Abby patted her hand. "I'm fine, Mom, so don't get hysterical."

"I get so angry when I think of what Brewster has done to my family."

"Me, too, but Jonas and I are hoping that tomorrow Mr. Brewster will tell us what this whole thing is about."

"He's an evil old man," Gail said, gathering dishes and carrying them to the sink. "I wouldn't believe a word he says."

"I want to know why he sent us on a wild-goose chase, and if he had anything to do with paying Rios to keep us away from Delores."

"It's all too horrible to think about." As Gail

picked up more dishes, Abby noticed her hands were trembling.

"Mom, I'm fine, really," she tried to reassure her.

Gail sank into her chair. "He's playing with your life the way he played with Abe's." Her eyes met Abby's. "I wish you'd go back to Dallas and your job and forget about Brewster. Then, he couldn't hurt you."

"I can't do that." She tried to make her mom understand. "I started this and now I have to finish it."

"Why do you have to be so headstrong?"

"Because that's the way I am."

"Yes, you've always been that way. Once you got something in your head, I could never change your mind."

"I have a head like cement."

Gail frowned. "What?"

"Jonas said I have a head like cement."

Gail fiddled with her napkin. "You and Jonas seem to have gotten very close."

"Yes, we have," Abby said without hesitation.

"I know it's useless to tell you to be careful, because you'll do exactly what you want...as you did with—"

"As I did with Kyle?" she asked shortly.

"I don't want to discuss that."

"Then, why are you always alluding to my marriage?"

Gail didn't say anything, and Abby went on. "My marriage is over—accept it. And I wish you'd give yourself a chance to know Jonas. He's more of a man than Kyle will ever be. He will never degrade or hit me. He's loyal, dedicated and responsible."

LINDA WARREN 185

Gail jumped to her feet. "This isn't about Kyle or Jonas," she shouted. "It's about Brewster and the hold he has over us. I want him gone—completely out of our lives."

Gail was visibly trembling again, and Abby got up and put her arms around her. "After tomorrow, we never have to see him again."

"Are you sure?" Gail brushed away a tear.

"Yes. If Delores shows up, we can get this whole thing straightened away. Then I'll tell him what I think of him."

"What about your father?"

Abby took a breath. "Mr. Brewster just used him as bait. I've accepted that he's not going to tell me a thing."

"And the letter?"

"I don't know. Earl said it was authentic, but he wasn't allowed to read all of it, so it's probably another lie."

"Then, why do you have to see Brewster tomorrow? Don't give him any more satisfaction."

"Because I plan to meet Delores at the mansion in the morning. And because I'm curious. I'm sure Brewster has all his bases covered, but it will give *me* some satisfaction."

"Why would Delores come here?" Gail asked skeptically.

"Because I offered to pay her."

"Oh, Abby, she'll say anything for money."

"I'm just paying her to tell Brewster that she didn't have his child—that's all."

"I wish this was over," Gail said, and started with the dishes again.

As Abby helped her mother, she remembered

something Delores had said. "Mom, do you remember any women that worked for Brewster thirty years ago?"

"No, why?" Gail wrapped the meat loaf and put it in the refrigerator.

"Delores said he had an affair with some woman who worked in his office."

"Oh?"

"Yeah. She didn't know the woman's name, but I thought you might."

Gail shook her head. "No, I can't recall anyone, and I wouldn't put too much faith in what Delores Alvarez says."

"I guess, but Jonas can check the employment records. That should tell us something."

"You're doing it again," Gail said.

"What?"

"Getting caught up in Brewster's lies."

Abby opened the dishwasher and began to put the dishes inside. Maybe she was, but she couldn't help herself. There were so many unanswered questions. Abby had told her mother that after tomorrow, she'd let it go. Now she was wondering if she'd be able to keep that promise.

CHAPTER TWELVE

JONAS WANTED A BATH and clean clothes, but he didn't go directly home. Instead, he drove to Mick's Tavern. Business was nil this time of day, and Mick was with a liquor salesman, which Jonas knew was a waste of time. Mick got most of his liquor from Mexico. Jonas went down the street to a café and ordered a meal. Afterward, he walked back to Mick's.

Mick was wiping down the bar. "Jonas, my boy. It's good to see you. Did you find Brewster's daughter?"

Jonas straddled a bar stool. "No, and I need information."

"I'll get you a Coke."

"No." Jonas stopped him, grabbing his arm. "I want to talk."

"Okay." Mick placed his hands on the bar. "What do you want to know?"

"Where can I find Victor Rios?"

"Aw, Jonas," Mick grumbled, rubbing his hands on his apron. "You don't want anything to do with that *hombre*. He's bad."

"Where can I find him?" Jonas persisted, knowing Mick knew everything about the Mexicans in Hope.

"Why do you want him?"

"Someone paid him to keep us away from Delores Alvarez, and I want to know who that someone is."

"That Duncan woman still got you all tied up, ain't she?"

Jonas's eyes narrowed. "Answer the damn question."

Mick rubbed a spot on the bar. "I don't want you to get hurt."

"Mick, I can take care of myself. Where is Rios?"

"He hangs out on Fifth Street, but you won't catch him there until early in the morning."

"Thanks. I appreciate it," Jonas said, and stood.

"Jonas?"

He glanced at Mick.

"Make sure your back is covered."

"Don't worry. I will." With that, Jonas headed for his truck and his apartment.

After taking a hot shower and putting on clean clothes, he called the mansion. He wanted to know if Brewster was home from the hospital. He was, so Jonas made his way to the big house to have a talk with the man himself.

Maria, the housekeeper, let him in, and he went upstairs to Brewster's bedroom. He heard Jules and Darby in the family room, but he didn't bother with them. He tapped on Brewster's door and went in. Brewster was lying in bed, hooked to an oxygen tank. Edna and a nurse hovered near him.

"This isn't the time, Jonas," Edna said, and tried to push him out the door.

But Brewster saw him. "Jonas, come in," he called.

"He doesn't need to be upset," Edna hissed.

"Everybody leave," Brewster ordered. "I want to talk to Jonas."

"Now, Simon, you can talk later," Edna told him.

"Get the hell out of my room," Brewster shouted, and both women left.

"So you're back," Brewster said, when they'd closed the door.

Jonas lifted an eyebrow. "Surprised?"

"No, why should I be?"

Jonas watched him and wondered—as he had so many times—what this man was about. Why was he so hell-bent on hurting people? Why did he have to be so hard?

"Where's Abigail?" Brewster asked impatiently.

"She's at home. She'll be here in the morning."

"In the morning?" Brewster roared. "Why in the hell isn't she here now? I want to know if she found my daughter."

"You have that down perfectly, don't you?"

Brewster frowned. "What are you talking about?"

"*My daughter.* You make it sound real."

"She is real, and I want to see Abigail. Get her—now."

Jonas sat down and crossed his legs. "She's worn-out from the ordeal we've been through, and I'm not bothering her."

"Ordeal? What ordeal?"

"Does Victor Rios ring a bell?"

"That bastard," Brewster spit out. "You'd better make damn sure he isn't on my property."

Jonas was taken aback. He knew that Brewster hated Rios, but he'd thought they'd reached some sort of truce that would benefit them both. From Brewster's response, it seemed that wasn't the case.

Jonas uncrossed his legs and rested his elbows on his knees. "Someone paid Rios to keep us away from Delores." He said the words slowly, watching for Brewster's reaction.

"No!" was all he said, but Jonas could see he was upset. Jonas decided to push further. "Rios hired two unsavory characters to block our every move, and what they had in mind for Abby would chill your blood."

"Goddammit, you didn't let them touch her, did you? Jonas, I want to see Abigail."

Brewster's breathing was coming in gulps, and Jonas walked to his bedside. Brewster actually cared for Abby. That was a shock. But then, Abby had a way of working her way into a man's heart. Jonas knew that for a fact.

He started to get the nurse.

Brewster stopped him. "I'm fine," he mumbled, then asked, "Is Abigail okay?"

At the sincerity in his voice, Jonas knew Brewster had had nothing to do with paying Rios. Then who? Who would do such a thing?

"Abby's fine," he finally answered. "She'll talk to you later."

"You find out who hired Rios."

"I intend to, and I'll start with Jules and Darby."

Brewster shook his head. "No, it's not them."

Jonas's eyes narrowed. "You seem very certain about that."

"I am," he said. "The sheriff came by the hospital. He found some prints on the file room door and on Abigail's car."

"And who did the prints belong to?"

Brewster brushed it off. "It doesn't matter. It's been taken care of."

"By whom?" Jonas asked in a guarded tone.

"By me, dammit, Jonas. Leave it alone."

"Like hell I will," Jonas exploded. "It *was* Jules and Darby, wasn't it." That made sense to Jonas. They were the only ones whom Brewster would protect.

Brewster didn't deny it. "They just got a little nervous about their inheritance. I put the fear of God into them, and they won't try anything else. I threatened to disinherit them if they didn't tell me the whole story. They just wanted to scare Abigail to keep her from going to Mexico. They didn't mention Rios, and they know better than to lie to me. So it's not them. It has to be someone else."

"And that's it?" Jonas asked in a barely controlled voice. "The sheriff's not going to arrest them or anything?"

"What good would that do? You can't arrest someone for being stupid."

Instead of telling Jonas or Abby about the prints, Sheriff Fisher had told Brewster. Jonas knew why. The sheriff took orders from Brewster, and Brewster had ordered him to back off.

Jonas glared at the man in the bed. "Do you know what Abby was like when I found her in that locked room? She was trembling and couldn't breathe and bathed in her own sweat. If I hadn't found her when I did, she might have died. That may not mean anything to you, but it does to me."

"They will pay." Brewster said threateningly. "Believe me, they will pay."

Jonas's anger cooled at the ominous tone. The future did not bode well for Jules and Darby.

"Did Abigail find Delores?" Brewster asked into the silence.

Jonas thought for a minute, then decided it was Abby's place to answer. He wouldn't steal the moment from her. "You'll have to ask Abby."

"Dammit, boy, you're trying my patience."

"It's not the first time."

A sly smile crossed Brewster's face. "Yeah, now get back to work. Two days off is more than you deserve."

Jonas nodded and walked out of the room. The words *more than you deserve* ran through his head. Brewster had made him believe that for years, but now Jonas felt differently...because of Abby. She made him realize that he deserved a hell of a lot more than Brewster's abuse. He could finally see the light at the end of the tunnel, and soon he'd have his freedom.

He saw Edna in the hall flipping through a magazine and decided to talk to her. If Jules and Darby had locked Abby in that room, then Edna had known about it. She had a good reason to make sure they didn't find Brewster's daughter. After her sister's death, she'd hoped Brewster would take an interest in Jules. There was no romantic involvement between Brewster and Edna, but she wanted Jules to take Brewster's son's place. That had never happened, but they were Brewster's relatives, and he put up with them. The same went for Darby, who was a distant cousin also on Brewster's wife's side. Brewster had no living blood relatives, so if a daughter showed up, those three stood to lose a lot. But did

Edna know Rios? Actually, she didn't have to know him. All she had to do was put out the word that she wanted a job done, and he'd show up on her doorstep.

When Edna saw Jonas, she put down the magazine and got to her feet. "I hope you didn't upset Simon with this daughter nonsense."

"What are you going to do if there really is a daughter?"

"There isn't," she snapped. "He's just delusional in his old age. But don't worry—I'll be here to take care of Simon."

"And his money."

She bristled. "How dare you talk to me like that."

"Who do you think you're fooling, Edna?" Jonas said curtly. "If Brewster didn't have money, you wouldn't even be here. You've been trying to get him to turn things over to you and Jules for a long time."

She patted her hair. "We're his relatives."

"That's a fact," Jonas conceded, and stared directly at her. "If I find out you had anything to do with Victor Rios, Brewster will disinherit you in a heartbeat."

Her cheeks flushed. "What are you talking about?"

"Victor Rios, Edna," he emphasized. "If you know him, you'd better start covering your tracks."

"You're talking crazy, and I'm not listening to any more of it."

"Heed my warning, Edna," he said, as she walked past him.

She shot him a piercing glance and disappeared into Brewster's room.

Now for Jules and Darby. He could still hear their

voices in the family room. Jonas had a surprise in store for them. He went into the kitchen and found Maria.

"Maria, do you have the keys to that closet in the downstairs hall?"

"*Sì*, Mr. Jonas."

"How many do you have?"

"Two. Why do you ask?"

Jonas held out his hand. "Let me have them."

"But, Mr. Jonas I—"

"Don't worry, I'll get them back to you."

"Okay," she said slowly, then walked to a desk in a corner. She picked up a large key ring, removed two keys and handed them to Jonas.

"Thanks, Maria, and I don't want you opening that door for any reason. Understand?"

She shrugged. "How can I? I don't have a key."

"Good," Jonas said, and went into the family room.

Jules and Darby were resting on the sofas, drinking beer, eating snacks and watching football on TV.

"Bet you a ten he doesn't make it," Jules said.

"Ten?" Darby laughed. "What the hell kind of betting is that? I'll bet you a hundred he makes this one and the next."

Darby was the first to see Jonas. "Jonas, my man, did you bring back the long-lost daughter?"

Jules snickered.

"No, afraid not." Jonas scratched his head. "But I have something I'd like you boys to see."

Jules turned down the TV. "What?"

"It's in the hall." Jonas turned to leave, but neither Jules nor Darby made a move.

"It'll be worth your while," Jonas promised.

"Why didn't you say so?" Darby got to his feet and so did Jules. They followed Jonas to the hall closet. Jonas opened the door.

"What's in there?" Jules asked.

"Something for both of you."

When they leaned in, Jonas gave them a push and locked the door behind them. They immediately began to yell and beat on the door.

"How does it feel, boys?" Jonas called. "Get used to it. You're going to be in there a while."

"You bastard," Jules screamed. "Let us out of here."

"How does it feel to be locked in a small space?" Jonas shouted back.

Maria came running from the kitchen, and Edna charged down the stairs.

"What's going on?" Edna demanded.

Jonas pocketed the keys. "Your son and Darby will be locked up for a while. When I feel like it, I'll let them out. It will give you and them some time to think about what you did to Abby."

Jonas strolled past her to the front door.

"Come back, Jonas Parker," she shouted after him. "You can't leave them in there. Simon will fire you. Come back here."

Jonas drew a deep breath and went to his office. He had to take care of business, but a smile kept threatening his composure. He'd go back soon and let them out. Maybe they'd think twice before doing something like that again.

TWO HOURS LATER—after Jonas and Stuart had gone over everything that had happened at Brewster Farms while he was gone—Jonas returned to the house and let Jules and Darby out of the closet. Edna was wringing her hands. When Jonas opened the door, they fell out coughing, cursing and breathing heavily.

"How could you?" Edna screamed at Jonas as she embraced Jules.

"The same way you locked Abby in that room," Jonas said. "It's not a good feeling, is it."

"Uncle Simon will fire you for this," Jules choked out.

"As soon as he does, I'll be outta here faster than you can say *slash my tires*." With that, Jonas turned on his heel and left.

"You smart-ass," Darby yelled after him.

It was after six by the time he got to his apartment. He lay on the sofa and stretched out. Damn, he was dog-tired. He noticed something on the coffee table and reached for it. It was Abby's clip. He'd forgotten to give it back to her. He rubbed it gently with his thumb and he could almost see the light in her eyes and hear the warmth in her voice. He closed his eyes as he let her presence wash over him. He had never dreamed he could care for someone so much. His eyes flew open. Care? Was that what he felt? Or did he just desire her? Could it possibly be the *L* word?

It was a tragic thing when a grown man couldn't even identify his own emotions. But somewhere between the little boy who had never known love and the adult who was afraid to love hovered an unfamiliar emotion. *Was* it love? He really wasn't sure.

All he knew was that he cared for her, wanted to protect her and longed to be with her in the worst way. He stared at the phone and resisted the urge to call her. She was exhausted and probably asleep; he wouldn't disturb her. His body ached for her, but the thought that they'd be together tomorrow night made the ache less intense.

In the morning, he'd find Rios and get some answers. Then he'd go with her when she confronted Brewster. By afternoon it would all be over, and he'd be there for her, no matter what happened. The night would be theirs. This time he wouldn't push her away.

He turned onto his side and thought briefly about the future. After tomorrow, would she go back to Dallas? How would he feel when she did? Suddenly his heart tightened in pain—real pain that he recognized. The type of pain he'd felt when they'd taken his sister. Pain he'd vowed he would never feel again.

He grabbed the remote control and turned on the TV. He pushed the volume button to high to block out everything he was feeling. But he couldn't keep the questions from niggling at him. Did Abby want something he wasn't willing to give? Or was it the other way around? Did he want something *she* wasn't willing to give?

WHEN ABBY WOKE UP, it was five o'clock in the morning. She couldn't believe she had slept all afternoon and all night. Sitting up, she pushed her hair out of her eyes and switched on the lamp. She stared at the phone. Was Jonas awake? Unable to resist, she dialed his number.

Jonas was headed for the door when he heard the phone. He wanted to catch Rios before he disappeared. He started to let it ring, but then yanked it up.

"Yeah," he barked into the receiver.

"Jonas?"

"Abby." He sank onto the sofa, melting into her sweet lilting voice and recognizing that his feelings for her were getting stronger and stronger.

"Did I wake you?"

He swallowed. "No, I've been up since about four."

"I went to sleep after I got in yesterday, and I'm just now waking up. I wanted to talk to you last night, but I slept right through."

He held the receiver closer. "You can talk to me now."

"Are you okay?"

"I'm fine. And you?"

"I'd be better if I were with you."

Me, too. "We still have a date tonight?"

"I'm looking forward to it, but first we have to deal with Delores and Brewster."

"Yeah, I talked with Brewster yesterday and he has me baffled. He seemed genuinely concerned that you were in danger."

"He was?"

Jonas heard the surprise in her voice. "He got so upset, I thought he was going to have another heart attack. He even ordered me to find out who paid Rios." Then he told her that Jules and Darby were the ones who'd locked her in the file room and slashed her tires.

"I can't believe it. When I talked to the sheriff, he said he hadn't found anything."

"The sheriff answers to Brewster first," he said. "Brewster said he'd taken care of them...whatever the hell that means."

"So Mr. Brewster didn't know what they were doing?"

"No, it was their own idea. I'm sure it was instigated by Edna."

"Do you think they hired Rios?"

"No, Brewster threatened to disinherit them if they lied to him. They'd be afraid not to tell the truth."

"I suppose," she murmured.

"They just wanted to scare you."

"God, that makes me so angry."

Jonas told her what he'd done to them.

"You didn't." She laughed.

"Yes, I did, and they won't be locking anyone in a room again."

"Oh, Jonas, I feel so much better."

"I'm glad, because I enjoyed doing it. I wish I was coldhearted enough to have left them in there a whole lot longer."

"But you're not that type of person."

He felt bolstered by the faith in her voice. She believed there was good in him, and he was beginning to think there might be, too.

He shook his head. "I hate to cut this short, but I want to catch Rios."

"Jonas, please don't do that," Abby cried. "The man is dangerous."

"Sorry, I'd already made up my mind to find him before Brewster mentioned it. That's where I was going when the phone rang."

"Then, I'll go with you. I can be dressed and ready in less than fifteen minutes."

"No. I don't want you near Rios. Besides, you have to meet Delores."

She gave in grudgingly. "Okay. But if Delores doesn't show, I'll need your shoulder to cry on."

"It will be there as soon as it can," he promised, "along with the rest of me."

"Please be careful."

"I will, because I'm not missing our date tonight."

"Jonas," she whispered.

"Hmm?"

"Tonight we'll talk about us."

He was silent.

"Don't panic, I'm not asking anything of you."

Why aren't you?

"Jonas?" she prompted.

He swallowed hard. "I'm not panicking," he assured her.

"Yeah," she said in a disbelieving tone. "I know this is hard for you, and I won't pressure you as long as you don't push me away."

"I'm not doing that, either."

"That means we're making progress."

Silence again.

Her soft voice wrapped around him and unfamiliar emotions surfaced. He wasn't denying them. He just didn't know how to accept them.

"Abby, I'd better go," he finally said. "I don't want to miss Rios."

She took a breath. "Be careful, because I need you, Jonas. I need you with me when I confront Mr. Brewster and I need you tonight." She had a feeling she would need him for the rest of her life, but how could she tell him that? She didn't want to scare him to death. How did you get a man to admit love when he'd never known love? She could only keep trying.

JONAS FOUND FIFTH STREET and waited. There was a small grocery store on the corner where he knew a lot of drug dealing took place. This had to be where Rios hung out. He parked some distance away and watched the store. He had driven one of the field trucks that didn't have the Brewster logo on the door. That way he wouldn't be recognized.

Soon he saw a green pickup pull up to the store. It was Rios. He recognized him immediately. Several Mexicans appeared as if out of nowhere and gathered around the vehicle. Packages and money changed hands. Rios was selling drugs out in the open, and the sheriff didn't make a move to stop him. He didn't dwell on it because he had other things on his mind right now. He wanted to talk to Rios, but he couldn't do that in front of all Rios's customers. Jonas had to wait until he could get the man alone.

The transactions over, Rios drove away. Jonas followed at a safe distance. He noticed it was almost eight o'clock. He didn't have much time, if he wanted to meet Abby. Rios headed to town, and Jonas couldn't imagine where he was going. Suddenly the green truck stopped at Brewster's Park. Jonas drove by and came up a back street to watch Rios from behind. Rios appeared to be waiting for someone.

Jonas was about to get out and confront Rios, when he saw a car drive up and stop behind Rios. Jonas settled back in his seat. He recognized the car and the person inside. Rios got out and walked over to the car. Jonas understood what was happening, and anger filled him. Rios started swearing and waving his arms. The two were arguing. Rios yanked an en-

velope from the person, and the car sped away. Rios
flung curses after it.

It took Jonas a split second to recover from his
shock, then he got out and hurried toward Rios. Rios
was getting into his truck with a scowl on his face.
Jonas caught the door before the man could slam it.
He grabbed Rios by the neck and forced him back
against the seat.

"Stay away from Abigail Duncan," Jonas warned.
He didn't have to ask who was paying Rios because
he already knew.

"Ain't got nothing to do with that bitch." Rios
choked, his face turning red.

"You'd better keep it that way." Jonas's hand
tightened around his throat. "Understand?"

"*Sí.*"

Jonas released his hold and noticed the small pistol
on the seat. Rios's hand edged toward it.

Jonas's mind clicked into action. Rios would shoot
him in a heartbeat. Mick had warned him. "Go
ahead," Jonas told him. "I'm not the only one
watching you this morning. One false move and
you're dead. You should watch your back a little
closer."

The bluff worked. Rios's hand stilled and his black
eyes darted around.

Jonas stepped away from the truck.

"Son of a bitch," Rios spat out as he slammed
the door. He gunned the engine and sped away.

Jonas let out a long breath and ran to his vehicle.
He had to get to Abby. He had to tell her before she
saw Brewster. It was almost nine o'clock. Dammit,
he had to hurry.

Jonas tried to make sense of what he'd just seen,

but he couldn't. Inside, though, he knew something bad was about to happen. Maybe Delores wouldn't show, he kept thinking. Then he'd have time to talk to Brewster and try to stop... What the hell was he thinking? There was no way to stop it now.

ABBY PACED by her car in front of the Brewster mansion. She glanced repeatedly at her watch. It was after nine. Delores wasn't going to come. Well, Abby could tell Brewster what Delores had said. If he didn't believe her, that would be the end of it. She couldn't upset her mother any more and she couldn't keep up the crusade to vindicate her father. He was at peace, and now she had to find some peace of her own.

She moved toward the steps, then heard a sound. A beat-up car came through the gates, smoke billowing from the tailpipe. A man was at the wheel. The passenger door opened, and Delores climbed out. She had on black stretch pants and a red tank top that showed off her full breasts. Brightly colored beads adorned her neck and wrist. She tottered on red high heels toward Abby.

"*Señorita,* I come for my money," Delores said as she reached Abby.

"First we talk to Mr. Brewster, then I'll give you your money," Abby told her.

"*Sì.*"

As Abby rang the doorbell, she added, "I'll do all the talking. You just follow my lead."

"What does that mean?" Delores asked.

"It means when I ask you a question, you answer it truthfully."

"*Sì, señorita.*"

Maria opened the door and let them in. Abby glanced toward the street, wondering where Jonas was. He should have been here by now. Had something happened to him? No, she wouldn't believe that. She said a silent prayer, and followed Maria up the stairs.

Edna was waiting at Mr. Brewster's door. She spoke sharply to Maria. "I told you not to let her in."

"Mr. Brewster said he wanted to see her. He's my boss," Maria replied staunchly.

"Simon is in no shape to see anyone." Edna's eyes settled on Delores. "You're not trying to pass her off as Simon's daughter, are you, Abigail? It's laughable."

Maria slipped around Edna and opened the door.

"Abigail, is that you?" Mr. Brewster called.

"Get out of my way," Abby warned Edna. "And you can tell Jules and Darby to stay out of my way, too."

Edna stepped aside. "You'll regret this, missy."

Abby ignored her and walked into the room.

Mr. Brewster was sitting in his rocker by the large windows. He had on blue pajamas and a blue silk robe. His short gray hair was sticking out everywhere, but his color was better and he looked like his old self except for the oxygen tubing in his nose. A nurse stood by his side.

"Ah, Abigail," he said, a slight smile on his face. "I see you found Delores."

Delores seemed to shrink a couple of inches beside Abby. She sympathized—Mr. Brewster had that effect on people.

"Out," he ordered the nurse and Edna.

"Now...Simon..."

"All right, stay," he shouted. "I don't give a damn. Now you'll see I'm not senile and that I do have a daughter."

Abby walked closer to him and tried to figure out what kind of game he was playing. Out of the corner of her eye she saw Jonas enter the room. Thank God. She turned and smiled at him. He didn't smile back. He had a worried frown on his face. Something was wrong.

"Come in, Jonas," Mr. Brewster said. "You're in time to hear the truth."

"I'm not sure you know the truth," Jonas replied.

"Yes, I do, and now Delores can tell everyone about my daughter."

All eyes stared at Delores, and Abby could see that she was very nervous and ready to bolt for the door.

"Delores did not have your daughter," Abby stated.

"I knew it," Edna said under her breath.

"I know she didn't," said Mr. Brewster.

Abby took a long breath, not sure why she was shocked. She'd known that Mr. Brewster was aware of what Delores would say. "Then, why did you send me to find her?"

"Because she is the only one who knows the mother of my daughter."

Delores was shaking her head, and Abby's shock turned to annoyance. "Delores doesn't know what you're talking about, and I'm tired of playing your games. You and I had a deal and—"

"I'm not reneging on the deal." He tapped the white envelope on the table beside him. "The letter's right here and you can read it anytime you want, but first I wish you'd listen to what Delores has to say."

Abby put a hand to her head, which was beginning to pound with the rhythm of a jackhammer. "Mr. Brewster, this is pointless. Delores doesn't—"

"Jog your memory, Delores," Mr. Brewster broke in. "Who did you see in this room—in this bed—with me?"

Delores shook her head, her eyes huge.

"She doesn't know," Abby said, reaching the end of her patience. "And you can keep the letter. I don't care anymore. My father was a good man, and most people know that. Those who don't...well, it's their loss. I've finally realized that, so it's over and you can stop this ridiculous hoax."

"It's not a hoax, Abigail," Mr. Brewster said quietly. "I'm surprised you're giving up so easily. I never thought you were a quitter."

"I'm not," she declared. "But enough is enough."

As Abby turned to leave, her mother stepped into the room.

Delores pointed a finger at her and said, "That's the woman I saw in your bed. She's older, but it's her."

"You see, Abigail," Mr. Brewster said into the silence. "You've been looking for yourself."

CHAPTER THIRTEEN

ABIGAIL LAUGHED. It was the only response she could make to such an absurd statement.

Jonas moved close to her. "Let's get out of here."

"Stay out of this, Jonas," Brewster roared.

Abby glanced from her mother to Brewster, then back to her mother. At the look in her mother's eyes, her world started to spin out of control. She took a couple of steps backward and came up against the solid wall of Jonas.

"Jonas," she whimpered. "What's going on?"

Before Jonas could answer, Brewster said, "Tell her, Gail."

"Shut up," Gail screamed at him.

Brewster stared directly at Gail. "I promised you I'd never tell her, but I didn't promise that someone else wouldn't. Delores has all but told her, so I'll give you the option of telling her before I do."

"You bastard," Gail said between her teeth.

The words didn't phase Brewster. His gaze swung to Abby. "You're my daughter."

"Oh my God," Edna muttered, and began to fan her face.

Gail ran to him and grabbed him around the throat. "I'll kill you, you bastard. I'll kill you."

Brewster was gasping for breath, and Jonas pulled

Gail away. "Stop it," he ordered. "You're no better than he is. Hiring Rios. What were you thinking?"

Gail began to tremble.

"She hired Rios?" Brewster choked out.

"What?" The word emerged as a squeak from between Abby's dry lips. She heard the voices in the room and saw the people, but she felt as if she were in a nightmare.

Gail hurried to Abby. "Let's go home, sweetheart, and we'll talk."

Abby repeated the last thing that had registered on her brain. "You hired Rios?"

"I was desperate for you not to find out, but as soon as *he* hired you to write his memoirs, I knew what he was up to. I had to do something. I didn't know those men would do those dreadful things. I didn't think…I just wanted them to keep you from finding Delores."

At the mention of her name, Delores came to life. "I want my money, *señorita*."

Jonas pulled out his wallet and stuffed one hundred-dollar bills into her hand, and without another word she left the room.

"You put our lives in danger," Abby said, as if there hadn't been an interruption. "Those men were going to kill Jonas and…" She trembled, unable to finish.

"I'm sorry, sweetheart, but I've been half out of my mind." Gail attempted to touch her, but Abby backed away.

"I'm…I'm Mr. Brewster's…daughter?"

"Yes, you are," Brewster said.

"Mama," Abby appealed with desperation in her voice, and Jonas moved to stand beside her.

Gail bit her lip, and tears ran down her cheeks.
"Mama?"

"Yes," Gail moaned. "Brewster is your biological father. That's all. He's nothing else. He's not even human."

"You didn't used to think so," Brewster quipped.

"Shut up," Gail screamed at him again.

A sob solidified in Abby's throat, and her legs were like rubber. *She was Simon Brewster's daughter.* The room and the people faded into a pearly gray light. She felt herself sinking, and she fought to control the weakness. Then two strong arms caught her. *Jonas.* She knew it was Jonas. His strength gave her courage to ask the question.

"Did Daddy know?"

Gail brushed away a tear. "He knew about a year before he died."

Abby held both hands to her trembling lips, remembering the kind, loving man who was her father. Gradually anger swept away all the other emotions. Slowly she lowered her hands.

"How could you? How could you do that to him?"

"Abby, try to understand. I was young and stupid. Your father and I were having marital problems. We couldn't have children, and I wanted to adopt. Abe wouldn't hear of it. He said we hadn't given it enough time. Things just got worse between us." She paused. "I had my teaching degree, but no job yet, so I started working in the office hoping that would draw Abe and me closer together. But then *he*—" she glared at Brewster "—took an interest in me, and I was flattered. Abe didn't seem to want me anymore, and I wanted to show him that... Oh God, I was so stupid.''

"But it happened," Brewster said.

Gail swung to look at him. "But as soon as your wife wanted to come back, you dumped me."

"I wanted my son in his rightful home."

"You have no right to Abby. She's Abe's daughter," Gail shouted.

"She's mine," Brewster shouted back.

Abby blocked out their bickering. "Why did you tell Daddy?"

Gail looked down at her hands. "Abe had to have a complete physical for insurance purposes. They sent the results to the office, and Brewster opened the package. He read that Abe was sterile and unable to father children."

"Then, Daddy knew all along?"

"No, he thought you were his. He considered you our miracle."

"So why tell him?"

"Brewster put two and two together and knew you were his, but he promised to never tell you, but he began asking Abe about you. As time went by, things got worse. Brewster wouldn't let up, and I knew he was going to tell Abe, so I told him myself. I didn't want him to hear it from Brewster. He took it hard...and immediately quit. Brewster didn't fire him. I thought Abe would leave me, but he didn't. Because of you he stayed. He couldn't stand the thought of hurting you."

Abby bit down on her lip, trying to still the turbulent emotions inside her. None of this was real. All that was real was the memory of her father's gentle face. She looked at the woman she called

Mother, and she didn't know her. Gail had hurt the most wonderful man on earth and then had done everything she could to keep the secret from coming out—even risking her daughter's life. Who was this woman?

"Abby, sweetheart, let's get out of here," Gail whispered. "We'll straighten all this out."

Abby shook her head. "No, I'm not going anywhere with you," she said vehemently. "I'm going back to Dallas, and I never want to see you again."

"No, Abby, no," Gail cried.

"This is your home," Brewster added.

"Home." She laughed sarcastically. "I don't even know where that is anymore. I only know that I have to get away from both of you. Don't call or try to get in touch with me, because I won't respond and I'll never come back. There's nothing here for me."

The pain in her voice was like a knife through Jonas's heart. He had wanted to shield her from whatever Brewster was up to. But he had never dreamed it was anything like this. He wanted to tear into everyone, to make them pay for what they'd done to her. But those were Brewster's tactics, not his. Now, he had to find a way to help Abby.

She ran from the room before Jonas could stop her.

"Abby," Gail called plaintively.

"Go after her," Brewster ordered Jonas.

Jonas glared at him. "I'll go after her, but not for you. She didn't deserve this. Your manipulative, controlling ways have driven her away. You'd better pray it's not forever." He glanced at Gail. "And you...how could you do this to your own daughter?"

Gail whimpered, and moved toward the door.

"No." Jonas stopped her. "Don't follow her. She

doesn't need another scene. Give her some time... that's the least you can do.''

Then he whirled on his heel and left the room.

JONAS RAN DOWN THE STAIRS and out the front door, in time to see Abby's white car drive away. Dammit. He immediately jumped in his truck and followed her. She went directly to her mother's house. He got out and hurried to the front door. It was unlocked, so he went inside. He found her in her bedroom, sitting on the bed holding a picture of Abe. A suitcase lay open on the bed. His heart twisted at the expression on her face, and he sat beside her. That was all he could do—be there for her.

"How could she, Jonas?" she asked in a tortured voice. "She broke his heart. How could she?"

Jonas didn't have an answer for her, and Abby didn't seem to expect one.

"Why did she have to tell him? Why couldn't she leave him with his pride?"

"He probably knew," Jonas said. "He'd read the reports, but the truth was something he couldn't admit because he loved you so much."

Her hand touched Abe's face. "Yeah," she murmured weakly. "When I started school, he thought I'd be afraid. I told him I wasn't, but he waited outside my classroom all day just in case I was. That's the type of person he was."

"Abe had a big heart, just like you."

"I thought I got all my good qualities from him, but I didn't. I don't have his blood in my veins. I don't have anything of his—" The last words came out on a choked sob.

"Yes, you do," he assured her. "You have all the

love and care he gave you. No one can take that from you."

"Oh, but they did," she said tersely, strength returning to her voice. "They took everything from me. I may look the same on the outside, but I don't feel the same. I'm different now."

"Abby..."

"It's true," she insisted, and turned and gently placed the photo into the suitcase. "Nothing's real anymore. I had all these wonderful feelings for you, and now I'm not sure about them. I'm not sure about anything." She brushed away tears with both hands. "You're probably very relieved."

"I'm not." The words came from the deepest part of his heart, but she didn't seem to hear them.

"I've always run headfirst into everything, but I got bruised this time. I'm so bruised that I—"

He slipped an arm around her waist, and she rested her head on his shoulder. "I have to get away from here and think...to come to terms with everything that has happened."

He kissed her forehead, and she turned her head to look at him. "I'll never forget you, Jonas Parker."

A lump formed in his throat and he couldn't speak. Dammit, why couldn't he do something to help her?

"What are you going to do, Jonas? Stay or leave?"

The blockage in his throat eased. "I'm not sure yet," he admitted. "Brewster and I have a lot to get through."

She got up and started putting clothes into her suitcase. "Don't let him take anything else from you. He's taken enough."

She amazed him. Her first thoughts were of her

father, not of herself, and now she was worried about him. She might not want to admit it, but she did have a heart like Abe...always giving and never taking. He'd never met anyone that caring before—and now she was leaving.

"If you ever make it to Dallas, look me up."

"Is that an invitation?"

Her eyes cleared. "Yes." Then they darkened again. "Because I'll never come back here."

"Give it time."

"I'll never be back," she stated with force, and he knew she meant it. He felt his heart wobble inside him, and for a moment he was locked in that pain he'd sworn he'd never feel again. Suddenly he could put a label on what he was feeling. He *loved* her. In that instant he knew it. He knew it by the agony in his gut, by the tears stinging his eyes and by the ache in his heart. This all-consuming emotion had to be love—and it was tearing him apart just like he'd known it would.

Gail appeared in the doorway. "Abby, please listen," she begged.

Abby snapped her suitcase shut. "I don't want to talk to you."

"You can't leave like this. Abby, please." Gail's voice grew desperate. "Let me explain."

Jonas noticed that Abby's hands shook as she placed the suitcase on the floor, and he recognized she was close to the edge. It was time for everyone to back off. This he could handle. He stood and pushed Gail out the door, then took her arm and led her into the living room.

"Jonas, please talk to her," she said.

"It's a little late for talk, Mrs. Duncan. You should

have done that weeks ago, when you knew what
Brewster was up to. Instead, you let him manipulate
the whole situation. Of the two of you, I'd say he
has more concern for Abby than you. Hiring Rios?
I'm still having a difficult time with that. Abby and
I could both be dead right now. Is that what you
wanted?''

"Oh God, no," Gail cried, sinking onto the sofa
and burying her face in her hands. "I didn't know
what to do. I tried talking Abby into going back to
her job, but she wouldn't listen. She misunderstood
everything I said, and I was at my wit's end. Then I
heard some cleaning people at the school talking
about a man who made problems go away for a price.
Out of desperation I called him and told him that I
wanted to keep Abby from finding Delores Alvarez.
I thought he'd hide Delores or send her deeper into
Mexico. I didn't realize he was so vile. I didn't. I
would never hurt Abby. She's my daughter, and I
love her.''

Jonas could see that she loved Abby, but Gail
Duncan now had to face the consequences of her
actions. She had made some stupid mistakes, and she
had to deal with losing what she valued most in this
world—her daughter. And like Jonas, there was nothing she could do about it. They had to let her go.

Abby came out of the bedroom with two suitcases
in her hands and a clothes bag over her arm. Jonas
went to help her. He took the cases from her, and
Abby walked through the living room into the
kitchen. She didn't even spare Gail a glance.

"Abby, please," Gail said, but Abby didn't stop
until she reached her car.

Jonas slowly followed. He put her luggage on the

back seat, hung the clothes bag and slammed the door. Abby had the driver's door open but she didn't get in. She stared at him sadly.

"I'm sorry I got you mixed up in all this."

He shrugged. "Don't worry about it. I have broad shoulders."

Her eyes caught his. "I know. You told me that once before. I want to thank you for—"

Jonas couldn't bear the pain in her voice. Unable to stop himself, he cupped her face and gently kissed her. She moaned and returned the kiss with an urgency that broke his heart. Her arms wrapped around his neck and trailed through his hair. He drew her against him, wanting to feel every part of her. It would be all that he would have in the days and nights ahead. The kiss went on—neither of them willing to end the moment. Finally Abby moved away and got into the car. They didn't speak. There was nothing left to say.

EVERYTHING INSIDE Jonas had crumbled into a hard ball of pain the moment Abby left. Now he drove to the mansion and charged through the front door without knocking.

"Mr. Jonas," Maria called, but he didn't pay her any attention. He entered Brewster's room. Edna and Jules were there.

"Get out," Jonas ordered.

Jules bristled. "You can't talk to us that way. Who do you think you are?"

"The man who's gonna kick your ass if you're not out of here in five seconds."

Jules's face turned red, and Edna appealed to Brewster. "Simon?"

"Get out." Brewster repeated Jonas's order.

"We'll be right outside if you need anything," Edna assured him as they left.

As soon as the door closed, Brewster asked, "Where is she?"

"Gone."

"Gone," Brewster echoed in a hollow tone.

"Yeah, you played your little game and you lost. You lost big."

"Go after her," Brewster thundered.

"No," Jonas replied tightly.

"I'm giving you an order." Brewster's voice was hard.

"And I'm refusing."

"You'd better—"

Jonas broke in. "No more orders or threats," he stated angrily, and walked closer. "Do you even realize what you've done? You've shattered her, just like this—" He brought his fist down hard on the small table. "And for what? To satisfy your gigantic pride. You had an affair with her mother and got her pregnant. Big deal. That makes you an adulterer, and Abby should never have known about the sordid tryst. You should have cared enough to let her keep her memories of her father."

"She still has those," Brewster muttered.

"But now they're tainted because she knows she's not Abe's daughter."

"She isn't. She's mine."

"And that makes you, what? A better man than Abe? Keep trying, Brewster, you'll never make it…not even in your own mind."

"She's mine," Brewster repeated stubbornly, and

anger swelled in Jonas. He could feel it boiling in his veins.

"I could kill you for what you've done to her." His breath burned in his throat.

Brewster shot him a cold stare. "But you won't."

"Don't be too sure of that."

"Oh, but I am," Brewster retorted. "You're nothing like your father. You don't have a violent bone in your body."

Jonas was taken aback, and all anger left him. For years he'd believed he was like his father. Abby had told him that he wasn't, and now Brewster was telling him the same thing. His anger frightened him at times, and he was afraid he'd do something violent, but he abhorred violence. He'd been raised in it and it sickened him. He took a hard breath. They were right. He wasn't like his father.

In that moment he made a decision. "I'm leaving," he said quietly.

"We have a deal," Brewster reminded him.

"Call the sheriff," he replied, and headed out the door.

"Jonas, come back here," Brewster ordered, but Jonas didn't stop.

He had a need for fresh air, the wind in his face and the sun on his skin. He drove to the warehouse and his motorcycle. He didn't know where he was going, but he knew he was leaving, and—like Abby—he wasn't sure if he was ever coming back.

SIMON BREWSTER STOOD by his window, staring down at Jonas with a somber expression. Edna and Jules entered the room.

"What are you doing?" Edna asked. "You shouldn't be up."

"Watching Jonas. He's leaving."

"Don't worry," Edna soothed. "It's time he left. Jules can run the farm."

Simon sank heavily in his rocker. "Yeah, he can run it right into the ground."

"You haven't given me a chance, Uncle Simon."

"And you won't get it, either."

"That's not fair," Edna snapped.

"Get used to it," Brewster growled. "Nothing in life is fair. It certainly isn't fair that my daughter hates me."

Edna glanced at Jules. "What are you going to do about her?"

"I think that decision has been made for me."

"You don't need her," Edna said. "You have us and Darby."

"Yeah, and where the hell is Darby? Shouldn't he be here sucking up?"

"He's in Vegas. He'll be back tomorrow."

"That's a big comfort," Brewster replied sarcastically.

"I can see you're in one of your moods, so we'll leave you to get some rest."

"Yeah, and you'd better pray that Jonas comes back, or it will be hell around here."

Edna didn't say another word as they left the room.

"You'd better come back, Jonas," Simon muttered under his breath. "You'd better come back."

ABBY DROVE STEADILY toward Dallas. At times she brushed tears away, struggling to keep from falling

apart. She stopped for gas in San Antonio, and saw
a motorcycle and thought of Jonas. His strength, his
warmth seemed to fill the car, and she drove on, each
mile taking her farther away from him. A choked sob
left her throat several times, but she didn't turn back.
Losing Jonas was a casualty of the devastating events
that had taken place. She would survive. She was
strong and independent—everyone told her that. So
why did she feel weak and needy.

Outside Austin, she stopped at a convenience store
and bought Coke and peanuts. Somehow it made her
feel closer to Jonas. But she wasn't close to Jonas.
He was in Hope, and she was suspended in a nightmare. Gail and Brewster had taken everything from
her...even her ability to love Jonas the way he deserved.

It was cloudy when she stopped in Waco for gas
again. As she got out and put the nozzle into the tank,
it started to rain. The heavens opened and heavy
drops pelted the pavement with a deafening sound.
She watched as water ran into a drainpipe. Suddenly
something in her broke and she started to cry, hard,
racking sobs that she couldn't stop.

The gas pump clicked, telling her that her tank was
full, but she couldn't move. She could actually feel
her heart bleeding, and she knew she was dying inside. Her father's face swam before her and then
Jonas's replaced it. She gasped as the pain consumed
her.

"Ma'am, ma'am, are you all right?"

The words penetrated the heavy fog that surrounded her. She jerked in the direction of the
strange voice.

"Are you all right?" a man asked.

Abby blinked and remembered where she was and what she was doing. *No, I'll never be all right again.* "Yes, yes, I'm fine, thank you," she said, and quickly removed the nozzle and retrieved her credit card.

The man eyed her strangely and walked to his vehicle. Abby quickly got into hers and drove into the pouring rain. She had to stop thinking, or she wouldn't be able to hold it together. *She had to stop thinking.*

It was late when she drove into her apartment complex, but she felt a moment of relief. This was her world, and now maybe she could get a grip on things. She paused at her apartment. Holly lived two doors down. Abby had the urge to pour her heart out, but she wasn't ready to do that. Anyway, she didn't see any lights on in Holly's place so her friend was probably out. Abby entered her own apartment, dropped her suitcases in the living room, flipped on the lights and locked the door. She walked into the bedroom and fell across the bed. Within minutes she was sound asleep.

JONAS RODE TOWARD LAREDO, then into the Panhandle. Soon he was in New Mexico and Colorado, then Kansas. The farther he went, the cooler the temperatures became. He lost track of the number of days that had passed. He slept in roadside parks and ate occasionally. He wanted to get as far away as he could.

He was so angry at Brewster, but with each mile the anger became less intense and he could think more rationally. Brewster and Abby became intermingled in his head. She was Brewster's daughter.

How could someone as compassionate as Abby be his daughter? Jonas thought about it over and over, until a few facts emerged. Facts he wanted to shut out, but couldn't. Brewster had his good qualities. He'd done a lot for Hope, Texas—the clinic and hospital, for example. Most towns that small didn't have those medical services. Hope owed him for that and for the good jobs he'd supplied to the area.

As the wind cooled Jonas's face, another truth hit him—he owed Brewster, too. That wasn't easy to admit, but the past reeled through his mind with a shocking reality. He had been on a fast track to prison. The accident and Brewster's weird proposal had saved him. Brewster had treated him shabbily at first, but Jonas had grown up and learned how to work. Brewster had also made sure he'd had an education…something Jonas wouldn't have done on his own. He remembered the first time Brewster had given him a paycheck. He'd never had so much money in his life. Every night he'd spread it out on his bed and counted it. He'd stored it away in a box, adding to it each week. Mick had encouraged him to open a bank account, which he did. Year after year Brewster had raised his salary, and now Jonas's earnings were comparable to those of a CEO of a big company.

He had money, so he could now leave Brewster Farms. Somehow the idea didn't appeal to him. For twenty years he had worked with Brewster to make Brewster Farms what it was today. Almost without his realizing it, the place had come to mean something to him. Even though Brewster was like a thorn in his side, it was a thorn Jonas was used to. His motorcycle seemed to make its own way back to Texas.

On the trip home, Jonas decided that things were going to change at Brewster Farms. He owed Brewster, but he didn't owe him his life. And he would tell the old man that up front. How Brewster responded to Jonas's demands would determine whether he stayed or left for good. He was gambling that loyalty and responsibility meant something to Brewster. It was a long shot at best, but Jonas would only stay on his terms.

Abby had a lot to do with his decision. She'd told him that he didn't owe Brewster anything else. With all his heart, Jonas hoped she would come back one day, and when she did, he'd be waiting. He'd wait forever if he had to. He was good at doing time.

CHAPTER FOURTEEN

JONAS PARKED HIS MOTORCYCLE on the drive in front of the mansion. He removed his helmet and hooked it onto the steering wheel. He ran his hands through his long hair. He hadn't had a bath or shave in over a week and he felt as grimy as hell, but it lifted his spirits to breathe the air of Hope again. It was good to be back. Things were changing, and definitely for the better...except for Abby. When he thought of her, an intense pain gripped his chest.

He marched to the house, up the stairs and into Brewster's room. The old man was sitting at the window as usual, and he was by himself.

"My God, you look like hell," he said, at the sight of Jonas.

"This is how it's going to be," Jonas said without preamble. "I will run Brewster Farms the way I see fit. I will not check every little detail with you. You will give me complete control. If you have complaints, you come to me and we'll talk, but you will not order me around anymore. My time here is up, and now I deserve the respect I've given you all these years."

"Fine," Brewster said.

What!

Jonas hadn't expected this. He'd expected an argument, a fight, anything but instant agreement.

"You run Brewster Farms," Brewster said, when Jonas remained quiet. "I don't know what the difference would be. You've been running it for years. You stick all those papers in my face, and I sign things I don't know anything about. I can't see squat without my glasses and very little with them. You see, Jonas, I've been trusting you longer than you think."

The words took the wind out of his sails. Brewster had played games to keep from looking like an ass. Jonas could see that now. He was just a desperate old man. Jonas felt a pang of sadness for him.

"Have you seen Abigail?" Brewster asked.

Jonas found his voice. "No."

"Why not? You've been gone long enough."

"Because she needs to be alone. She needs time."

"That's something I don't have," Brewster murmured in a quiet tone and Jonas wondered what had happened to this man since he'd been gone. Brewster seemed almost human.

His eyes caught Jonas's. "Bring her home."

Jonas held up a hand. "No, that has to be her decision."

"Dammit, Jonas."

"And no more orders, remember?"

"Well, you'll pardon me if I say go take a bath and get rid of that hair on your face."

Jonas rubbed his beard. "I was planning on doing that, and I'll probably sleep for the next twenty-four hours."

"Fine, just get back to work soon, because this place is falling apart, and I'm tired of listening to everyone whining."

"Yes, sir." Jonas saluted and started out of the room.

"Jonas."

He stopped.

"I'm glad you're back."

The words threw Jonas into a tailspin. This definitely wasn't the Brewster he knew. Maybe the old man was in shock or something, but Jonas wasn't going to look a gift horse in the mouth.

He nodded and ran down the stairs. Yep, he was back and ready to go to work. He didn't like idleness. He liked having something to do. He enjoyed the workers, the camaraderie, and he liked being in charge. He felt a sense of pride in what he'd achieved. As he straddled the bike, his thoughts turned to Abby and he wondered how she was, if she'd returned to work. He also wondered if she'd ever be able to forgive Gail and Brewster. Maybe her strong spirit would help her see past the cheating and the lying. Then maybe she'd find her way back to Hope, Texas.

ABBY THREW HERSELF into her work. That was all she had now. At night she talked to Holly. She told her everything, even about Jonas. She had to talk to someone. It was the hours between bedtime and morning that got to her...the loneliness, the thinking. She tried to rationalize, to put the events into perspective, but all she felt was the betrayal to her father and her anger toward her mother.

Jonas was never far from her thoughts, but she couldn't make any decisions about him, either. Every day there were calls from her mother and Mr. Brewster on her answering machine. She never returned them. If the phone rang while she was home, she checked the caller ID and didn't answer if it was either of them. She didn't hear a word from Jonas, and that was just as well. Hearing his voice would only make the torment inside her worse.

Tonight she and Holly had made salads and were eating at her place. Usually they worked late. Tonight they had a spare evening.

"You working on the Coleman piece?" Holly asked, as Abby poked at her salad.

"Yeah." Abby pierced a tomato and stared at it. "It's very interesting. They had a baby in order to get a bone marrow match that would save the life of their other child. It's very touching, very moving. It should be a good article."

"I wish I could have done the photos, but Ted got the call."

"It's not award-winning stuff like you do."

"What do you mean? I keep picturing this little girl with no hair and a bright smile holding the baby brother that saved her life. It could be huge."

"I suppose," Abby mumbled, and got up and dumped her salad into the garbage disposal.

"That garbage disposal eats better than you do," Holly remarked.

"I'm not hungry."

"You're never hungry, Abby. You can't keep this up. You have to eat or you'll make yourself sick."

"I'm fine," Abby said, and sat down.

"No, you're not." Holly waved a hand. "Look at you. You don't wear makeup and you scrape your hair back. You take no time with your appearance. It's like you're in a catatonic state. I don't know this Abby."

"I don't, either," she choked out, feeling the pressure of walls that were closing in on her.

"Then, for God's sake do something about it."

"Like what?"

"Like reviving that spirit and fire that was such a big part of you."

"I'm not that person anymore."

"Yes, you are. What is it you used to say in college?" Holly was thoughtful for a second. "Yeah, you'd say, 'I'm Abigail Duncan—no middle name. My father's Abe and my mother's Gail. I was named after them.' You're the same Abby you've always been and you're stronger than this. I know you are."

Abby didn't say anything—she just stared at the blue napkin on the table.

"Your mother had an affair. She's human."

Abby raised her head, her green eyes fiery. "I'm the result of that affair."

"So what? Your parents have loved and cared for you all your life. You had a childhood that kids dream about. I was shuffled back and forth between my divorced parents like an old shoe. My father's been married three times, my mother twice. I have half sisters and brothers, not to mention stepsisters and brothers. I need a score card to keep track. I envied that closeness and love you shared with your parents. That love hasn't changed. It's still there."

"It's different, though," Abby insisted. "I can get past what she did to me, but I can't get past what she did to him."

Holly watched her for a moment, then asked, "Did your father leave her when he found out the truth?"

"No."

"Why didn't he?"

Abby shrugged. "I don't know. He should have."

"He didn't leave because he loved her."

When Abby didn't answer, Holly went on. "He forgave her. They tell me that's what love's all about."

Abby felt a jolt to her heart, and she held her head with both hands to stop the current surging through her. "Stop it, Holly," she cried. "You're driving me crazy."

"Call this Jonas guy," Holly said softly.

Abby shook her head. "No, I can't call Jonas."

"Why not?"

"If I hear his voice, I'll...Holly, please, let's drop this."

Obviously sensing her distress, Holly relented and started cleaning up the kitchen. Abby helped. They worked in silence.

Holly folded the dish towel and laid it on the counter. "I hate to bring this up, but Kyle called me again today."

Abby's face muscles tightened. "Tell him not to call you."

"I have—repeatedly, but he seems intent on getting a message to you. He wants you to know how good his life is going and that all he wants to do is apologize. There, I've given you the message. My job is done."

Abby bit down on her lip. "I'll call him and make sure he doesn't bother you anymore."

"You don't have to do that."

"Yes, I do. I have to close that door for good, and the only way to do it is in person."

"Are you sure?"

"Yes," Abby replied, and she was. She was confused about so many other things, but she had to get Kyle out of her life and the lives of her friends—of that she was positive.

Holly gave her a brief hug. "I've got to go. I've got a six o'clock shoot in the morning." At the door, she added, "Call Jonas."

"Holly." Abby sighed.

"What?" Holly shrugged. "I want to meet this guy. You make him sound like Brad Pitt, George Clooney and Clint Eastwood all rolled into one—with a heart of gold. *Perfect* is the word that comes to mind." Holly laughed and disappeared out the door.

Jonas *was* perfect, and he probably never wanted to see her again. She couldn't blame him. She didn't want to see herself. When she looked in the mirror, she didn't know the woman staring back at her and she didn't care to find out who she was. She didn't care about anything but the pain that was ripping her apart. She knew it was controlling her, and she was powerless to stop it.

JONAS WORKED from daylight to dark, exhausting his body and his mind, but he couldn't exhaust his heart. Every day he waited for a call from Abby—none came. Days turned into weeks. Thanksgiving came and went and still there was no word. He took several trips into Mexico, looking for the old lady who made the jackets. On the third trip he found her and purchased one similar to the one Abby had bought. The old lady wanted to give it to him because he'd been so generous before, but he couldn't let her do that. Again he paid her a hundred dollars and enjoyed the smile on her face. He had the jacket in his apartment.

He'd give it to Abby one of these days. When? He had no idea.

Brewster kept his word. He let Jonas run the farm without interference, but Jonas was worried about him. That was a new twist in Jonas's life. He was now concerned for Brewster. The old man's health was deteriorating. That was obvious from his pale skin and frail body. Jonas went each day to the house on the excuse of business, but he needed to see how he was doing. Brewster was hurting. He was hurting like hell, and Jonas couldn't help him. Brewster had brought it all on himself.

Jonas was on the way to the house one morning, when Mrs. Duncan stopped him. She handed him a piece of paper. "This is Abby's number and address," she said. "Please, call her. She'll listen to you. She won't take any of my calls."

"Mrs. Duncan, I've been through this with you and Brewster. Abby has to do this on her own. I can't force her to come back here."

"Just call her. She needs someone."

Jonas fingered the paper.

"I'm her mother and I will never stop loving her."

Jonas looked at her and saw the same hurt he saw in Brewster's eyes. "I'm sure she's aware of that," he said gently. "But that love has received a severe blow. It needs to heal first." Where those words had come from he had no idea, because he didn't know a thing about love. He only knew he wanted all the hurting to stop.

Gail choked back a sob. "Call her, Jonas. I can't stand the thought of her going through this alone."

"I'll think about it," was all he'd say.

"Thank you," she said, and walked to her car.

Jonas went into the house wondering if this nightmare was ever going to end. Brewster was in bed as he had been for the past few days. The nurse was taking his blood pressure.

Jonas sat down and twirled his hat in his hand. "How are you doing?" he asked, when the nurse had finished.

"Not good—even I know that," he replied in a weak voice that seemed so at odds with his stronger character. "My days are numbered."

Jonas realized that, too, and he couldn't believe the sadness that filled his heart. He'd hated this man for so long, but Mick had always told him there was a thin line between love and hate. He now knew that to be correct.

"Everything going okay?" Brewster asked.

Jonas blinked. "Yes, everything's fine, and as you know things slow down this time of year."

"Maybe you ought to take some time off...go to Dallas."

Jonas rubbed his thumb over his hat. Everyone had the same person on their minds—Abby. As much as he wanted to, he couldn't do what they were asking. Abby had to... Dammit, he was tired of using that excuse. If he wanted to see her, then...why couldn't he? What was stopping him? The *L* word now had him by the throat, and he was either going to die loving her or—

Brewster's voice penetrated his thoughts. "I want you to read something."

Jonas had been lost in his own inner pain, and it took a while for Brewster's comment to register.

"What?" he managed to ask.

He pointed to a paper that lay on his nightstand.

"I had that drafted by my lawyer, and it's running in the *Hope Herald* and several big newspapers across Texas."

Jonas stood, placed his hat in the chair and picked up the paper. It was titled "A Good Man" and it told of Abe Duncan's life at Brewster Farms. It told of his service, loyalty and honesty as an accountant. It was a moving story signed by Simon Brewster. Finally Brewster was telling the truth.

Jonas carefully laid the paper back in its place and took his seat. "Abby will be pleased."

"I didn't do it for her," he muttered in his old gruff voice, then relented. "Well, not completely. I'm dying, Jonas, and before I meet my maker, I have to atone for a lot on this earth."

Jonas had guessed as much. Simon Brewster had been a different man these past few weeks, and Jonas wished that Abby was here to at least get a glimpse of the man who was her father. That was asking a lot of her. But the wounds had to heal…eventually. Brewster, Mrs. Duncan and Abby couldn't go on like this.

"And I want to talk to you."

Jonas moved uncomfortably in his chair. "About what?"

"The accident."

Jonas's hand gripped his hat. "I think we've talked that one to death."

"No, we haven't. You don't know the whole truth."

"What truth?" Jonas asked in a guarded voice.

Brewster looked through the windows to the sky, as if he needed to see wide-open spaces. "My son…my son wasn't the angel I made him out to be.'' A slight pause, then he said, ''He was in trouble all the time. He wouldn't study or stay in school. He thought that since his father had money, the world was his playground. He spent eight years in college, and I finally had to buy his diploma.'' He stopped. ''That night we argued, and I told him if he didn't marry the girl he was dating and settle down, I was going to disinherit him. He'd been drinking all day, and he blew up and ran out of the house before I could stop him. The last thing he said to me was *I hate you.*'' He paused for a second. ''His alcohol level was higher than that of any of the teenagers, but I had the reports destroyed.''

Jonas's vocal cords closed up. He hadn't expected this, and for a moment he was back in the body of that young boy who'd felt so lost and afraid.

''I hated you because you lived and he didn't, and I took out my grief, my anger and my guilt on you. The truth is, the sheriff couldn't do much to you. You were a kid in the wrong place at the wrong time, but I never let you believe that. I wanted you close so you could pay for my son's death. I needed someone to pay.'' He took a breath. ''I drove you hard that first year and I treated you badly. I'm sorry for that, but I never broke your spirit. If there was any weakness in you, Jonas, I never found it. You became the man my son would never have been.''

Jonas was waiting for his anger to overtake him, but nothing happened. Why wasn't he consumed with rage? This old man had used him unscrupulously to justify his own guilt. But all Jonas felt was a release. It was as if a steel band had popped around his heart and he could breathe normally for the first time in years.

He hadn't killed Brewster's son. No one had. It had been a horrible accident.

"I realize you don't want anything from me," Brewster added as an afterthought.

Jonas stood, his hat in his hand. "No, I don't."

"I've seen your accounts at the bank. You've saved just about every dime I've paid you over the past twenty years, except what you've spent on that motorcycle and your apartment and given to workers when they needed money. It's grown into a hefty amount, so when I die I know you'll want for nothing."

Except for Abby, he thought.

"That leaves me the problem of what to do with Brewster Farms. My family's nothing to brag about, but they're all I have. And Abigail doesn't want anything from me. She's made that very clear."

"Yes, she has," Jonas had to admit, and he had to say something else. "What you do with Brewster Farms is up to you, because when you do...when you go...I'll be leaving, too." He could see that clearly. There would be nothing for him here—just a lot of bad memories. But now that the time for him to leave was at hand, he felt little joy.

He'd thought that everything would be complete if Abby was here. But Abby was never going to live here. Her home and job were in Dallas. He had to finally admit that he was living in a fool's paradise.

"I figured as much." Brewster sighed regretfully. "Would you do one last thing for me?"

"I'll try."

"I've made you executor of my will, and I'd appreciate it if you'd carry out my last wishes. That's all I ask."

Jonas swallowed. The thought of dealing with Edna, Jules and Darby was daunting, but he said, "I'll do my best."

Brewster took a ragged breath as if he was at peace. Of its own volition, Jonas's hand reached out and touched the gnarled one lying on the bed. Brewster's hand gripped his with a strength that surprised him.

"That's all you've ever given me," Brewster said, his voice cracking on the last word. Jonas walked out of the room in silence.

He stood outside the door and brushed away a silly tear. He hadn't cried in years and he wouldn't now. He put his hat on his head and went back to his office.

ABBY HAD ARRANGED to meet Kyle at a restaurant. She wanted people around. She knew that she didn't have to see him, but she wanted to make sure he understood that their marriage was over. He seemed to think that since he'd straightened out his life, she should fall back into his arms. She had to disabuse him of that idea.

She put on makeup and did her hair. Not for Kyle, but for herself. Holly was right. She'd been wallowing in self-pity. It was time to stop.

She walked into the restaurant and spotted Kyle at a nearby table. He waved and she went over. He tried to take her in his arms, and she backed away.

"Please, don't touch me," she said, more sharply than she'd intended.

Kyle held up his hands. "Sorry, it was just a reflex action."

Abby sat down before he could pull out her chair.

She stared at him briefly. He wore a dark blue suit and a matching tie and handkerchief. He was an impeccable dresser. That was one of the things that had attracted her to him. That and his blond hair, blue eyes and an athletic build. His attractiveness did nothing for her now. It was all superficial. She'd learned that the hard way. Underneath, Kyle had a temper that frightened her. Jonas also had a quick temper, but she'd never been afraid of him and she never would be.

"What would you like to drink?" Kyle asked.

He must have seen the shock on her face.

"It's all right, Abby," he said. "I'm not drinking, but I know you like to have wine occasionally. It won't bother me. I can handle it."

Abby linked her fingers in her lap. "I don't drink anymore."

Kyle lifted an eyebrow. "Since when?"

Since I met Jonas. "It's just a choice I made," she said. She saw the hope in his eyes and added, "It has nothing to do with you."

"I see," he said moodily, and asked, "What would you like to drink?"

Coke and peanuts.

Suddenly Jonas was controlling her thoughts, and she didn't know why. Maybe it was the obvious contrast between the two men. Jonas had substance and character, and he didn't need clothes or anything else to make him a man. Kyle was the complete opposite, and she wondered how she had ever thought she loved him. And she wondered why she'd put up with so much, trying to make that a reality. She answered her own question: foolish pride. She never liked to fail at anything.

"Abby?" Kyle tried again.

She collected her thoughts. "Tea, please."

Kyle signaled the waiter and, after he left, said, "You look wonderful."

She had to swallow the bitter taste in her mouth before she could say, "Thank you."

"I'm so glad you agreed to see me."

"You haven't left me much choice."

"I'm sorry for all the phone calls, but I wanted to apologize and I wanted you to see how I've changed. I'm working now...for your rival paper. I never miss my AA meetings." He paused. "I'm so sorry I hit you, but I was drunk and I didn't know what I was doing. The thought of you with another man made me crazy."

The waiter placed iced tea in front of them, stopping conversation. Abby touched the cool glass with her fingers. "I know you're sorry, but it doesn't change anything. It doesn't change the way I feel."

He closed his eyes briefly. "Don't say that."

"It's true," she stated. "I don't love you and I haven't for a very long time."

"You never gave our marriage a chance," he said in a spiteful tone, and she knew the old Kyle was just below the surface. "It made me so angry when you wouldn't have a child. It would have changed so many things."

She knew she had to say some things he didn't want to hear. "You thought I refused because I didn't love you, but it wasn't that, as I told you. A child should be brought into a solid family with love, happiness and stability."

The way I was.

That thought was another jolt to her heart, and this

time she couldn't ignore it. Her parents had given her so much love, so much—

"We could have had those things if you had tried harder."

His words had her full attention. "Excuse me?"

"Your job was all-important to you, and you had very little time for me, but you had time for all the other men at the paper."

She didn't know why she'd made the effort. Kyle hadn't changed at all. She started to push back her chair.

He reached out and grabbed her hand. "I'm sorry, but you make me crazy. Oh, Abby, I love you and I miss you."

She was never going to be free of Kyle unless she ended it right now. She slowly removed her hand. "We've been divorced for four months now. We didn't have much of a marriage before that. So does that mean you've been celibate all this time?"

He drew back. "What?"

"You say that you love me and miss me, so I'm assuming that means I'm the only woman for you and that you haven't been with anyone else."

The tips of his ears turned red. "Well…"

"Who do you think you're fooling? You slept with other women while we were married." It was just a guess, but she had her suspicions.

His ears turned completely red, and her suspicions were confirmed. All those nights when he was out drinking, she'd wondered where he was. Now she knew.

"Abby."

"No, Kyle, you listen to me. Our marriage is over…completely. Stop calling me and my friends.

Tell your mother to stop calling, too. Our association ends now. Get on with your life because that's what I'm doing.''

She stood and walked away.

ON THE WAY to her apartment, she stopped and bought a paper. She hadn't read today's edition. That was the trouble with being a reporter—she never had time to read.

She laid the paper on the seat and drove toward her apartment. She was glad she'd seen Kyle. That door was closed, locked and sealed for good. Now she could admit that one of the reasons she'd seen him was that she wanted to see if she could find any of the old Abby—the one who didn't know she was Simon Brewster's daughter. But that woman was gone...as was her love for Kyle. She now had to deal with the fact that she was Simon Brewster's daughter. Somehow, someway...

She stopped at a red light and glanced down at the paper. "A Good Man" caught her attention and she picked it up. As she read, her whole body began to tremble. "Oh my God, oh my God," she moaned, and tears poured from her eyes.

Cars began honking behind her, and she realized the light was green. She wiped her eyes with the palms of her hands, held the paper to her chest and drove on.

CHAPTER FIFTEEN

JONAS PACED IN HIS APARTMENT. He had made up his mind to call Abby and he didn't know why it was so hard. She'd had enough time for the wounds to start to heal. If he and Brewster could find a common ground, then there was hope for them all.

Before his courage failed, he grabbed the phone and punched in her number. A feminine voice answered, but it wasn't Abby's.

"Hello, is anyone there?" the voice asked abruptly.

Jonas was about to hang up, thinking he'd dialed the wrong number, when the voice said, "Kyle, is that you? Abby should be at the restaurant by now, so why are you calling? You got what you wanted."

Jonas slowly replaced the receiver and stared off into space. Abby was seeing her ex-husband. Why? Why would she do that? He remembered how angry she'd gotten when her mother had suggested she hadn't tried hard enough to make her marriage work.

He went into his bedroom, pulled out his suitcase and packed. He knew Dallas was his destination. He had to go see Abby. He should have gone weeks ago, but he'd wanted to give her some time. Later his stupid pride held him back. Now nothing would keep him away from her. All it took was a little old-fashioned jealousy, and his pride went right out the window.

He couldn't leave immediately. He had to wait for a flight to Dallas out of Brownsville. It was the fastest way. He told Stuart where he was going, and Stuart thought it was great. Brenda and several of Abby's friends were worried about her. He debated whether to tell Brewster, and then decided not to. He didn't want the old man to expect too much. Maria had Jonas's cell number in case anything happened while he was gone.

ABBY WALKED INTO HER APARTMENT feeling numb. She held the paper in her hand. She vaguely noticed that Holly was there.

"I left my earrings over here the other day and I came to..." Holly's voice trailed off as she noticed Abby's expression.

"Abby, what's wrong?"

She handed Holly the paper. *Wow*, Holly mouthed as she read.

"I've been working on the Coleman piece for two days. I haven't been in to the office. Why didn't someone tell us?"

Holly shrugged. "It's a big paper, and I'm sure the decision to print this came from high up. Someone who didn't connect the story to one of its reporters."

Abby sank onto the sofa. "I can't believe how many nice things Mr. Brewster said about my father."

"Yeah," Holly said as she continued to read. "Seems like he's reaching out to you."

Abby didn't say anything. She was locked somewhere between the little girl that was Abe Duncan's child and the grown woman who knew herself to be Simon Brewster's daughter.

Which one was she? Would the real Abigail Duncan stand up? *Please.*

"I'm sorry." Holly put down the paper. "I've got to run. I have a late date with Brent, the accountant. That's why I was looking for my earrings."

Abby still didn't say anything.

"Are you gonna be all right?" Holly asked.

Abby found her voice. "Yes."

"Abby, I—"

"Don't worry about me." Her voice was stern, and Holly got the message.

"Okay, then, I'll talk to you in the morning." At the door Holly stopped. "Did you meet Kyle tonight?"

Abby nodded.

"Strange, the phone rang earlier, and I answered it. The other person wouldn't answer and I thought it was Kyle. The battery was out on your caller ID. I replaced it for you. See you later."

Could it have been Jonas? Was Jonas trying to reach her? She curled up on the sofa. Oh God, Jonas. I need you.

Abby didn't know how long she lay there with feelings threatening to overwhelm her. Soon she got to her feet and went into the bedroom, searching for her carryall. She found it in the back of the closet and pulled it out. Inside were all the tapes Mr. Brewster had dictated to her. She sat on the floor listening to each one…learning about his poverty as a boy, his service in the war, his struggle to start Brewster Farms and his heartbreak over losing his only son.

By morning she was still sitting on the floor—the
tapes all around her. She had thought that Simon
Brewster was a cruel and evil man who didn't care
about other people. But he wasn't. He'd cared for his
mother and made sure she never had to go hungry.
He'd amassed an empire from nothing but a few
acres of farmland. As his profits grew, he bought
more land. He needed laborers to work the land, so
he offered good jobs to the people of Hope—better
than they could have gotten anywhere else. His ob-
jective was to boost the economy and keep people in
Hope. He also offered the Mexicans a better way of
life than they had across the border. He paid them
fair wages and gave them housing. He built the clinic
and hospital so everyone could have access to medical services. He'd loved his son and that love drove
him to take Jonas in, under devious means, but it
gave Jonas a direction, a focus in life. Something he
didn't have on the streets. Simon Brewster had many
facets and...and *he* was her father.

For the first time, the words didn't feel like a betrayal to the man whom she loved as her father. They
were just a statement of the truth. A truth that didn't
burn or hurt until she couldn't breathe. It was a truth
she had to live with.

She put the tapes away and went to take a shower.
When she came out, the phone was ringing. She
glanced at the caller ID and saw that it was her
mother. It rang a couple more times, then Abby
reached out and picked up the receiver.

"Mama," came out as a strangulated sound.

"Abby, sweetheart, oh, Abby," Gail murmured.
"Thank you for answering."

Abby took the phone and sat on the bed. "It's time

we talked," she said, knowing Gail had given her total love and support. She'd given her the space to develop her own ideas and opinions. She'd taught her to be independent and strong. Abby owed her, at the very least, a chance to explain.

"Did you love him?"

"Oh, Abby, I wish I could say that I did, but I didn't. I've always loved your father," Gail replied honestly, and Abby was glad she wasn't going to lie to her. "As I told you, we were having a rough time. We'd been married four years and I wanted a baby, but nothing was happening. I guess I became obsessed with it. When I mentioned adoption, Abe became furious. That did something to him. He started sleeping on the sofa, and later he moved in with a friend. He said he couldn't take the pressure anymore and that he'd be filing for divorce. I was devastated. While I was waiting for a teaching job to open up, I took a job at Brewster Farms to be near him, to try to change his mind, but it only made matters worse. He wouldn't talk to me. I started taking papers and forms up to the house for Simon to sign. His wife had left him, and he was distressed over it. We began talking, and gradually it led to other things. He was older, exciting and different from Abe. He made me feel attractive."

A long pause.

"You and Daddy were separated during this time?" She had not known her parents had spent any time apart.

"Yes."

Her mother had said that he'd moved in with a friend, and Abby didn't ask who. If it was another woman, she didn't want to know. She knew too much already. She remembered her mother saying something about her father not being a saint, and Abby was willing to leave it at that.

"The affair lasted about a month, then Simon's wife came back and he said it was over. I was so depressed that I quit my job and stayed in my bathrobe for days. I felt used and I didn't know what I was going to do. Then Abe showed up one morning and said he still loved me and missed me and wanted to come home. I suddenly had my world back and I wanted to tell him about Simon. I was so afraid he'd leave me again, so I kept my mouth shut. Then I realized I was pregnant and knew it couldn't be Abe's. I struggled with my conscience, but Abe was so happy that I couldn't tell him. He never even questioned when you were born early. He just loved you with all his heart."

Abby knew that. She'd felt it every day of her life.

"When did Mr. Brewster find out?"

"A couple of years ago. When he read that report on Abe's desk, he came to me wanting answers. I told him that you weren't his, but I could see he didn't believe me. He kept coming back until I told him the truth. He swore he'd never tell you. He promised me."

"That's why he planned that elaborate ruse about Delores Alvarez," Abby said. "Delores was the only one who'd seen you together."

"Yes. That's why I did those crazy things. I never wanted you to know. I'm sorry about Rios. Everything got out of hand. Oh, sweetheart, I never meant for any of this to happen. Please forgive me."

"Did Daddy forgive you?"

Silence stretched, and Abby asked again, "Did Daddy forgive you?"

Quietly her mother said, "He wouldn't talk to me for two days. Then one day he came into the kitchen and wrapped his arms around me and said that I had given him the greatest gift of all so he had nothing to be angry about. I had given him you. He was hurt that I had slept with someone else, but he said he'd get over it. I was grateful for his loving generosity and I thought all our problems were over. Then he became ill, and we found out about the cancer."

Abby remembered Gail's devotion to her father during those difficult months. She had never left his side. And when she stepped out of the room for a moment, Abe would ask for her, and Abby knew he had completely forgiven her. Those last days proved their love for each other.

"I'm telling you the truth, Abby, and it's hard," Gail added. "I'm sorry, but I don't regret having you. I did a lot of stupid things, but I can't regret that."

Abby swallowed and blinked back tears. "I've got to go," she muttered.

"I love you, Abby. No matter what I do or what you do, nothing will ever change that."

"I know, Mama. I'll talk to you soon." She quickly hung up because the waterworks were about to erupt.

She had known her parents as people who loved her and were always there for her. Now she saw them as human beings with faults, desires and weaknesses. The revelation didn't overwhelm her or shatter her. It gave her an insight into two people who had truly loved each other. And she got a glimpse of herself—

a woman who was strengthened by their weaknesses. Slowly she could feel Abigail Duncan emerging from the dark mist that had surrounded her, and she knew she'd soon be able to embrace life again. She'd be different, but that was what life was all about... changes.

SHE DRESSED AND HURRIED to the paper to turn in the Coleman story. She thought someone would mention the article in the paper. When they didn't, she realized no one had connected it to her, just as Holly had said. They worked together as colleagues, but they knew very little about each other's personal lives, unlike her and Holly, who had known each other for years.

Abby went back to her apartment and fell into a deep sleep. She woke up to the sound of Holly's voice.

"Abby? Abby? Are you ill?"

Abby pushed herself into a sitting position. She'd been dreaming a wonderful dream of Jonas, and now it was gone. "Why are waking me?" Abby muttered crossly.

"It's seven o'clock in the evening and I was worried when you wouldn't answer the door. I saw your car outside."

Abby frowned. "You've been knocking?"

"Yes."

"I haven't heard a thing. I must have been completely wiped out."

"I'll say," Holly said, then her eyes narrowed. "You didn't take anything, did you?"

Abby shook her head. "Stop worrying and hand me my robe. I'm hungry."

Holly threw a white silk robe at her. "That's a twist. You've hardly eaten a thing in weeks."

Abby slipped from the covers into the robe. All she had on was her bra and panties. She had been so drained when she got in that she hadn't bothered with a gown. Now she felt refreshed and hungry.

Holly followed her into the kitchen. Abby opened the refrigerator and glanced inside. There wasn't much to eat. Then she spotted a Coke and smiled. Jonas was still on her mind. She grabbed it and rummaged in the pantry. She didn't have peanuts, but she found a Snickers candy bar. Sitting on a bar stool, she popped the top of the can.

"You're having Coke and Snickers?" Holly asked in disbelief.

"Yeah, and it's pretty damn good. Want some?"

Holly held up a hand. "No, thanks, but why don't we go out to dinner and a movie? I'm free for the rest of the evening."

"Sounds great," Abby said, taking a bite of the Snickers. "Let's see a love story. A gooey, mushy love story that will make us want to grab the first man we see."

Holly watched her closely. "Are you sure you didn't take something?"

"Will you stop worrying." Abby sighed. "I didn't take anything. Besides, what would I take—aspirin?"

"You're different...almost like your old self," Holly commented.

"Yes, I'm finding my way back," she admitted. "Abigail Duncan's going to be fine."

"You talked to your mother," Holly guessed.

"I did, and we got through a lot of stuff."

"That's great, Abby," Holly said. "Did you talk to Jonas?"

"No, not yet, but I will soon." It felt good to say the words, and her heart beat faster at the prospect. She wasn't confused anymore. She loved Jonas. That feeling hadn't changed.

She slipped off the bar stool. "I'll be ready in a jiff."

As Holly threw the empty can and candy wrapper in the trash, the doorbell rang. "I'll get it," she called to Abby.

Holly swung open the door, and her eyes widened. Jonas removed his hat. "Howdy, ma'am," he said. "I was looking for Abigail Duncan's apartment."

Holly eyed him from his boots to his long, long legs, perfect in jeans, to his cotton shirt to his handsome face and sun-bleached hair. She placed a hand on her hip. "Howdy yourself, cowboy, and you've found Abby's apartment."

"Is she here?" he prompted, when Holly didn't say anything else.

"Oh." She quickly collected herself. "Yes, do come in. I'm Holly, a friend and neighbor."

Abby pulled out a pair of slacks and stopped. She heard a deep masculine voice and her toes curled into the carpet. *Jonas.* No one but Jonas had that effect on her. She dropped the slacks and ran into the living room.

"Jonas," she whispered, staring at him across the room, her heart beating so fast that she had to catch her breath. He looked even better than she remembered. Oh, how she loved him.

"Abby," he said hoarsely, taking in her disheveled appearance. Her hair was longer, and he liked it. He liked everything about her.

"How are you?" he asked.

She ran across the room and threw her arms around his neck. He dropped his hat, and his arms enfolded her body against his. His mouth opened over hers, and they kissed hungrily.

"I guess the movie's out," Holly joked, picking up Jonas's hat and placing it on a table. "Don't mind me. I'll be leaving now. No, don't bother. I'll see myself out." The door clicked behind her, but Jonas and Abby didn't notice.

"Oh, Abby, Abby." He kissed her cheeks, her nose, her forehead, his hands coming up to tangle in her hair. "Are you okay?"

She drew back slightly to smile into his eyes. "I'm great now."

His lips twitched into that beautiful grin she loved, and she kissed him and kissed him until their breathing became labored. She pushed her hands through his hair, her fingertips needing to feel everything that was Jonas.

"Abby," he groaned, when she began to unbutton his shirt.

"No, don't even think about stopping," she warned, her lips following her fingers down his chest.

"It never crossed my mind," he said against her hair. "I just thought we should talk first."

She shook her head. "I'm tired of talking and thinking. Right now, all I want is you." As she spoke, she brought her lips back to his.

"Where's the bedroom?" he asked between kisses.

She started walking backward, undoing his belt as

they moved down the hall and into her room. Slipping the shirt from his shoulders, she reveled in the muscles that rippled under her fingers. She stepped back and let her robe slide to the floor, then she eased onto the bed.

He watched as if mesmerized. Then in slow motion, he removed his boots and socks. Abby waited impatiently for him to remove the rest, but he didn't. Instead, he knelt and picked up her foot, gently kissing her instep. The sensitive touch sizzled along her leg, making other areas of her body hum for attention.

His lips trailed up her calf to the back of her knees to the inside of her thigh. By then she wasn't breathing, she was only feeling...pure, sensual pleasure. He removed her panties with little effort and unclipped her bra. She slid backward on the bed, and he moved over her, his lips continuing the delicious onslaught they had started. She groaned and dug her nails into the bedspread. As if sensing her weakness, he relented and found her aching breast. He suckled one, then the other, until she thought she would scream from the exquisite torture. When she couldn't take any more, his lips found hers again and an explosion of senses bolted through her, demanding more and more.

He rolled her over until she lay on top of him, and her lips and hands went to work on him. Then she helped him shimmy out of his jeans and shorts. She sat and stared at him. She'd never seen such a perfect male form. His broad shoulders and narrow waist enhanced a masculinity that took her breath away. He was fully aroused, and she felt her body answering with an urgency that she couldn't ignore.

Going on pure instinct, because she'd never been this bold before, her hands, lips and tongue caressed, stroked and massaged every inch of him. She didn't want to leave any place unknown or undiscovered. She had to experience all of him.

Suddenly Jonas rolled her onto her back again. She parted her legs, and he settled between them. He stared into her eyes as he slowly entered her, then his lips covered hers with a passion that she never wanted to end.

She wrapped her legs around him, holding him deep inside her, and he began to thrust against her, harder and stronger. Her hands ran down the whip-cord muscles in his back as each thrust took her higher and higher, to a place she'd never been before. As her body convulsed with unforgettable pleasure, she cried out, "I love you," and gave herself up to everything she knew Jonas could make her feel. A moment later she heard his cry of release and felt it encompass them both. Jonas eased to his back holding her on top of him.

She thought she had known about sex and love, but she didn't know a thing. She knew she had never given herself to Kyle as completely as she had just given herself to Jonas.

Even though he hadn't said *I love you*, that was okay. He'd just showed her with his body how much he cared about her. She felt loved and adored. She rested on his body in an unashamed languidness.

Jonas had always prided himself on his control, but he'd lost it the moment she'd touched him. He'd had sex before, but not like this. This time he'd made real love. It was the coming together of two hearts, two souls and two bodies—even he knew that. When he heard her say *I love you,* his body had exploded with a brilliant array of emotions that surged from him into her...a union that left him complete. He wanted to say the words back to her, but they were locked away so deep that he couldn't bring them to the surface. It would take time, but eventually he would tell her. While he waited for the miracle to happen, he'd show her in ways that he understood. He hoped she knew he'd given her something he'd never given anyone else—himself.

They had to talk, but right now, all he wanted was her in his arms and to savor this feeling that he didn't want to lose or diminish in any way. This feeling of being loved. He'd finally taken that big step, and now all he had to do was see it through—with Abby.

CHAPTER SIXTEEN

THEY HADN'T SAID A WORD during the passionate lovemaking, and Abby still wasn't ready to talk. She just wanted to hold on to the joy she was feeling. How had she existed before he'd touched her? Her hand began to trail down his side, loving the way his skin felt under her fingers.

"Abby, I can't think when you do that."

"You don't need to think," she said wickedly, as her tongue found his flat nipple and teased it. With him she was brazen and daring; he brought out the sensual side of her personality—a side she was beginning to enjoy to the fullest.

"Ab-by," he groaned.

She turned her head to look at him. "You like that? You want me to stroke any other places?"

He grinned. "I don't think you have to."

A bubble of laughter escaped her as she felt his hardness against her.

"That's what you do to me," he murmured raggedly. "When you first came to Brewster Farms, all I had to do was look at you and that would happen, so I kept my distance and made a point of speaking to you as little as possible."

"That's why you were so mean to me?" She pouted her lips, then rained kisses along his chin. "That's a pity, because every time I looked at you I thought about ripping your clothes off. I'd sworn off men, but I had all these naughty thoughts concerning you.''

She stretched along his body and felt every muscle in him tighten. She giggled in delight and found herself on her back, smiling into his desire-filled eyes. His mouth took hers as he slid inside her, and all laughter disappeared as she gave herself up to the erotic pleasure of making love with Jonas. He began to move slowly, their breath and tongues mingling and their hearts beating rapidly against each other as waves of ecstasy grew, then washed through them.

This climax was swift and powerful. Abby moaned and writhed beneath him with abandonment. She would never grow tired of this. Her heart and body had been waiting for him forever. ''I love you,'' she whispered.

Totally replete, he lay beside her, hearing those words over and over. It was like a needle stuck in a groove and the sound wouldn't stop until he acknowledged his own feelings. He felt his heart open and the words surge to his throat, but his vocal cords wouldn't work.

Abby soothed his roughened cheek with her finger, and he took it into his mouth and stared into her eyes, hoping to convey what he was feeling.

Abby saw the struggle in his eyes and knew how hard it was for him to voice his emotions. She understood and she would be patient.

Jonas scooted up against the headboard and pulled her back against him. His arms locked so tightly around her that she thought her ribs were going to crack. She didn't mind, though. She didn't mind at all.

Abby stroked the hands around her waist. "You okay?"

"Yeah." He kissed the side of her face.

She rubbed the back of her head against his chest, and they were silent for a while. Then Abby spoke. "I talked to my mother today."

"Oh, Abby. I'm glad."

"We talked about that time," she went on, needing to tell Jonas everything. "I never realized my parents were separated and thinking of getting a divorce."

"Really?"

"Yeah, my dad had moved out. Mom said that he was tired of her pressuring him to have a child. He told her he'd be filing for divorce because he'd had enough. He moved in with a friend. I didn't ask who and I really don't want to know, but I have a suspicion it was another woman."

Jonas didn't answer.

"I always saw them as parents, that's it. Two people who were perfect and had a solid marriage, but now I see them as humans with desires, drives and needs. It's so different, and I'm trying to understand." She paused. "You know what?"

"No, what?"

"I keep thinking that if I had met you while I was married to Kyle, I'd probably have cheated on him like he always accused me of doing."

"No, you wouldn't have," he assured her. "Your conscience wouldn't let you. I know you well enough to know that."

"I'm not sure. I'm shameless when it comes to you."

He nuzzled her hair. "We'll keep that our secret,"

he said, then added. "You're not like your mother, Abby. You probably got your strength from Brewster. Your mother doesn't have that. She was weak and made bad choices. She was human, like you said."

"I suppose."

"It's not your fault," he told her. "You're the victim in all this."

"Yes," she agreed. "Now I have to go on."

Silence stretched.

She played with his fingers. "I saw the article in the paper. Why did he do that?"

"I think he felt he owed it to you, and he's getting his affairs in order. He's dying, Abby, and he knows it."

Abby's heart constricted with something she didn't expect...an ache. Her father was dying.

Sensing her distress, Jonas told her how he and Brewster had drawn closer together the past few weeks. He told her of their many talks and the revelation about Brewster's son.

"I'm glad you weren't angry, because as much as you don't want to admit it, I believe Mr. Brewster saved you from a life of crime."

"Yep." Jonas took a long breath. "I finally realized that. And Brewster apologized for the way he'd first treated me. He vented his grief, anger and guilt on me, and I took it because I felt I deserved to be treated like that."

"And now you've resolved everything and forgiven him?"

"Yes," he replied without hesitation. Somehow he and Brewster had found a bridge from the past to the present. Now he had to help Abby do the same. They had no future until that happened.

"It's time to come back to Hope, Abby," he said softly.

She inhaled deeply. "I know and I can do it now…and I will."

Jonas felt a moment of relief. He didn't know what he would have done if she'd refused. "I'll be right beside you," he promised, and kissed her. He pulled the covers over them and they sank into the softness of the bed. Abby reached over and turned off the light.

She was quiet for a moment, then asked, "What made you come to Dallas?"

He shifted uncomfortably. He couldn't escape her questions, and he certainly didn't want to escape her. So he had to tell her the truth. "I called yesterday and I guess your friend answered." He stopped as something occurred to him. "Your friend was here earlier. Where did she go?"

"She lives two doors down. I'm sure she went home. You were saying?"

"I was shocked to hear another woman's voice, and when I didn't answer, she thought I was your ex-husband. She started speaking to me as if I was him. She said you'd gone to the restaurant to meet him and something about how he'd got what he wanted. I couldn't imagine why you'd be seeing him, and before I realized what I was doing, I was packed and on my way. I was gonna make damn sure he didn't hurt you again."

She kissed his chest. "I had to finish with Kyle, once and for all. He thought since he'd straightened out his life that I should be willing to come back to him. He wouldn't stop calling me and my friends.''

His arm tightened around her. "How did it go?"

"He won't be calling me again...ever."

"Good, because I'd hate to have to look him up and get the point across—man to man."

She smiled in the darkness and caressed his face. "Were you jealous?"

"No. Yes. Maybe a little."

"It's all right to be jealous...a little," she told him.

He held her tight, and they drifted into blissful sleep.

THEY HAD PLANNED to be up early to make plane reservations for Brownsville. But the moment they opened their eyes with their naked bodies pressed against each other, that plan went south. They made passionate love again. After a lengthy shower together that surpassed any sensual fantasy she'd had of this event, they managed to get dressed. It felt natural to have Jonas in her apartment, in her bed, sharing all the little intimate pleasures with him. She wished they could stay here forever and shut out the rest of the world. She knew once they walked out the door that things would change. She had to go, though. There was no other way.

Jonas held her hand on the plane, and when she leaned over and kissed him, a woman across the aisle whispered, "Newlyweds."

They weren't, and Abby couldn't help wondering what the future held. She wasn't sure, but she knew she wasn't leaving Jonas again. She wanted marriage and a family, and they hadn't talked about any of those things.

"Are you still planning on leaving when Mr. Brewster...dies?"

"Yes, Brewster and I talked about it. There'll be nothing there for me when he goes. He understands that."

"I see," she said dismally.

He must have caught that note in her voice. "Abby."

"Hmm?"

"You sound distant."

"I was thinking about the future."

He rubbed her hand. "I know it's difficult for you, but you have to resolve things with Brewster and your mother."

He'd completely misunderstood her. She wasn't thinking about Mr. Brewster or her mother.

"What will you do when you leave here?"

"I don't know. I thought I'd hang out in your apartment for a while. Do you think that's a possibility?"

She smiled. "Most definitely." As long as she was in his future, that was all that mattered. But she knew that Jonas was used to wide-open spaces, fresh air and sunshine. A tiny apartment would stifle him. They'd talk about it later, she decided, and work it out.

They landed in Brownsville. It took a while to find their luggage and get through the airport, but soon they were headed for Jonas's truck.

As they drew nearer to Hope, Abby's nerve began to weaken. "I'm not sure I can do this."

Jonas glanced at her, then reached out and caught her hand. "If you don't try, I think you'll regret it."

"I keep thinking that, too, but I have this bitter feeling I can't seem to shake."

"Once you see him, maybe that will change. He's so different, and I think you'll notice that and respond in kind."

"I hope so," she murmured. "How long does he have?"

"I don't know. The doctor's with him every day. He said it could be a matter of days."

When she didn't say anything, he said, "Abby, if you don't want to see him, you don't have to. Let's wait until we get to the mansion before you make that decision."

"Okay," she replied, and stared out the window. She knew they were getting close to Hope when she saw the flat agriculture fields of plowed-under crops. Farmers were preparing the land for spring planting. The smaller farms didn't do business during the winter season, but Brewster Farms never shut down. They operated all year. The winter months dictated a smaller scale of crops due to weather conditions.

She wondered how Jonas was going to leave here. Farming was his whole life. He knew how to produce crops, harvest and market them. He did it better than anyone. That's why Brewster Farms was so successful.

"Do you want to go to your mom's first?" Jonas asked, interrupting her thoughts. She realized she was trying to think of anything but what she had to.

She brushed her hair back. "I'd rather not." She could only handle one thing at a time.

They drove through the iron gates to the mansion.

It seemed forever since she'd come here to write Mr. Brewster's memoirs.

Jonas reached into the back seat and brought out a gift bag. He handed it to her. "I have something for you."

For a second she was disconcerted, but she took it and pulled out something wrapped in white tissue paper. Carefully she folded back the tissue and gasped. It was the denim jacket she'd lost in Mexico.

"Oh, Jonas, I can't believe you did this," she cried, holding up the jacket. "You went back and found it."

"No, the other one is long gone. I found the old lady and bought another. She makes each one a little different."

She threw her arms around his neck. "Thank you, Jonas."

He groaned. "When you say *thank you* like that, I want to do one thing."

"What?" She gazed into his eyes.

"This—" he answered a moment before his mouth covered hers. They kissed over and over. Finally they came up for air, and she slipped on the jacket.

"What do you think?"

"Beautiful, like the woman wearing it." She went into his arms, and they held each other.

"Ready?" he whispered.

She nodded and got out of the truck. There were several cars parked in the drive. Abby recognized Edna's and Darby's.

"The doctor's here," Jonas remarked as they walked up the steps. At the front door he stopped and turned to her. "You okay?"

"Yes," she said, and she knew she was. Mr. Brewster was dying. It was an ending, and she had to see him one more time—that was the only way she'd have a new beginning.

Edna, Jules and Darby sat in the hallway outside Mr. Brewster's room. Edna got to her feet when she saw Abby.

"What's *she* doing here?"

"Don't start, Edna," Jonas warned, "or you might find yourself on the outside looking in."

"Don't threaten me," she snapped indignantly. "We've been here for Simon. Where has she been?"

Before Jonas could reply, the doctor came out. A short, thin man with wire-rimmed glasses. "Oh, Jonas, I'm glad you're here. He's been asking for you," the doctor said.

"How is he?" Jonas asked.

The doctor shook his head. "I don't know what's keeping him alive. His kidneys have shut down, his heart beats for a while then it stops, but he's still coherent. He just won't let go. I've never seen anything like this. It's like he's waiting for something. Maybe he's waiting for you."

"No, I think he's waiting for someone else." Jonas glanced at Abby, then asked, "Is it all right if we see him?"

"Sure," the doctor answered. "I'm going to my office, but I'll be back later."

"Let me see him first," Jonas whispered to Abby. "I'd better prepare him."

"Okay," she said, feeling a knot form in her stomach so tight that she had trouble breathing. She was glad when the others didn't speak to her. She couldn't handle their barbs at that moment.

Jonas stepped into the room, and his heart constricted. The old man was so pale and still that Jonas wasn't sure he was breathing. He moved to the bed, and the nurse busied herself in another area of the room.

Suddenly Brewster turned his head as if he sensed someone was there. "Jonas, is that you?" His voice was weak and low.

Jonas swallowed before he could answer. "Yes, it's me."

"Where have you been? I've been worried. Thought you left."

"No, remember we have a deal," Jonas told him lightly. "I'm not going any where until..." He couldn't finished the sentence.

"Until I die," Brewster finished for him. "You can say it, Jonas. I know it's happening."

"I brought someone to see you," Jonas said quickly, to change the subject.

Brewster shook his head. "I don't want to see anyone."

"I think you'll want to see this person." Jonas went over and opened the door.

Abby took a shuddering breath and walked inside. Jonas led her to the bed. The moment she saw his frailty, all the bitterness, anger and resentment faded away. This was her father, she kept thinking, and she barely knew him. Oh God, oh God, this was her father.

Brewster opened his eyes and stared at her. A light burned bright in the inner depths. "Abigail, Abigail, oh, Abigail," he moaned in distress.

Jonas stepped closer. "Yes, it's Abigail. She's come to see you."

Tears rolled from his eyes onto the pillow, and Abby had to bite her lip to keep emotions from overpowering her.

"Thank you, Jonas, and thank you, Abigail. I don't deserve this."

Jonas pulled up a chair for Abby, and she was grateful because her legs were wobbly.

"I'm sorry," Mr. Brewster said, his voice weakening. "I got selfish. I wanted you to know, but I should have left you with your memories. Sometimes that's all we have."

Abby wasn't sure what to say. It was very clear Mr. Brewster was seeking forgiveness and atonement for everything he'd done. In that instant she knew she'd already forgiven him.

She held her hands tightly. "Thank you for the article."

"You're welcome." He sighed tiredly.

Without thinking, she quickly added, "I've been listening to the tapes you dictated, and if you want, I'll finish your memoirs."

Mr. Brewster held out a hand and slowly she placed hers in his. His fingers moved, but that was the only strength he had. As his hand fell to the bed, a sob rose up in her throat.

Frantically she glanced at his chest, afraid that he'd stopped breathing. Suddenly his chest started to move. She let out a long sigh of relief. It was too soon. He couldn't die just yet. *It was too soon.*

Jonas gently helped her to her feet, and they made their way out the door past the others and onto the front veranda. Outside, he folded her in his arms, and she allowed herself to cry silent, aching sobs. After a while she brushed away the tears.

"I never realized it would be like that," she choked. "I just felt so...I can't explain it, but I wanted him to stop hurting. I wanted him to know so many things, and I didn't know how to say them. I'm a writer and I was at a loss for words."

"You did fine," he assured her. "He understood."

"You think so?"

"Yes." He helped brush away tears with his forefinger. "He's not asking a lot. He just wanted to see you before he died."

"He's so different. I once thought he was evil, but I didn't see any of that just now."

"That part of him is gone, and soon the rest will be, too. Life hasn't been too kind to Simon Brewster."

"It's so sad and I...I..."

He slipped his fingers through her hair and held her head. "What?" he asked softly.

"I wish I didn't feel this guilt about my father...the man who loved and raised me."

"Oh, Abby." He kissed her forehead. "It will get better with time. Abe loved you all the years when you were a little girl, an active teenager and a young adult. No one can take those memories from you or him. Abe took those memories to the grave, and nothing will ever change that—not even knowing that Simon Brewster is your biological father."

She wrapped her arms around his waist and rested against him. Jonas was right. She couldn't change a thing. She had her memories, and she cherished that.

"I think I'd like to see my mother now," she whispered.

Hand in hand they walked to the truck. Before she got in, she glanced back at the house one more time. How much time was left? she wondered. How much time was left to know her father?

CHAPTER SEVENTEEN

WHEN THEY REACHED her mother's house, Jonas said, "You want me to come in with you?"

"No, but thanks for asking. I need to talk to her alone."

She stared at the house with a melancholy expression. "I grew up in this house," she said in a distant voice. "I learned to ride a bike in that driveway. My dad ran alongside of me huffing and puffing to make sure that I wouldn't fall. I told him I wouldn't, but he wanted to be there if I did. I roller-skated on this street and busted my knee. He carried me to the house and bandaged it. I got my first kiss on that front porch and I knew he was watching through the window." She glanced distractedly at him. "I'm rambling, aren't I?"

"You're being human and dealing with a lot of raw emotion right now."

"I'm just trying to put it all together...trying to understand my parents," she replied. "This house has always been a cocoon where I felt safe and warm. That's how my parents made me feel. I was so naive as a child. I didn't understand fights and argument or drugs and drinking. There was none of that in our house. I thought they had the perfect marriage." She chewed on her lip. "When I was about eleven, I went to spend the night at a friend's house. I got sick to my stomach, and my friend's mother brought me home. I walked in the back door and I could hear soft music playing. My parents were on the sofa. My dad was in his underwear and my mom had on a skimpy nightie I'd never seen before. She was lying between his legs, and he was brushing her hair. I didn't know what they were doing, and they were so embarrassed when they saw me. I told my friends, and they called me a doofus. They said my parents were having sex. I felt so stupid. My mother had told me about the birds and the bees, but I didn't pay much attention. I did after that. It was the first time I became aware of sex.'' She took another breath. ''I don't understand how all that love my parents had could have gone so wrong. How could my father move out? How could my mother turn to another man?''

Jonas didn't have an answer for her and he knew she wasn't expecting one. But he wished he could take that look from her face.

Finally, she swallowed hard. ''Thanks for the jacket.'' She fingered the embroidery on the lapel. ''It means so much.''

''I'm glad you like it,'' he said, and yearned to say a lot more, but he didn't know what she was ready to hear. He wanted to ask her to stay at his place. He cursed that part of him that couldn't express his true feelings.

She reached for her suitcase and quickly got out. ''I'll talk to you later,'' she mumbled.

Jonas gazed after her with a perplexed frown. She hadn't kissed him goodbye. Funny how he'd gotten used to that. Was she pulling away from him? No. She just had too much on her mind. She'd call later.

ABBY OPENED THE FRONT DOOR and set down her suitcase. Her mother was vacuuming and had her back to her. Abby stared at the wall that had photos of her from the day she was born. There she was as a baby, a little girl, a teenager and a young woman. In all of them she was smiling. Her whole life was on that wall. Her life as Abe Duncan's daughter, and it depicted everything he'd given her: love, happiness and security. Jonas was right. No one could change that. In that moment she knew who she was. Mr. Brewster may have given her life, but Abe Duncan had given her everything else...everything that mattered. She was Abe Duncan's daughter.

Suddenly she felt light-headed and she knew it was because a burden had been lifted from her shoulders. The sense of betrayal disappeared, and she didn't feel guilty about her new feelings for Mr. Brewster. Her father would understand. If he had taught her anything, it was compassion. Mr. Brewster needed her now, and she'd go back as soon as she'd talked to her mother.

Gail turned and saw her. She let go of the vacuum and ran to Abby. The vacuum propelled itself into the wall and hummed louder. Gail didn't notice as she hugged Abby.

"Abby, you're home," she cried. "Thank God. Oh, sweetheart, I'm so glad you're home."

Abby hugged her back and went to turn off the vacuum cleaner. She looked at her mother and didn't know what to say. The years of her mother's love and support filled her. When life got rough she could count on Gail to understand. Kyle was the only thing they'd ever disagreed on, and Abby wondered whether that had something to do with Mr. Brewster.

Her mother had wanted her away from Hope. She didn't want Abby to get hurt. As always, her mother was trying to protect her. The Rios thing had just backfired. Abby could see that now.

"I love you, sweetheart," Gail said softly.

"I know, Mama," Abby replied, and sat on the sofa.

Gail sat beside her. "I wish I could go back and change things, but I can't. Besides, I would never change your birth. You're the best thing that ever happened to Abe and me."

Abby picked a speck from her black pants. They had said these same words on the phone, but now Abby had to go deeper. "Was it hard keeping it a secret all these years?"

"Not really," Gail admitted truthfully. "I considered you Abe's child and I never even thought about Simon until he confronted me with what he knew. Then it all began to fall apart, and I was so afraid...afraid of losing everything I loved. That's what made me do such stupid things."

Abby studied her slacks. "I've been trying to figure out who I am."

"You're our daughter," Gail said immediately. "You're strong, independent, daring, smart, brave, beautiful and compassionate. Doesn't matter who your biological father is, you're still all those things. You're still Abigail Duncan."

"Yes, I've finally figured that out." Abby glanced again at the pictures and knew that was true. So many memories. So much love. Those feelings gave her the strength to admit that a small part of her heart was with Mr. Brewster.

"I saw Mr. Brewster before I came here. He's...
dying."

"I heard that in town."

"It was so strange. When I looked at him, all the
bitterness and resentment left me. He's just a lonely
old man who's..."

Gail wrapped her arms around her. "It's all right,
sweetheart, to have feelings for him. I wouldn't expect any less of you."

Abby rested her head on her mother's shoulder.
"At first I felt such a betrayal to Daddy, but now I
don't. Mr. Brewster can't take anything from me. He
can only add to it."

"That's true," Gail said.

Abby drew back, and they sat in silence.

"Did you drive home?" Gail finally asked.

"No, Jonas flew to Dallas, and I came back with
him."

"Thank God for Jonas."

Abby raised an eyebrow.

"I have to apologize for what I said about Jonas.
He's a good person, but I didn't want you involved
with anyone here. I was trying to make you go back
to Dallas. That's why we argued about Kyle. I was
desperate."

They talked for a while longer, then Gail fixed
supper. It was good to be with her mother again.

Over supper, she asked, "How are Aunt Sybil and
Earl?"

Gail rolled her eyes. "Please, don't mention that
sister of mine. She now thinks I'm the loose woman
of Hope."

Abby laughed.

"But Sybil has her own problems. Earl moved in

with that woman he's been dating, and Sybil is beside herself. The man is thirty-five years old, and she still can't let go.''

"Good for Earl," Abby said. "I hope he doesn't give in to Aunt Sybil."

"I don't think he will," Gail replied. "He's really in love."

Abby toyed with her food. "How do you know that love will last?" She asked the question that had been tormenting her.

Gail placed her hand over her heart. "In here, sweetheart. You know in here."

"But you loved Daddy—and look what happened."

"Love is also deaf, blind and stupid, and you have to make sure not to get caught in any of those traps." She watched Abby for a second. "You're strong, Abby, and you won't do any of the stupid things I did. I've never had your strength."

Jonas had told her the same thing, and maybe there was a grain of truth to it. Abby drew a deep breath. "I love Jonas, Mama."

"Yes, I know," Gail said.

"I'm concerned about the future."

"Why?"

"He says he's leaving when Mr. Brewster passes away. Brewster Farms has been his whole life. I'm not sure it's the right thing for him to do."

"Sounds like you two need to talk."

"Jonas isn't very good at talking."

"Well, then, you *make* him, because that's what happened to Abe and me. Our pride wouldn't allow us to talk, and we hurt each other. Don't let that happen to you. If you love Jonas, go after him and tell him how you feel."

She didn't tell her mother that she'd already told Jonas she loved him and hadn't gotten a response. She'd gotten one from his body, but she wanted it from his heart. If he couldn't tell her he loved her, what kind of future did they have?

JONAS SAT BY Brewster's bedside watching him draw each ragged breath. The nurse checked his vital signs, and Jonas got up and walked to the windows. Brewster Farms lay before him like a patchwork quilt—warehouses, barns, equipment sheds, citrus groves and field after field of agricultural crops. He knew exactly what grew in each field and if it was harvested or not. He knew everything about the place and the laborers that worked the fields. Brewster had made sure of that.

As he watched, Stuart came out of the office and got into his truck. He was going home to Brenda and the kids. Family. That was important, but Jonas knew very little about family. He glanced toward the bed. Brewster was probably the only real family he'd ever known. On holidays Brewster had insisted that Jonas eat at the mansion with the family. It wasn't idyllic, but it was his life.

The years rolled back and Jonas remembered other things...like the young boy that had come here so scared and lost. Brewster drove him from the hospital to the warehouse and showed him the storeroom where he'd sleep. There was a bed, a dresser and an area rug on the concrete floor. Clean sheets were on the bed and clothes were in the dresser drawers. That night he lay awake thinking of running away, but he was sure the sheriff would catch up with him. The next morning he looked at the room a little differently. It was better than any place he'd ever lived and there was a small bathroom down the hall. When a maid brought him breakfast, he didn't know what to think. Food on a regular basis was a luxury he'd never had.

Brewster took him to the fields and he loaded onions onto a trailer until his muscles ached and his back hurt. At lunchtime Brewster brought him a sandwich and something to drink. Jonas rode back to the warehouse with the other laborers, and a maid again brought him supper. He fell into bed exhausted. That daily routine continued for the next year. Each night he marked the day off on the calendar. One day closer to freedom. He wasn't sure when he stopped marking days. Work, school and good grades began to occupy his mind. He didn't want to give Brewster anything to gripe about because Brewster was always there watching him, pushing him, and Jonas was determined to never let the man break his spirit.

Looking back, Jonas could see that Brewster had shaped him into a man and somewhere along the way they had become attached to each other. Jonas had hated him at first, but even as a kid he recognized that three meals a day, clean clothes and a place to sleep was better than the streets.

The old man had given him a life, and as he gazed out at Brewster's valley he knew that Brewster was the reason he'd stayed and Brewster would be the reason he'd leave. He would leave behind him his childhood, his teenage years and the years he'd spent working here. It would be over, and he'd be free to start a new life with Abby.

He was glad Brewster understood that he had to go. His life would be different, but he had Abby, and somehow he had to find a way to tell her how he felt. He wasn't going to live without love anymore. He glanced toward the bed. He and Brewster were two people who'd needed each other in a troubled time. Now that time was coming to an end.

ABBY KEPT WAITING for Jonas to call. When he didn't, she borrowed her mother's car and went to the mansion. Maria let her in, and Abby made her way upstairs. There was no one in the hall so she opened the door and went in.

The room was almost in darkness, but she could see Jonas sitting by the bed just watching Mr. Brewster's face. No wonder he hadn't called. He'd probably been here since he'd left her at her mother's.

He noticed her and immediately got to his feet. "Abby, I've been waiting for you to call."

And she'd been waiting for him to call. They definitely had a communication problem...something she intended to rectify. She stared at Mr. Brewster's still body.

"How is he?"

Jonas shrugged and came over to her. "He hasn't said a word in over two hours. I don't think it's going to be much longer."

Abby's throat closed tightly and she was glad she'd come—for Jonas and herself.

Jonas took her arm and led her to the bed. He bent down and whispered in Mr. Brewster's ear. "Abigail's here."

Mr. Brewster moved his head slightly, and Abby noticed his right hand twitching. She reached out and covered the hand with her own. His skin was cold and clammy, but it gave her a warm feeling. The twitching stopped and a contented look came over his face.

So many emotions welled up in her. Through the sadness and heartache, one thing rang true. None of the other stuff mattered. It all came down to a basic thing—human emotion. In her heart she had found a place for Mr. Brewster. She didn't even have to think about forgiveness and the past. It didn't make a difference to the way she felt inside. It didn't make a difference at all.

She didn't know how long she stood there holding the hand of the man who had given her life. She became aware that Jonas had pulled up a chair for her, and she sank gratefully into it. He sat beside her. Neither spoke. They just waited. Jonas got up several times to check Mr. Brewster's breathing, as did the nurse who had come back into the room. Mr. Brewster kept hanging on, just the way he had lived his life—breaking all the rules with a fierce strength.

Abby rested her head on Jonas's shoulder.

"Why don't you go home and get some rest," Jonas suggested. "I'll call you if anything happens."

She moved her head. "No, I want to be here."

"Abby."

"I'm fine, really."

Mr. Brewster passed away in the early hours of the morning, with Abby and Jonas by his bedside.

Abby thought she was prepared, but when it happened, a dam broke in her. Agonizing sobs shook her body and she couldn't control them. Jonas held her, unable to take the tortured cries.

"Abby." He stroked her hair. "He's at peace now."

"But I feel so cheated," she said. "I never had the chance to know him. I never—"

"That's probably why he dictated all those tapes. He told you everything about his life...the good and the bad."

CHAPTER EIGHTEEN

THEY BURIED HIM TWO DAYS LATER. Dignitaries came from all over the state of Texas to pay their last respects. Mr. Brewster was very well-known. Abby stood with Jonas at the graveside and she saw a tear ooze from his eye. He quickly brushed it away, still holding all his emotions inside.

Maria and her staff had prepared a meal for after the funeral. The mansion was packed. Her mother had attended the funeral, and Abby appreciated her presence. The past was fading into an unclear future.

She searched for Jonas in the crowd. She hadn't seen too much of him in the past two days. He had been busy making funeral arrangements and getting Mr. Brewster's affairs in order. She saw him across the room, talking to a congressman who represented the Rio Grande Valley. He seemed to be on speaking terms with all the dignitaries here. That didn't surprise her. Jonas had been at the helm of Brewster Farms for a long time. She wondered how it could be so easy for him to leave.

She wished they had talked about the future in her apartment, but they had been too busy discovering and enjoying each other. She loved being with him and would do anything to be with him. That thought got her. Her job meant the world to her, but if Jonas asked, she'd give it up. Now she knew what her

mother had meant when she'd said that Abby would
know when love was real. That she'd feel it in her
heart. She'd given Jonas her heart the first moment
she'd looked at him. Her divorce and her parent's
problems had her questioning her feelings. But love
didn't come with a guarantee. It only came with faith
and trust. And in her heart, she knew she and Jonas
would be together forever. They just had to get
through the days ahead.

Brenda and Stuart came up to her. "How are
you?" Brenda asked tentatively, and Abby could see
that she was nervous about speaking to her. The revelation about her biological father had been a shock
to the whole town, and no one was sure what to say
to her.

Abby smiled. "I'm fine, really, and thanks for the
letter. It meant a lot at a very difficult time."

Brenda and several of her high school friends had
written her a letter saying they loved her and she was
still Abby to them.

Brenda visibly relaxed. "Gosh, Abby, I've been
wanting to call you, but..."

"You didn't know what to say," Abby finished
for her.

"That's about it. Brit, Candy and I were worried
about you."

"Thanks, Brenda. I'm adjusting."

"I'm sorry about Mr. Brewster," Brenda said.

"He's at peace now." Abby repeated the words
Jonas had said to her, and it was the way she felt.
Mr. Brewster had led a long and full life. Abby
planned to write his story. It would be her personal
gift to him...a gift from his daughter.

Brenda leaned closer and whispered. "I'm so glad

about you and Jonas. I've been trying to fix him up for years.''

"You can stop now," Abby said in a teasing tone.

"She'll move on to someone else," Stuart put in.

Brenda poked him in the chest. "Don't start."

Stuart shook his head, then said, "I'm happy about you and Jonas, too. I wish he wasn't set on leaving. I don't know if I can work for Jules."

"Everyone feels that way," Brenda added.

"Now that Mr. Brewster is gone, Jonas doesn't feel that he can stay here."

At that moment, Jonas walked over to them. He looked different today. He wore a dark suit, white shirt and a multicolored tie. She liked him in a suit. She liked him in jeans and chambray shirts. In fact, she liked Jonas in anything he wore—or didn't wear. Her blood started to heat up at that thought.

"Hi," he said to everyone.

"The service was beautiful," Brenda said.

"Yeah, you did him proud," Stuart added.

"I hope so," Jonas replied. "I wanted everything just like he requested."

Stuart shoved his hands into his pockets in a nervous gesture. "I was just telling Abby, I don't know if I can work for Jules."

"Sure you can," Jonas insisted. "He'll be one of those absentee bosses, and you, Perry and Juan will basically run things."

"I don't know, Jonas. I have a feeling Jules will jeopardize all our jobs."

"I have to go. Please understand that," Jonas said in a firm voice. He knew his friends didn't understand his reasoning, but it was personal and he couldn't explain it any further than that. As long as Abby understood, that was all that mattered.

Stuart and Brenda walked away, and Jonas stepped in front of Abby. "You do understand why I have to leave, don't you?"

She fingered a button on his jacket. "I know it's been your goal since you were fifteen and that it's important to you, but…"

A man walked up and offered his condolences, interrupting her. After he left, Jonas turned back to her. "There are so many people here, and we need to talk."

"Yeah," she replied, glancing around at the crowd.

Edna whizzed past them giving instructions to a waiter. She was making sure everyone had enough food and drink. She was acting as Lady of the mansion and was obviously in her element.

Jonas stepped so close to her that Abby could smell his aftershave. "Let's go somewhere more private."

It's what she'd been waiting for. "I'd like that."

He took her hand and headed for the foyer. Mr. Foster, Mr. Brewster's attorney, stopped them.

"I'd like to get the will read as soon as everyone leaves," he said to Jonas.

"This evening?"

"Yes, Mr. Brewster wanted it read right after the funeral."

"I see." Jonas glanced at Abby, then back at Mr. Foster. "I guess it's just as well to do it now. I'm ready to get out of here."

Abby watched his face. He'd earned his freedom

and he would take it. Again she hoped it was the right thing for him…and her.

"I'll meet you in the dining room in ten minutes," Mr. Foster said. "I'll tell the others."

"There's no need for me to be there, so I'll—"

Mr. Foster turned back. "Ms. Duncan, Mr. Brewster requested that you be there."

She shook her head. "No, I don't want anything from him."

Jonas heard the anxiety in her voice and nodded to Mr. Foster. "Don't worry, Abby," he said, as Mr. Foster walked away. "Brewster knew how you felt. We discussed it a few days ago. The bulk of his estate will go to his family. He said they weren't anything to brag about, but they were his family. He made me the executor, and I promised to carry out his wishes, which—" he sighed "—will probably be to make sure they don't squander every dime."

The tension inside her eased. She didn't want anything of monetary value. He'd given her what she wanted: the article in the paper. That was all she needed—to know he cared enough to have done that.

A thought struck her. If Jonas was the executor, that meant he couldn't leave right away. He'd have to take care of Mr. Brewster's affairs. She wondered if he'd thought of that. Oh, damn, she wanted to talk to him…

As the last person left the mansion, Abby, Jonas, Edna, Jules and Darby made their way to the dining room. Mr. Foster was already there, with his briefcase and papers strewn on the table. He motioned for Jonas to sit next to him. Abby sat beside Jonas, while the other three took seats across the table.

"I'll make this short and simple," Mr. Foster began, adjusting his glasses. "Mr. Brewster wanted this done after the funeral so everyone could get on with their lives."

"That's a very good idea," Edna said, shifting in her chair.

"Mr. Brewster thought so." Mr. Foster picked up a legal document. "It's really very simple. He left monetary amounts to several members of his staff who have been with him for years. He left monetary amounts to the hospital and clinic so they can continue to operate without difficulty." He pushed papers to the center of the table. "Here are the amounts, if anyone would like to read them."

Edna immediately snatched up the papers.

Mr. Foster started to read. "'To the following people, I bequeath one million dollars each—Edna Kline, Jules Kline and Darby Combs.'"

"What!" Edna shoved the other papers away in anger. "Who gets the—?" Her eyes settled on Abby. "Oh God, that stupid bastard."

"Mrs. Kline, please," Mr. Foster appealed.

Edna waved a hand. "Go ahead. I'd love to hear the rest of this nonsense."

Abby's stomach felt like one big knot, and she couldn't shake a sense of foreboding.

Jonas was confused. From his talks with Brewster, he had assumed that the bulk would go to Edna, Jules and Darby. Evidently he'd been wrong. He'd told Abby she didn't have to worry, but it seemed that Brewster had changed his mind. Jonas didn't know how she was going to react to this.

Mr. Foster focused on the document in front of him. "'To my daughter, Abigail Duncan...'"

Oh, please, no, don't do this to me. She clenched

her hands so tight that she felt her nails dig into her palms. She wanted to get up and run from the room, but she couldn't move. She could only listen to Mr. Foster's words.

"'I would like to say I'm sorry. I know you don't want anything from me, but I could not leave this earth without acknowledging you in some way. You have so much talent, and the only way I could think of to encourage that talent was to give you a voice to explore and expand your capabilities. So I bequeath to you the *Hope Herald* and its monies to use as you see fit. Use it wisely, Abigail.'"

Her insides trembled. It wasn't what she'd expected at all. Mr. Brewster had given her the one thing she couldn't refuse. How could he know her so well?

He is my father. We have the same genes and the same stubborn pride, her heart answered.

"Now for the bulk of the estate," Mr. Foster said, withdrawing a long legal document.

Everyone waited. Mr. Foster cleared his throat. "Mr. Brewster has written a letter that he's instructed me to read. Please remain silent until I finish." He glanced at Jonas. "The letter is to you."

Jonas swallowed. "I'd much rather read it in private."

"I'm sorry, Mr. Brewster wanted it read aloud."

Jonas nodded, knowing Brewster had planned everything to the end, in control as always. Somehow Jonas knew that the words he would hear now would touch his very soul. He braced himself.

Mr. Foster began to read. "'Jonas, you and I started out on shaky ground, but over the years that ground has become solid and secure. We have worked together, argued together and built Brewster Farms into what it is today. You learned everything I taught you with an eagerness and intellect that always surprised me. All the laborers respect you and the locals admire you. You became the man I wanted my son to be.

"'I know you have toiled each day with one goal in mind—freedom. At fifteen you used to mark each day with a big X on the calendar. You did that for a whole year, then you went back to school and began to learn and grow, and the calendar was put aside. It's in my safe if you'd like to have it.

"'Even though you didn't mark the days any longer, you were still marking time in your head. Each day meant you were closer to freedom, closer to leaving Hope and me behind. That never changed, and I hate to take that away from you, but I want to do what's best for you and for Hope.

"'At this point I know you're getting angry, but please try to hear what I'm saying. Over the past twenty years you and I have argued on numerous occasions. A couple of times you left, but you always returned. This last time you left because I had hurt Abigail, and I didn't think you were coming back. But you did. There's a reason for that. You return because Brewster Farms is your home. It has been for a long time.

"'Love is an emotion that's not easy for me. We are much alike in that, but I've loved you as much as anyone in my life. So forgive me for what I'm about to do, but I feel it is only right. This is my last bequest. The rest of my estate, my monies and holdings in land, especially Brewster Farms, I bequeath in its entirety to the man who deserves it, Jonas Parker.'''

Abby glanced at Jonas. His sun-browned skin was white, and he gazed straight ahead with a dazed expression. She wanted to reach out and touch him, to reassure him, but he was in a place she couldn't reach. She recognized that he had to handle the contents of the letter in his own way.

Jonas stared across the room, seeing nothing, but hearing those words over and over inside his head. He wasn't breathing or moving. He was only hearing a jumble of phrases that had him caught in a vortex of emotion.

You became the man I wanted my son to be.... The calendar is in my safe if you'd like to have it.... Brewster Farms is your home. It has been for a long time.... I want to do what's best for you and for Hope.... I've loved you as much as anyone in my life.

The words held him, and he could feel his heart beating with the same intensity as that scared, lonely fifteen-year-old's. His hand tightened with the same excitement as when he'd marked off each day on the calendar. His eyes burned with the same emotion as when he'd received his diplomas and Brewster had sat in the front row. All those feelings jolted through him, and freedom became something he could see clearly. He *was* free. He'd been free for a long time. His stubborn pride was the only part of him that wouldn't admit it. God, he'd been free all along. Why hadn't he seen that before?

Everyone's eyes were on him. He got up and slowly walked out of the room.

"Jonas," Mr. Foster said, but he didn't respond.

"What's the matter with him?" Edna asked sharply. "You'd think he'd been given a death sentence."

Abby quickly followed him. "Jonas," she called, but he kept walking. She was still in a state of shock herself, but she knew Mr. Brewster was right. This was Jonas's home. That's why she'd had so many doubts about his leaving. She'd said she didn't want a thing from Mr. Brewster. Now she did. She wanted Jonas's happiness. And happiness was here at Brewster Farms—with her. In a flash she knew that. She was Abe Duncan's daughter and she belonged in Brewster's valley...as did Jonas.

Jonas stood at the bottom of the steps and glanced beyond the mansion, to the gates and fields of vegetables and fruits, to the workers settling back to their jobs after the funeral.

I want to do what's best for you and for Hope.... Brewster Farms is your home. It has been for a long time.... I've loved you as much as anyone in my life.

He suddenly realized why he'd wanted to leave. It had nothing to do with freedom. It had to do with his feelings for Brewster. Over the years, they'd had their ups and downs, but Brewster was always there, always a guiding force in his life. The truth behind those words surged through him. Without Brewster...without him... Oh God, he loved that old man. That's why he'd been so set on leaving. He didn't want to face these feelings, but now...

"Jonas."

He heard her voice and turned toward it. He blinked. Where was he? He hadn't even realized he'd left the room.

"Jonas, are you all right?"

"No." He shook his head. "I..."

"He loved you," she said softly. "And he's right. This is your home and it's where you belong."

"But he's not here, Abby. He's gone." As he said the words, tears began to roll down his cheeks. "Oh God, he's gone."

Abby ran down the steps and held him. Jonas clung to her and allowed himself to cry—to grieve— for Brewster, the man he had loved.

They stood for a long time just holding each other. Finally Abby whispered into his shoulder, "You were like a son to him."

He sucked air into his raw throat. "I know." He rubbed his face against hers. "I just wish he had told me what he was planning to do."

"He knew that if he did, you would refuse his gift. I think he hoped that after his death you wouldn't be able to do that."

This place had been Jonas's whole life. It was a part of him, just as Brewster had said. But how did he accept this? How did— "I can't be happy here without you," he uttered in a miserable voice.

She drew back and looked into his eyes. "Why is that?" she asked.

He gazed into her eyes and the words rose up from his heart without any difficulty. "Because I love you."

A smile lit her face, and she quickly brushed away tears. "I love you, too."

He kissed her deeply, passionately, until the world spun away, leaving only this wonderful feeling of love and being loved. After a moment, he rested his forehead against hers. "How do we handle this? Your job's in Dallas. I've waited a long time to have these feelings I have for you, and I can't stay here unless you're with me.''

''I don't think that's going to be a problem.'' She smoothed the lapel of his jacket.

''Why?''

''I suddenly have this newspaper to run and I can't do that from Dallas.''

Brewster's other gift—the *Hope Herald.* ''That means you're coming home?'' *Home.* It was such a beautiful word, he thought.

''Yes,'' she said brightly. ''To you, to Hope and to our future.''

He held her tightly. ''Oh, Abby, I love you.''

''As long as I know that, we'll be fine.''

He gazed into her bright eyes. ''I do, so much.'' He cupped her face and kissed her gently. ''I'm sorry it's been so hard for me to say that.''

She kissed his chin. ''Well, you've said it now, Jonas Parker.'' She smiled at him. ''Maybe we'd better go back inside and ease Mr. Foster's mind.''

''In a minute,'' he said as he gazed at Brewster's valley. Things looked so different now. He had mistakenly thought that without Brewster there was nothing here for him. But this was his home. It always had been. He glanced up at the sky and murmured a word of thanks to the old man who had given him more than he had ever dreamed possible...including Abby.

EPILOGUE

Four years later

"PERFECT, JUST PERFECT," Abby said as she studied the front-page layout for the *Hope Herald*. "The picture is spectacular. Steve, you did a wonderful job. You captured the essence of my story. The image of the little girl hanging from the international bridge fence with one hand and begging with the other is so poignant. And that look on the American tourist's face tells all. She's trying not to look at the child, but you can almost see her hand coming out of her pocket."

"Thanks, Mrs. Parker, I'm glad I did your story justice," Steve said.

Abby glanced around at the staff. The paper had come a long way. When she'd first started, there'd been three people who'd been with the *Hope Herald* for years. Now she had a staff of ten. It had been hard at first, but Abby had purchased new equipment with the money Mr. Brewster had put into the *Herald* account. His generosity had made her determined to turn the *Hope Herald* into a competitive newspaper. She was succeeding. In the past four years, the circulation had quadrupled and several articles were being picked up by the Associated Press. One of her